Editing by Amy Gamache @ Rose David Editing

Cover Design by Melissa Gill Designs

M000087705

Table of Contents

Chapter One
Finley

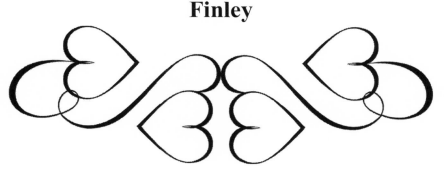

Have you ever had a dream so vivid that you swore it was real? A nightmare so terrifying that you felt like it was a part of you, even long after you woke?

What if you woke up and realized that your nightmare was actually your reality? That everything you thought would never happen to you already has?

We go through life thinking the worst only happens to other people. Until one day - you are that person.

****

I'm sitting in a sterile office, the distorted voice of a doctor pulsing in my ears. I can no longer understand his words. All I can manage is to stare at his degree on the wall and wish for myself to wake up. Wish for my mind to stop playing such a sick and awful trick on me.

He says it's a malignant brain tumor.

A brain tumor?

Cancer?

I'm only nineteen.

Thirty minutes ago I thought I had my whole future ahead of me and now this doctor's telling me my life is basically over. Instead of trying to process anything he's telling me, I continue to stare at his degree, my eyes scanning the bold letters printed across it over and over again.

When he stops talking I finally look at him, still convinced he's made some kind of terrible mistake. *Maybe he mixed up my scans with someone else's.* When he begins to speak again it sounds like he's talking down a tunnel. The words echo and dance around me.

He says he'll need to remove the tumor right away, with chemo starting almost immediately after. He's gone over all of the available options, even though it's a blur in my mind. He said sometimes they do it the other way around, but given the size and position of the tumor I only really have two options. Take it out now and have a thirty percent survival rate or die within months. At least if I have the surgery I have a chance, albeit a very small chance. But the smallest chance is better than no chance at all… Isn't it?

I don't know why I'm so surprised to be meeting my demise at such a young age. It's totally my luck. My mom didn't want me enough to fight for me. My dad never wanted me, leaving my mom when I was just an infant. And now the world apparently doesn't want me either.

"Did you hear me, Miss Roberts?" Dr. Newton questions, pulling me from my haze.

I know I need to acknowledge him, at least in some way. "Uh huh." It's all I can manage.

"Do you have any questions about your procedure?"

What are you supposed to say when someone tells you they're going to cut into your brain and you only have a thirty percent chance of survival? And a zero percent chance if you decline.

"No." My voice sounds like it belongs to a complete stranger.

Thirty percent...

I look down at my fingers knotted in my lap as I repeat it over and over in my head, trying to make it make sense. *Thirty percent.*

God, I want to get out of here. If I'm possibly going to die in less than forty-eight hours, I don't want to spend what little time I have left sitting in this office with a doctor who looks like he's completely unphased by my dying.

Well, *I'm phased, asshole!*

"Ms. Murphy will give you your paperwork on the way out. It will have all of the instructions regarding the preparation of your surgery. If you think of anything between now and then, please do not hesitate to reach out. You have my number."

"Okay." I stand, my legs numb beneath me, yet somehow still able to hold my weight.

"Are you sure I can't call someone for you?" he offers for the second time since he hit me with the worst news a person can get.

"I don't have anyone to call."

Okay, so that's only partly true. I do have a sister. She's quite literally the only person in the world who cares about what happens to me. But I don't want her to find out like this. Of course she knows about the horrible headaches and dizziness that prompted me to see a doctor in the first place. But to find out the grim diagnosis, I think that's something she needs to hear in person. Just the thought of going home and telling the only family I have that I'm probably going to die curdles my stomach.

"I'll see you at the hospital Thursday morning." The doctor cuts into my thoughts.

"Okay."

I grab my coat off the back of the chair and slide it on before quickly exiting the office.

The fog that has surrounded me for the past forty minutes seems to lift slightly when the bright sun and frigid breeze hits my face as I step outside. Suddenly it all feels too real. I take a few deep breaths of the cold Chicago air, willing myself not to fall apart.

Shoving my hands deep into my coat pockets, I turn left, heading in the opposite direction of the apartment I share with my sister.

I don't want to go home yet. I don't want to look at Claire and utter the words that seem too unreal to even digest.

So instead I walk.

I walk for what seems like forever.

I walk until my toes are numb and my cheeks burn from the cold. I walk until I feel like I can't walk anymore, yet I still have no desire to stop.

I'm finally seeing things as if it were one of my last days on Earth, because it very well may be. I walk around the park; appreciate the sights, the sounds, and smells. I go to my favorite coffee shop and order my favorite muffin. And even though I have absolutely no appetite, I eat it anyway so I can taste it one last time.

I walk block after block, trying to commit a tiny part of the city to my memory as if somehow I will be allowed to take it with me into the afterlife.

I've been walking for nearly two hours when I come across a small, trendy looking bar sitting on the corner and have the overwhelming urge to go inside.

The sun has begun to set and my nose is so cold I feel like it might fall right off my face, but that's not why I want to go inside. Maybe it's because bars are where people go when they're at their lowest or maybe it's because I've never actually been inside one. And this very well might be my last chance. *I guess there's no better time to check it off my bucket list.*

I push through the front door and walk right in like I've been there a million times. I briefly look around the lightly crowded space as I head directly for the bar located at the back of the open room. I pass a few empty tables and stools before claiming a seat at the very end of the bar where it curves into an L shape, placing my back to the wall and giving me a view of the entire room.

Sliding off my coat, I hang it on the back of the chair before taking my seat. Less than a minute passes before a woman, maybe in her late twenties, who has more tattoos than she has visible skin, approaches, eyeing me warily. I've never wished that I could order a hard, stiff drink more than I do right now. *And I might never be able to...* I settle for a water and wait a few short seconds for her to set the glass in front of me.

It's so strange, because as I watch her walk away, all I can think is I'm never going to be as old as she is right now. And man is that a depressing thought.

I take a small sip of the cold liquid, fighting against the sudden surge in my throat that threatens to bring it right back up.

I take a deep breath and try to focus on anything else. On the sound of the music playing in the background. The bustle of conversation that floats all around me. On trying to pretend I'm not totally falling apart on the inside.

Thirty minutes pass and I've barely moved. I'm still staring at the water in front of me like it's some magical object that's going to spring to life and make all my problems disappear.

I've run it all over in my head. My childhood. My mom. Everything that's happened. How unfair it all seems. Self-pity doesn't even begin to describe how I feel right now. It goes way beyond that.

"You okay?" A smooth voice fills my ears, startling me from my thoughts. I look up, momentarily stunned by a pair of big blue eyes.

"Huh?" I stutter out, realizing he must be speaking to me.

"I was just asking if you were okay." A long stretch of silence passes between us, and even though I tell myself to look away, I can't. I can't turn away from those eyes. Eyes the color of ocean waves. Eyes I could spend my entire life getting lost in if I had any life left.

"Uh huh." I nod slowly, not sure what else to say. What *should* I say? *Actually I'm not. I just found out I have cancer and am likely going to die, but thanks for asking?*

He studies me for a long moment and for a second I think he might say more, but instead he nods and turns his attention to the bartender.

While his focus is elsewhere, I take the opportunity to study the rest of his face. I'm immediately taken aback by how good looking he is. Short, light brown hair, firm jaw covered with the slightest amount of scruff, perfect nose, and one dimple. A deep imprint on his left cheek that peeks out when he smiles at the woman standing on the other side of the bar. Oh god, that smile. I feel a flutter run through my chest. And did I mention his eyes?

I open my mouth, as if my mind could possibly form words right now, as if I could possibly think of a single thing to say to him, but I quickly snap it shut when he speaks to the bartender, ordering a round of beers.

I study his profile, taking in the curve of his face and the bob of his Adam's apple as he swallows before allowing my eyes to sweep lower.

I'd guess he's in his early to mid-twenties, dressed in a dark v-neck shirt that stretches over his broad shoulders with jeans that hang perfectly on his narrow hips. He's fit but not overly muscular. And one arm has a full sleeve of tattoos while the other appears completely bare.

If drooling was something people actually did, other than in their sleep, I'd definitely be drooling right now.

Unfortunately, the bartender returns all too soon with his drinks, and before I know it, he's gathering them from the bar and turning to leave.

Reality slams back into me.

How many times have I looked at an attractive man and thought *one day*? One day a man like that will love me. One day I'll get married and have children. One day I will have all the things I never had growing up. Love. Stability. A real home. People who love me. One day...

Knowing that I probably won't live to see that day is one hell of a pill to swallow. We live life thinking there's always more. More days. More time. More chances. But I know better. I know that things can change on a dime and that nothing – absolutely nothing – is guaranteed, especially not tomorrow.

Our eyes meet again as he turns. My skin tingles from looking into those eyes a second time. He gives me a soft smile and then, just like that, he's gone. I watch his backside as he walks away, wondering how on earth God could have ever created something so perfect. If God even exists, which right now I'm questioning more than ever. I think it's safe to say I'm having trouble believing in anything right now.

I mean, if there's a God then where has he been my whole life?

When I was younger I used to pray every night. I would pray so hard. I'd pray for my mom to get her life together and finally break free of her addiction. I'd pray that my dad wasn't who my mom said he was and that one day he would come find me and take me away. I'd pray for food and shelter when my mom would go on a two month bender and we'd find ourselves, *once again*, out on the streets. I'd pray to go home when I'd find myself in yet another foster home with people who saw me as nothing more than a paycheck.

Needless to say, my prayers were never answered. Had they been, maybe the one person I need more than anything right now, my mom, would be here with me. I could pick up the phone and call her and she'd comfort me and tell me everything was going to be okay. But instead I'm sitting here alone, unsure if my mother is alive or dead.

It's been nearly a year and a half since I left. It broke my heart to leave her but I had to. I had to escape. Otherwise I was going to end up stuck, just like her. I couldn't do that to myself. I couldn't sit there and watch her slowly kill herself. I'd done it my entire life. Watched drugs steal her away, watched her fade further and further into the distance. Truthfully, I'd be surprised if she even remembers she has a daughter. That's how bad it had gotten.

Her face filters through my mind – her sunken in eyes and the hollow expression she wore the last time I saw her.

I shake away the thought and refocus on the man, watching as he crosses through the various high top tables positioned a few feet away from the bar. He stops at a table next to the far side windows where three other guys are sitting. All of them seem a little older than the blue eyed man, and while none of them are quite as attractive, all three are still good looking enough for me to take notice.

He sets the drinks on the table and then to my surprise, glances back in my direction, causing my stomach to twist in the best possible way. One brief moment is all I get before he's taken his seat, his back facing me.

I watch him and his companions for several minutes, thankful for something to focus on other than the hollow pit in my stomach and the deep ache in my chest.

I watch the muscles in his back flex as he laughs, his shirt stretching across his broad shoulders every time he leans forward even the smallest bit. I imagine what they must be saying to each other, envision how incredible his laugh sounds. I bet it's deep and delicious, just like the rest of him.

I watch different women approach the table throughout that time, ignoring the pang in my stomach when the blue eyed man wraps his arm around one particular woman with blonde hair that hangs inches from the waistband of her too tight jeans.

I couldn't be more different than her if I tried. She's all lean legs and perfectly highlighted hair while I'm about as basic as they come. Petite, dark shoulder length hair, sporting my usual attire of leggings, an oversized sweater, and fluffy boots. Nothing about me screams sexy. Whereas this woman oozes it from every pore.

I bet this is the kind of woman he usually goes for. The kind that looks like they exist in an alternate universe from the rest of us plain, ordinary folk.

She leans in close and my gaze narrows, watching as her head falls back as she laughs at whatever the man says. For a moment I think she might join them, but she ends up sauntering away a few seconds later, a satisfied smile on her pretty face.

Not long after that all four men gather their coats, talking as they empty the remainder of their drinks before walking out the front door.

And just like that, my world comes crashing back down. I feel like I've been punched in the stomach. All the air leaves my body in one quick movement and I'm left chasing after it, trying to pull in a breath.

It's silly, really. How something like an attractive man could make me forget what I'm about to face and likely not survive. But there's something about him. Something I can't quite put my finger on.

I lean forward, wrapping my hands around the glass of water in front of me as my mind spins off into some fantasy world. A world where I'm not sick. A world where I would have the courage to grab my coat and walk right out of this bar after him. Ask him for his number or out to grab a bite to eat. It's absurd, of course. Something I would never in a million years do, but it still doesn't keep me from thinking about it. I'm so consumed by the thought that I don't even look up when I sense someone take the seat next to me.

"I don't think I've ever seen someone so mesmerized by a glass of water." The deep voice vibrates straight through me.

I look up, completely caught off guard to see the same blue eyed man sliding into the stool next to me, a twinkle of amusement in his eyes.

It takes me several long moments to gather my thoughts enough to form a coherent sentence.

"Yeah, it's really not that interesting." I laugh to myself, realizing how stupid I must look.

"If it's not that interesting then why does that water seem to be the only thing you care about in this entire bar?" His left dimple makes an appearance causing my heart to beat a little faster.

"Nothing better to do, I guess." I shrug, releasing the glass as I sit back in my seat.

"Certainly there's somewhere you could be; something you could be doing besides sitting here staring at a glass of water."

"Afraid not." I can't help but smile when his eyebrow shoots up in question.

"Abel Collins." He extends his hand, waiting for me to take it.

It takes me longer than it probably would with a normal man, but this guy is anything but normal. *Abel.* God, even his name is sexy.

"And you are?" he prompts when I take too long to do, well, *anything*.

"Finley." I take his hand, ignoring the zing that shoots up my arm.

"Finley?" He smirks, clearly hinting for my last name.

"Just Finley," I confirm.

"I've never seen you here before, *just* Finley." He shifts in his seat, not pressing the matter further.

"You come here often I take it?"

"Here and there." He grins and all I can think is that my mother, if I had a real one that is, would probably kill me if I ever brought a man like this home.

No matter how good looking he is, it's clear he has bad news written all over him. Or maybe that's the perception he's trying to put off because I swear he has the softest, kindest eyes I've ever seen.

"I could tell," I state, finding it hard not to get lost in the depths of those eyes and hold my composure.

"So you were watching me then?" His lips curl in what can only be described as a cocky smirk.

My god, I bet this man has women eating out of the palm of his hand. He's sure doing a good job on me right now.

"I was not watching you," I object, swiveling my stool toward him when he does the same.

"Is that what you call staring at someone for the better part of an hour."

"I was *not* staring." I feel my blush flood my cheeks and embarrassment creeps up my spine.

"That's not what I heard." His voice is full of amusement.

"Is that what your friends told you?" I gesture toward the door where all four of them had exited minutes ago.

"Brothers, actually. And yes."

"There are four of you?" I ask, my cheeks getting even warmer.

"Five actually. My oldest brother lives in California."

"Wow, I can't imagine having four brothers." I nervously sip my water, not sure what else to say. If I tell him his brothers were lying to him and continue to insist I wasn't watching him – which I totally was – it will only make me look guiltier. Not that salvaging my pride is really all that important at this point.

"It's not so bad." He shrugs. "I'm the youngest so they've taken it pretty easy on me over the years. And by taking it easy on me I actually mean they've pretty much made life impossible." His smile widens, making it clear he finds humor in this.

"I take it you're pretty close to them," I say the only thing I can think of to fill the space.

"We have our moments. They're closer with each other. I'm a bit of a black sheep." He chuckles to himself and I'm left wondering what it is he finds amusing about that fact. "What about you?" he inquires. "Any siblings?"

"Me?" I question, not continuing until he nods, leaning in like he's genuinely interested in what I'm about to say. "One sister."

"Older or younger?"

"Older."

"You fight a lot as kids or were you close?"

"I didn't know her when I was a kid." I shrug, taking another long drink of water.

"Parents divorced?"

"You ask a lot of questions." I eye him warily.

"Only way to get to know a person." He shrugs.

I think over that for a long moment before answering his initial question.

"My parents were never married. I never met my father; he left when I was a baby."

"Sorry to hear that."

"I'm not. Clearly he wasn't a very good guy to begin with." I shrug, twirling my straw around in my glass. "Anyway, he's my sister's father, too. Hence why we didn't grow up together."

I'm not sure why I'm divulging all this to him, but I can't seem to stop the words from pouring out of me.

"Did you grow up around here?" he continues his inquisition and I'm thankful not to have to linger on the conversation of the father I never knew.

"South Carolina."

"You're a far ways from home."

"That's kind of the point."

"Did you come to Chicago for any reason specifically?"

"It's not South Carolina," I quip.

"Fair enough." He chuckles, the sound deep and sexy. Exactly as I had pictured it would be. "I guess that's as good of a reason as any." He smiles, tilting his head as he stares back at me.

"Anyway, my sister lives here. Which I guess is the real reason I decided to move *here*."

"Do you still have family in South Carolina?" he asks.

"None that I claim."

"You always so talkative?" His eyes give away his humor.

"Are you?" I fire back.

He falls silent next to me, watching me so intently it's like he can see right through me. If he doesn't stop I might explode under his gaze.

"What are you doing tonight?" His question has my heart lodging somewhere in my throat.

I wish I could say that there is no way in a million years I would go anywhere with a complete stranger, but the truth is, it's all I've thought about since the moment he sat down next to me.

"You tell me?" I shrug, not even sure where the hell that came from. His smile spreads and it's all I can do not to let out an audible moan at the sight.

Oh my god, could this man get any sexier?

"Well, I can think of a lot of things, but maybe we could start with a drink?"

"Considering I'm not old enough to drink, that may cause a problem." I watch his brows draw up.

"How old are you?"

"Nineteen. How old are you?" I lean back in my stool, crossing my arms in front of my chest.

"Twenty-five," he answers quickly.

"Old man," I tease.

"Baby," he taunts back. "If you're not old enough to drink, why come to a bar?"

"Best water in town," I deadpan, reaching for my glass on the bar before taking a quick sip.

He tilts his head back and lets out a deep laugh.

"Water simply will not do," he says, his smile still firmly in place. Turning, he signals the bartender.

"What are you doing?" I ask curiously.

"Ordering you a drink."

"Did you miss the part where I'm not old enough to drink?"

"Since when does that stop anyone?" He winks, turning his attention to the approaching bartender. "Hey, Lucy. Can I get another beer and a..." He turns his attention to me. "What's your poison?"

"Um," I stutter, put on the spot. "A Sex on the Beach?" I phrase it like a question, saying the first drink that comes to mind. I've never actually had one but I know Claire loves them.

Truth be told, I'm not much of a drinker. Mainly because I'm not old enough, but also partly because anything that alters your mind scares me. Not the feeling per se, more the addiction aspect. I guess that's what happens when you grow up with an addict as a parent.

"Sex on the Beach." He flips his gaze to the bartender.

I hold my breath, waiting for her to ask for my I.D., but to my surprise she nods only once, her ponytail bobbing as she does, before she walks away.

"On a first name basis with the bartender, I see."

"She's an old friend."

"Uh huh." I nod slowly.

"So you like sweet cocktails?" he asks, turning to watch Lucy make our drinks.

"No idea. Never had one," I admit.

"You've never had a drink?" His eyes widen.

"I didn't say that. I've just never had a mixed drink before."

"Well *just* Finley, glad I could be your first," he says, his eyes on the bartender as she steps back in front of us and slides our drinks across the bar.

He waits until Lucy walks away before picking up his beer off the bar and swiveling back toward me.

I mirror his actions and do the same.

"So, what should we toast to?"

I think on that for a moment before I blurt the first thing that comes to mind. "To living."

"I like that." He lifts his beer. "To living." He taps the bottle against my glass before lifting it to his lips.

"To living," I repeat, fighting the swell of emotions that swarm me as I lift the glass and take a long gulp.

Chapter Two
Abel

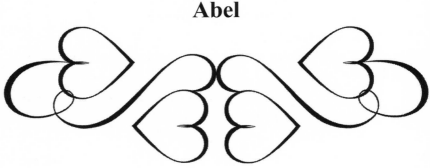

"So, how is it?"

"It's really quite good, actually." Finley smiles at the drink in her hand.

"Good, I'm glad you like it." I chuckle when she goes in for a second drink almost immediately.

I don't know what possessed me to come back into this bar, but there's something about this girl. Something that instantly intrigued me the moment we locked eyes earlier. Had it not been for my brothers I'd likely have sat down right then and there. It sure as hell would have been better than listening to them lecturing me about how I need to grow up and get a real job for the better part of an hour.

They've never understood my love of music. I'd rather play in a dirty bar for a couple hundred bucks a night than get a real job any day. At least then I'm doing what I love.

"So, tell me about yourself, *just* Finley." I tilt my beer bottle to my lips and take a long pull.

"Not much to tell." She shrugs, setting her drink on the bar.

"Now why don't I believe that? Pretty girl like you, sitting all alone in a bar in the middle of the week. There has to be a story there."

"No story. I'm about as uninteresting as they come." She smiles but it doesn't quite reach her eyes.

"I doubt that. Come on, tell me something."

"Like what?"

"I don't know, what do you like to do for fun? Where do you work? How do you take your coffee?"

"My coffee?" She cocks a brow, her green eyes giving off an almost glow under the dim bar lighting.

"You know, so I know what to order when I run out for coffees in the morning," I joke, the statement coming across more arrogant than I intend for it to. "I'm sorry. I didn't realize how bad that would sound until I said it out loud." I shake my head, laughing at myself.

To my relief, an amused smile slides across her lips. "Black, two sugars."

"Black, two sugars," I repeat.

"How do you take your coffee?"

"I don't drink coffee." I shake my head. "I'm more of an energy drink person."

"Those things are awful for you," she points out.

"Isn't everything?"

"Good point." She sighs, shaking her head in agreement.

"And for fun?"

"You mean what do I like to do for fun?" she clarifies, reaching for her glass.

I nod, watching her take a slow drink.

"Read." She draws slightly into herself before her eyes come back to mine. "Told you I was boring."

"Reading doesn't make you boring," I disagree. "What kinds of things do you like to read?"

"Everything." She smiles, and for the first time it seems genuine. "I love romance and suspense, paranormal and drama. Pretty much, if it has a good story line, I'll read it."

"Who's your favorite author?"

"God, that's too hard. I love so many."

"If you had to pick just one."

"If I *had* to pick only one it would be Tam Thompson. Her Confession Series is probably the best thing I've ever read."

"I've never heard of her."

"That doesn't surprise me. You don't strike me as much of a reader." She gives me a long once over.

"And why is that?"

"I don't know. You just don't seem like the type."

"I didn't realize there was a *type*."

"There's not, but if there were, you're not it." She gives me a pointed look.

"Okay, well you've got me there. I'm not much of a reader. Not to say that I don't enjoy reading, I just always have other things I'd rather be doing."

"Not me. I would read over just about anything. There's something so freeing about being able to live in another world. In another life."

"Have you always liked to read?" I ask, feeling like I could listen to her talk about books forever. From the way her eyes light up it's clear how much she loves it.

"Always. It's the one place where I can escape."

"Escape what?"

"Life." She shrugs. "I guess that makes me sound even more lame."

"Not at all. I get it. That's how I feel about music," I offer. "No matter what's going on or how shitty I feel, all I have to do is pick up my guitar, strum out a few chords, and it takes me to a whole other reality. Everything else kind of fades away and I lose myself in the lyric, in the picture I paint, in the story I tell. And for that brief moment, life doesn't seem quite so hard."

"You play music?"

"Have since I was little. It's always been an outlet for me. As I got older I decided it's what I wanted to do with my life. It's nothing fancy. Most nights I play for less than twenty people, half of which can't remember their own names by the time they leave, but that's not the point. The point is, I get to play. I get to do what I love for a living. I don't need fame and wealth. I just need a guitar and a stage. That's enough for me."

"So do you play around the city?"

"Yep. I've played about every bar there is to play in this city, most of them multiple times. I still get a rush every time I step up on a stage, too. No matter how many times I've played there before or how few people are actually there to hear me. Every time is like the first time."

"I wish I had that. That one thing I knew I was born to do. I've never really known what to do with my life. I feel like most of it I've spent wandering in the dark." I can tell the moment she says it that she wishes she could take it back. There's something so vulnerable about her admission and to say it to a complete stranger no less.

"There has to have been something. Something you dreamed about doing when you were younger?"

"Well, there was *one* thing. But it's silly."

"What is it?"

"It's nothing."

"Oh come on. I practically laid out my entire life story," I jokingly exaggerate.

She lets out a long sigh.

"When I was little I wanted to be a dancer. A ballerina to be more specific. I know, how completely unoriginal, right?" She rolls her eyes.

"There's nothing unoriginal about doing something you love. As long as you're doing it for you and for no other reason than it makes you happy. I mean, I'm a musician, come on. That's about as cliché as they come."

"Whatever." She shakes her head.

"So did you ever try it? Ballet I mean?"

"My mom couldn't afford the classes, not that it mattered much. I was never built to be a ballerina."

"Why do you say that?"

"Ballerinas are tall and slender and perfect. Not short and curvy with two left feet."

"I don't know; I'd pay good money to see you twirl around in a tutu." I grin, letting my eyes travel the length of her.

Finley is one of those rare beauties. The kind that seems to have no idea just how beautiful she is. The kind that steals the spotlight from every other woman in the room without realizing she's even doing it.

Dark hair. Intense green eyes. Full pouty lips. She's a show stopper on every level. I mean hell, she had me with only one look.

"Such a guy thing to say." She rolls her eyes.

"But still true." I chuckle. "So, what do you do? I mean, where do you work?"

"Here and there."

"Here and there?" I give her a curious look.

"I've dabbled in many things since coming to Chicago."

"Now I'm intrigued."

"Don't get too excited." She shakes her head, her shoulder length dark hair swaying as she does. "Waitressing. That kind of thing. Nothing glamorous, that's for sure."

"There's a lot to be said for someone who can waitress and not murder people."

"Gotta earn an honest living somehow."

"That you do." I tip back my beer.

"And since my dance career didn't pan out." She grins slyly.

"I don't know. Perhaps there's still hope for you yet." I set my beer on the bar. "Why don't you show me some of your moves?" I gesture to the empty dance floor a few feet from where we're sitting.

"Pretty sure I have no moves." She shakes her head.

"I bet you're better than you give yourself credit for."

"Or maybe you're giving me too much credit. You don't know me. When I say I have two left feet, I'm not joking."

Standing, I extend my hand to her.

"What are you doing?" She looks to my outstretched hand and then back up to my face, a slow pink hue creeping across her cheeks.

"Calling your bluff." I smile, tilting my head toward the dance floor.

"Oh no. There is no way I'm going out there with you." She shakes her head.

"Oh come on, live a little." Her eyes dart to mine, something passing over her features that I can't quite pin point.

She looks down at my hand again for a brief moment before taking it and allowing me to pull her to her feet and lead her away from the bar.

"I can't believe I let you talk me into this," she says once we reach the center of the small dance floor.

The pink returns to her cheeks when I drop my hand to her hip and wrap my other around her back, pulling her close. She has to look up to meet my gaze, standing a good six inches shorter than me.

"Hey, Lucy," I call over Finley's head toward the bar. "Turn up the music. And play me a slow one, would ya?"

"'Cause I'm not trying to work or anything," she hollers back, shaking her head at me. I flash her a smile and a wink, knowing she'll do it anyway, before looking back down at the beauty in my arms.

"I thought you were calling my bluff. Everyone can slow dance." Finley narrows her gaze at me and I have to fight the urge to laugh.

For someone who comes across so sweet, I'm learning very quickly this girl has no problem calling me on my shit.

"Not everyone." I grin, pulling her in closer until her body is resting flush against mine. The sweet smell of honey and vanilla invades my senses and I pause, breathing in the intoxicating scent.

The music kicks on moments later and I can't help but smile at the opening chords of Van Morrison's "Into the Mystic." I should have known Lucy would choose this song. She knows I'm a sucker for a good Van Morrison song.

Resting my face against the side of Finley's head, I begin to move, swaying much slower than the tempo of the song, which isn't very fast to begin with.

She melts into my embrace and allows me to lead, laughing when I step back, give her a little twirl, before pulling her back into my arms. I swear her laugh is the most incredible sound in the world.

I've never met someone like Finley. Someone, who after only a few short minutes of conversation, has me completely smitten. I don't know what it is about her. What it is that makes her so different from so many countless others. But I do know one thing – I sure as hell plan to find out.

Chapter Three
Finley

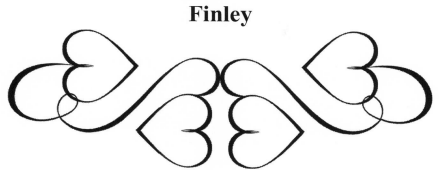

I let Abel move us along the dance floor. One song turns into two and before I know it, the third starts to play.

I'm completely out of my element. I've never danced this intimately with someone before, especially not a guy like Abel. A man, who in the span of thirty minutes has almost made me forget the heaviness of this day. *Almost.*

The thought is still there of course. The worry and anxiety. It's balled tightly in my chest and refuses to budge. But my mind is focused on him. On the way he smells, on the way he feels against me, on the way he keeps pressing his face into my hair and holding me like I'm the most precious thing in the world to him, even though we've only just met.

"For what it's worth," Abel pulls back slightly as the third song enters the chorus. "I think you're a very good dancer." He smiles down at me.

"Not sure walking around in slow circles is considered dancing, but I'll take it." I find myself smiling, and for the first time in a very long time feeling like I mean it.

I've forced so many smiles over my life, faked my way through so many things. It feels refreshing to feel like my actions meet what I'm feeling inside.

"Well, you didn't step on my feet, so there's that." He smirks.

"You're being easy on me. I'm starting to think you might genuinely be a nice guy."

"As opposed to what, not being a nice guy?" He smirks.

"An asshole pretending to be a nice guy," I tell him bluntly.

"Well, thank you. I think. You know, you might be the first girl that's ever called me a nice guy."

"Well, maybe that should tell you something about the girls you surround yourself with."

He thinks on that for a minute, a softness moving over his features. "You know, I think maybe you're right."

"I know I am."

"And what makes you so sure? You don't even know me." His words are playful.

"No, but if the girl that was hanging all over you earlier was any indication, pardon my bluntness, but you don't have the greatest taste in the female sex."

"And you said you weren't watching me," he teases.

"I wasn't. It's not my fault she made a spectacle of making sure she was noticed."

"For the record, she's not the kind of girl I like." He reaches out, tucking a strand of my hair behind my ear.

I suck in a sharp breath, my entire body feeling the effects of that one small, innocent gesture.

"Is that so?"

"It is."

"So what kind of girls do you like?" I ask, not sure I really want to know the answer.

"A girl who knows who she is."

"Does anyone really know who they are?" I argue.

"Some more than others." He grins. "Take you for example. While maybe a little unsure of yourself, you strike me as the kind of girl who knows exactly what you want."

"I'm glad you think so." I give him a disbelieving look, thinking he's got me pegged all wrong.

"A girl who knows exactly who she is and what she wants but, forgive me for saying, is maybe too afraid to reach out and take it when it's standing right in front of her."

"You act like you know so much about me when in truth, you couldn't be more wrong." I pause, trying not to lose my focus in the depths of his incredible eyes. "I haven't got a clue who I am. Let alone what I want. I'm just trying to stand on my own two feet and not get trampled on by the swarm of people moving around me."

"Tell me something then." He tips my chin up so I'm forced to meet his gaze. "If I know nothing about you then why do I feel like I've known you forever?"

"Maybe because you're delusional," I tease.

"Or maybe it's because I see you more clearly then you see yourself."

"You see me so clearly?" I challenge. "Then tell me what else you see."

He stares at me for a long moment, thinking it over.

"I see someone who doesn't realize her own beauty."

"Superficial." I shake my head. "Try again."

"Tough critic." He chuckles. "Okay, how about this… You had a rough childhood and carry a lot of resentment toward your parents, but you don't quite know how to compartmentalize your feelings." He pauses, reading my reaction. Something must tell him he's on the right track because he quickly continues, "Instead of dealing with your problems, you fled the first chance you got, hoping for a fresh start. You're incredibly smart, but not in a smug way. You care a lot. Sometimes too much, which has led to you being taken advantage of more times than you care to admit."

I stare back at him in stunned silence, wondering how the hell he got me so spot on.

"Am I close?" He grins, knowing based on my reaction that not only is he close, but he's got me pegged so clearly I'm not sure if I should be scared or amused.

"My turn." I avoid the question, needing to take the focus off of me.

"Do your worst." His smile widens.

"Spoiled rich kid. Youngest of five siblings. You want to prove you're different so you made yourself stand out, never following the obvious path. You have the love of a family who cares what happens to you, yet for some reason you resent them for it. You're desperate to prove you're more than they think you are, and even though you're happy being just who you are, they're acceptance weighs more heavily on you than you'd ever admit."

His smile falters. "Please tell me I'm not that transparent."

"Truthfully." I stop moving. "I took a wild guess."

"Pretty good for a fucking wild guess." He shakes his head, his smile sliding back into place. "What do you say we get out of here?" The abruptness of his question should surprise me but for whatever reason it doesn't.

"And do what?"

"I've got an idea. But you'll have to trust me."

"No offense, but I've only just met you."

"True. But in all fairness I've only just met you, and I'm willing to take the chance." His smile widens and that damn dimple makes an appearance. "What do you have to lose?"

I open my mouth to list all the reasons why leaving this bar with him is a bad idea, but then the reality of my situation hits me like a sledgehammer to the face and suddenly those reasons seem like nothing more than pointless excuses.

Cancer. Cancer. Cancer. The one word is so loud it's deafening and yet makes no sound at all.

"What do you say, *just* Finley? Wanna go have an adventure?"

"I guess that depends on what you mean by an *adventure.*"

"Let's see where the night takes us." He drops his hold on me and takes a full step back. "You in?" He extends his hand to me.

I think over his proposition for a long moment before realizing I really don't have anything to lose.

"I'm in," I concede, placing my hand in his.

Chapter Four
Finley

"It's cold out here." I cross my arms, rubbing my hands up and down the outside of my coat sleeves, trying to warm myself.

"Welcome to Chicago," Abel teases. "Given the time of year, I don't think the temperature is half bad."

"This isn't my first winter in Chicago," I tell him with a pointed look. "But it's still cold."

"This is nothing."

"Maybe for you, but for me this is freezing," I stutter, my teeth chattering slightly.

"That's the Carolinian in you. It'll take you a few years to adjust."

"Says the person who's lived here his whole life. How would you know how long it will take me to adjust?"

"I never said I grew up here." He looks down at me.

"Oh, I just assumed."

"I'm just messing with you. I grew up about fifteen minutes outside of the city."

"Such a brat," I mutter under my breath. "So are we almost there? I'm starting to regret our decision to walk."

"Taking a car would have been a waste of money. We're nearly there."

"And where exactly are we nearly there to?" I ask, still having no idea where he's taking us.

"You'll see." He grins at me before dropping an arm over my shoulder and pulling me to his side.

I try to pretend like the action has zero effect on me, when in reality it sends a whole other kind of chill straight through my body.

"Taking me to a dark alley so you can off me?" I bump my hip into his, trying to hide my reaction to him.

"*Off you*?" He laughs, the sound rumbling through him. "Pretty sure if all I wanted was to *off you* I would have done so five blocks ago."

"Maybe you just like watching me suffer," I quip.

"I hate to disappoint, but I'm not trying to off you. And," he pauses, his gaze sweeping in front of us. "In case you haven't noticed, we're hardly alone."

"I guess you've got me there," I say, looking around the busy walkway.

"Besides, we're here," he announces seconds later, pulling me to a stop directly across the street from the *House of Blues*.

"House of Blues?" I question.

"One of the best concert halls around. So many great bands have played here. It's one of my favorite places. You ever been?" He drops his arm from my shoulder and turns toward me.

"I haven't." I shake my head. "Who's playing tonight? Anyone I might know?"

"Guess that depends on what kind of music you like."

"Guess what kind of music I like," I challenge.

"Hmm." He taps his chin dramatically as he stares at me. "I'm going with Pop."

"Wrong." I shake my head.

"Country?" he guesses again.

"Nope."

"Rock?"

"You're getting warmer." I pull my bottom lip between my teeth to contain the ridiculous smile that threatens to take over my mouth at how freaking cute he looks right now. "Indie alternative is my favorite."

"Man, I was way off base." He shakes his head. "But it just so happens that tonight's headliner is one of the best Alternative bands around, at least in my opinion."

"Who is it?"

"Nothing but Ordinary."

"Shut up!" I practically squeal.

"I take it you approve?"

"Approve? Oh my god, I freaking love them!"

"Well then I guess I did good." He looks pleased with himself.

"Are we actually going to see them?" I ask, trying to contain my excitement.

"We are," he confirms. "I mean, if you want to that is."

"I want to," I answer too quickly.

"Then that's what we're doing."

"Wait, don't we need tickets? There's no way this show isn't sold out."

"Oh it is, but lucky for *you* we don't need tickets." He winks.

"We don't?" I ask, waiting for him to clarify.

"I still can't believe I was so far off on your music choices. I thought for sure you were a pop kind of girl."

"Well, in all fairness you'd be hard pressed to find a style of music I don't like."

"Jazz?" He arches a brow.

"Okay, I take that back." I giggle.

He stares at me for a long moment without saying a word, making me feel self-conscious.

"What?" I ask, feeling squeamish under his stare.

"You're adorable," he announces, sliding the back of his hand gently down the side of my cold cheek. "Come on, let's get you inside." He turns, sliding his hand into mine like we've held hands a hundred times before. I try to push past the swarm of butterflies that take over my stomach when his fingers squeeze around mine but it's impossible to ignore.

Pulling me alongside him, he quickly leads us across the valet lanes toward the entrance. Passing the line of people waiting to enter the venue, he approaches a middle aged security guard who's standing off to the side, monitoring the scanning of tickets as people make their way in.

"Abel." He smiles the moment he sees us. "It's been a spell." He abandons his post to reach out and shake Abel's hand. "How've you been?"

"Doing good." Abel releases his hand and takes a step back. "How about you? How's Caroline?"

"As crazy as ever." He chuckles to himself.

"And that's why you love her," Abel interjects.

"Lord help me, but it's true." The man's eyes slide to me. "And who do we have here?"

"Joe, this is Finley."

"Well hello there, Miss Finley." He gives me a toothy grin.

"Hello." I smile politely.

"You two better get inside. The show starts soon." His attention returns to Abel as he steps to the side and gestures for us to pass.

I give Abel a questioning look.

"Thanks, Joe. We'll see you later."

Abel pulls me past the security guard and inside the venue before leading me down a hallway that opens into the main concert hall. Several people have already begun to gather around the stage.

"Okay, so you're on a first name basis with the security guard and you didn't need tickets to get us into a sold out show. What are you not telling me?"

"Perks of knowing people." He winks, gesturing around the room. "So, what do you think?"

I look around the incredible space, taking in the gold accents and eclectic décor.

"It's awesome," I say, smiling as my eyes scan the room.

"It is, isn't it?" He steps around me and quickly helps me out of my coat before draping it over his forearm. "I'm gonna take our jackets to coat check. You want something to drink?"

"Sure." I nod.

"Anything in particular?"

"Surprise me." I shrug.

"You got it." He flashes me that incredible one dimpled smile before turning to walk away. I keep my gaze on his backside longer than is probably acceptable before forcing myself to look away.

Making my way closer to the stage, I turn and look behind me where two balconies wrap the back of the room.

I feel so completely out of my element, but in a weird way it's oddly comforting. It feels good, doing something simply because I want to and not overthinking the why or what happens next.

It's so different from how I've lived my life up to this point. I don't know if it's because I just found out I have cancer or Abel, but suddenly everything feels different. And weirdly enough, I'd bet on the latter. Because while yes, I know I'm sick, I think deep down I'm still in denial about the whole thing. It doesn't seem real. I mean, I feel fine. How can I be dying when I feel completely normal?

"Hey." I jump slightly when Abel appears next to me, a fruity looking cocktail in one hand and a beer in the other.

"Hey." I smile, taking the drink when he extends it to me. "Thank you." I hold the glass up to inspect the contents. "What is it?"

"Blue Hawaiian," he tells me, gesturing to the drink. "Thought you should expand your horizons."

"Did you now?" I smirk, pressing the straw between my lips before taking a long sip, humming the instant the sweetness hits my tongue.

"Good?"

"Delicious." I nod enthusiastically.

"Next you should try a Long Island. I bet you'd really like those."

"Are you trying to get me drunk?" I smart playfully.

"One can only hope." He laughs, the sound rumbling through his chest.

I ignore the way the sound makes my pulse quicken and take another drink.

"So, how did we get in here tonight, really?" I gesture around the space.

"I've played here a few times." He shrugs like it's no big deal.

"I thought you played dive bars."

"I never said I *only* played dive bars. You assumed. I said I've played every bar in the city. House of Blues is included in that. One of my brother's friends manages the place. Whenever there's a band that fits my genre he usually hooks me up and lets me open the show if there's space for me. Some bands have two opening acts. Others have one, and when they do, the club recruits local bands for the other spot. That's where I usually come in."

"That's really cool. So have you met a lot of famous musicians?"

"I've met my fair share." He presses the beer bottle to his lips and takes a drink.

"Are they all assholes?"

"On the contrary, actually. Most of them are pretty down to earth. Don't get me wrong, there's definitely a few not so great ones. But most are genuinely good people just doing what they love to do. Play music. You'll have to come the next time I open. I can get you backstage."

"I'd love that," I say, a wave of sadness washing over me knowing I'll probably never get the chance.

Why did I have to meet him now? When everything is so uncertain? Where was he a year ago? Or six months ago? I try not to let the emotion I feel seep to the surface but apparently it shows on my face just the same.

"You okay?" Abel asks, his brows furrowing.

"Yeah. Of course." I force a smile and lift the straw to my lips.

How easy it is to forget with him. How effortless. When he smiles at me it's like the rest of the world melts away. But that doesn't change the reality of my situation. If anything it makes it more real. Because it reminds me of what I'll never have.

It would be so easy to give into the panic and fear that's gripping my chest like a vice. It would be so easy to let myself fall apart. But what good would that do? At least being here with Abel I'm able to enjoy what little time I have left.

You could survive... the tiny voice in my head reminds me. And while yes, there is a thirty percent chance I will – and I want to believe in that thirty percent more than anything in the world – the fact still remains that there's a seventy percent chance I won't. I'm not a pessimistic person, but I am a realist. And realistically I know that this could very well be one of my last nights on Earth. And the last thing I want to do is spend it doing anything other than living.

Abel starts to say something but the words die on his lips when my cell phone buzzes to life in the small handbag draped over my shoulder. I immediately reach for it.

My heart picks up speed when I see my sister's name flash across the screen. I've avoided calling her all evening out of fear that she would know just by the sound of my voice that something is off.

Tomorrow. I will tell her everything tomorrow. But for tonight I want this. I want to live my life like a normal nineteen year old girl. I want to laugh and dance. I want to get lost in the eyes of the incredible man standing in front of me. Tonight, I want to forget.

"You gonna answer that?" Abel asks as I stare at the screen for several long moments.

"It's my sister," I say, silencing the ringer. "I'll call her later." I wait until my phone signals a missed call before sliding it back into my bag.

I look around, realizing that several more people are now standing around us. One minute the place was vacant and the next there were hundreds of people, all crammed together and somehow it wasn't something that even registered on my radar. Then again, not much has. Abel is too distracting, too consuming, to really focus on anything else.

"Looks like the show is about to start," Abel informs me, pointing to the stage right as the lights dim. Sure enough, within seconds the band filters out and there's an instant shift in the crowd as everyone surges toward the front. "You wanna move closer?"

"Not yet. I think I'd rather enjoy it back here for now," I say, feeling like I've got a pretty good view of the stage.

"Good choice. When you get up close it becomes harder to see, anyway. Especially for someone of your stature."

"My stature?" I grin.

"I just mean, you're not very tall. It can become hard to see when you have people taller than you standing directly in front of you."

"So you're calling me short?" I pretend to be offended even though I can tell he knows I'm just messing with him.

"Would you prefer vertically challenged?" He laughs when I narrow my gaze at him.

"I'm going to pretend you didn't just say that." I whip my hair over one shoulder and turn my gaze forward. "Who are these guys?" I ask, having not thought to ask who the opening act is.

"Naughty Water."

"Naughty Water?" I arch a brow in his direction, not able to fight the smile that slides across my lips.

"Is that funny?" He seems amused.

"Just reminds me of a movie."

"What movie?"

"You know, when the world slips you a Jeffery, stroke the furry wall."

"Get Him to the Greek." He smiles knowingly.

"Yep." I nod, impressed he knew exactly what I was talking about. "Just a little sip of naughty water," I say in my best Russell Brand voice.

"You're something else, you know that?" He raises his voice to be heard over the opening guitar riffs that bellow from the massive speakers surrounding the stage.

"I'm going to pretend you meant that as a compliment."

"Oh, I did." He keeps his eyes locked on mine long after the singer croons out the opening lines.

I should look away. I should be looking up at the stage like every single other person in this room is, but I can't. The air crackles and pops around us and for a brief moment it's like we're the only two people in the room.

Abel turns, sliding one arm around my waist before pulling me against his chest. Sliding my hair away from my face, he leans in and he presses his lips to my ear.

"I've never met anyone quite like you, *just* Finley," he says, the feeling of his breath on the side of my neck causing my skin to prickle. "Would you be freaked out if I told you how badly I want to kiss you right now?" He pulls back just enough to gauge my reaction, his gaze dropping to my mouth before moving back up to my eyes.

Every single hair on my body stands to attention and the swarm of butterflies that have been flapping inside my stomach since the moment he sat down next to me at the bar go spiraling in every direction, making me feel like I'm seconds away from taking flight.

Without really thinking, I reach up with my free hand and slide it around the back of his neck, pulling his face closer to mine.

It's completely out of character for me. I've always been the shy, backward girl. The one who felt like she was never good enough therefore always lacked the confidence to do, well, *anything*. But Abel makes me feel different. He looks at me and suddenly I'm not that scared little girl anymore. I feel powerful and beautiful. It's a feeling I've spent my whole life chasing.

His face dips and I hold my breath, waiting as each painfully slow second passes before his lips touch mine. And when they finally do, when I finally feel the softness of his mouth pressed to mine, nothing could have prepared me for the surge of energy that accompanies it.

My heart thrums violently in my chest. My hands tremble and my knees shake. Every emotion I thought I would feel I do. Only it's so much more intense than I anticipated it would be and I'm not quite sure how to process it.

When his tongue slides along my bottom lip before dipping inside my mouth, an entirely different feeling takes hold, tightening my core and warming me from the inside out.

Abel isn't just a good kisser. He's an incredible kisser. Hard but gentle. Sweet yet demanding. It's the perfect combination of push and pull and I swear I feel it *everywhere*.

I don't know if minutes pass or mere seconds. All I know is that when he pulls back and those incredible eyes meet mine, I'm a goner.

Chapter Five
Abel

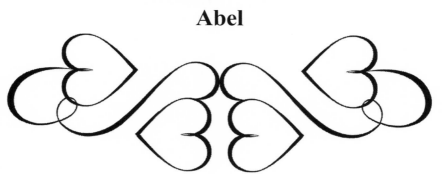

I can't take my eyes off of her. The band is on fire. The show is electric. Yet she's the only damn thing I can see. She's swaying and singing along to every song. When I'd told her who the headlining band was, and she said she liked them, I didn't realize just how much she liked them until they took the stage nearly an hour ago.

The way her eyes lit up and a smile spread across her lips when they started to play was enchanting. I couldn't stop looking at her then and I certainly can't stop now.

She's absolutely intoxicating. Even more so now that I know what she tastes like. What she feels like against me. How her body trembles under my touch. I could kiss her all night and never tire of it. I'd venture to say there are a lot of things I could do with this girl all night that I'd never tire of.

I can't help but think about how this night was supposed to go and this was nowhere even close. No, it's a million times better.

Had I not met Finley I would likely be at Heather's place, or Amber's, depending on what mood I found myself in. Neither would have made me feel even an ounce of what Finley has and I've barely scratched the surface with her.

She blinds me with a light I feel like I've spent my whole life searching for and have never been able to find. The physical attraction is undeniable but this runs far deeper than simply physical. It's like I've found a part of myself I didn't even know I was missing until tonight.

She senses me staring and turns her big green eyes on me, her smile only widening when she meets my gaze.

Fuck me.

I suck in a sharp breath, having to resist the urge to lean in and kiss her again. I want to, more than anything, but I also don't want to push her too hard, too fast.

I've always been a jump first, ask questions later type of guy, which has come back to bite me in the ass more times than I care to admit. And the thought of scaring her off and never seeing her again bothers me a hell of a lot more than it should've after only knowing her for a few short *hours*.

"Stop staring," she mouths, giving me a knowing look.

I lean in and run my nose along the curve of her neck. "I can't help it," I tell her, my lips stopping just shy of her ear.

Her body shudders under my touch and it damn near brings me to my knees.

What is this girl doing to me?

Chapter Six
Finley

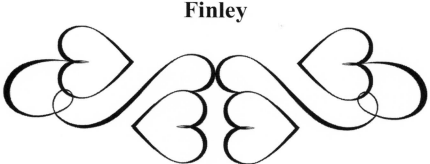

The way he looks at me makes me feel stripped bare. Like he can see every part of me with just one sweep of his eyes. It's unsettling and yet so refreshing – to feel like someone can see you for the first time. I mean, *really* see you.

It's like I've been invisible my entire life. Until now.

"So what's the verdict?" Abel pulls my back to his front, his forearm pressing across the top of my chest, as he lets a large group of people pass us.

The concert ended moments ago and while some people are still standing around talking, most have begun to make a mad dash for the door.

"They were incredible," I say, turning when he releases his hold on me. "Best first concert ever."

"This was your first concert?" He hits me with a surprised look.

"It was." *First and probably last*, the voice in my head reminds me, causing my stomach to twist.

I push the thought away. Tomorrow I can deal with what happens next. Tonight I want to live in this moment with Abel. A perfect moment. One I couldn't have dreamt up even if I'd tried.

"Well I wish I would have known that." He entwines his fingers with mine and pulls me alongside him as we head for the door.

"Wouldn't have changed anything, would it have?" I question.

"I guess not," he admits, lifting our joined hands to lay a light kiss to the back of mine.

My heart flips inside my chest.

We stop at coat check on our way out and Abel helps me into my jacket before sliding on his own. I swear, right when I think I've got him figured out he throws me another curve ball.

He screams player, with his sultry smile and bedroom eyes. But then he does the most unexpected and sweet things; like helping me into my coat, holding open the door for me, and kissing the back of my hand like we're part of some cheesy old movie where chivalry is still very much alive. And when he looks at me? My god, I can't even begin to process the way that makes me feel.

I could spend years trying to break it down and dissect it and even then I don't think I'd have an answer. I feel like I'm living in one of the many stories I've read, because men like Abel only exist in fiction. But he's here and he's real and I want to pinch myself to make sure this isn't some kind of wild and crazy dream.

"So *just* Finley." He waits until we step out into the cold night air before turning toward me.

"So," I breathe out, rocking back on my heels. "Where to next?"

"You mean you aren't sick of me yet?" he teases.

"Not quite." I crinkle my nose playfully. "Got any other surprises up your sleeve? I gotta say, it's gonna be hard to top this one." I gesture back toward the building we just exited.

"I might have a few ideas." He winks, pulling me toward the curb where a bright yellow taxi is sitting. "Your chariot awaits." He grins, pulling open the back door.

"When did you have time to call a cab?" I give him a questioning look as I climb into the backseat.

He slides in next to me and shuts the door and I'm thankful to not have to stand out in the cold any longer. Less than two minutes and already the tips of my fingers are numb.

"I did it while you were in the bathroom. Figured you'd rather not walk."

"Good call." I smile, snapping my seat belt in place right as he does the same. "Any chance that our next stop includes food?" I add when my stomach grumbles loudly.

Based on the humor that floods his face I'd wager he heard it too.

"Hungry, are we?"

"Starving, actually," I admit, realizing that other than the muffin I ate earlier, I've put nothing in my stomach other than water and three sugary cocktails.

"How does a burger sound?"

"Like heaven," I groan, my stomach grumbling again.

"I know a place on the other side of town that has the best burgers in Chicago."

"If you say Jefferson's I'm going to throw you out of this car," I warn. "My sister swears by that place but I can't justify paying twenty dollars for a freaking hamburger that's not even that good."

"Jefferson's is overrated, for sure," he agrees. "The place I'm talking about puts Jefferson's to shame."

He turns his attention to the driver, an older man with thinning hair and a small stud in his right earlobe. "Can you take us to 81st and Vine?"

"What's at 81st and Vine?" I ask, not knowing the city well enough to have any idea where that even is.

"You'll see." He winks.

"Do you do that a lot?" I shift toward him, knotting my hands together in my lap.

"Do what?"

"Make people wait, leave them trying to guess your next move?"

He lets out a light laugh, thinking it over for a moment.

"You know, I can't say that I do."

"So just me then?" I huff playfully.

"Just you." He leans over and squeezes my leg right above my knee, causing me to jump.

I swat at his hand, laughing.

"Lucky me." I stick my tongue out at him.

"No, lucky *me*." He snags my hand, looping his fingers through mine before relaxing back into the seat.

We spend the next ten minutes in silence. I keep my gaze out the window, watching the city pass through the tinted glass, but Abel's eyes stay on me. I don't have to look at him to know he's looking at me. I can feel his gaze like a hot branding iron against my skin.

"We're here," Abel announces when the driver pulls up to the curb outside of what looks like a run-down diner.

"We are?" I question, leaning forward to look out of his window.

"Trust me, it may not look like much, but Jack's has the best food in town."

"Guess I'll have to trust you." I unbuckle my seatbelt.

"Guess you will." He does the same, pushing open the back door seconds before sliding out.

Instead of using my own door, I scoot across the long bench seat and exit directly behind Abel, catching a whiff of his masculine scent as I do. It's a combination of cologne, laundry detergent, and something distinctly Abel. And it has quickly become my absolute favorite smell in the world.

After handing the driver some cash, Abel closes the door behind us and leads me to the run down establishment. There's a neon sign reading *Jack's Diner Open 24 Hours* across the top, but only half the lights are working so it looks more like *Jac iner pe 24 H us.*

A bell above the door sounds as we enter, announcing our arrival and I let my eyes scan the small restaurant. The room is long and narrow and kind of reminds me of the shot gun style house my friend, Sabrina, lived in when we were kids. There are five booths on one side of the restaurant and five on the other, all of which are lined in a straight row along the windows.

Other than a younger couple in one booth and an older gentleman sitting at the bar area, the restaurant is completely vacant, which doesn't surprise me considering it's close to midnight on a random Tuesday in the middle of January.

"Come on." Abel takes my hand and leads me to the booth in the far right hand corner, waiting until I take a seat before sliding in across from me.

I remove my coat and set it next to me, and when I look up at Abel I see he's done the same. I can't keep my eyes from sweeping across his broad shoulders before they finally make it back to his face.

"Okay, you've got me here. Now what?" I rub my hands together nervously under the table.

"Now, we eat." He smiles at me, reaching over to a small caddy next to the wall that houses the menus along with a few condiments. Sliding one of the plastic menus in front of me, I've only just looked down when our waitress approaches.

"Now there's a face I haven't seen in a while." I look up to see the middle aged woman's gaze locked on Abel, a wide smile on her tired looking face.

"Hi, Claudia." Abel returns her smile. "How have you been?"

"Oh you know." She shrugs. "Living the life." She gestures around the diner.

"I didn't expect you to be here so late," he tells her.

"Our third shift waitress called off."

"You left Jack at home all alone?" There's a hint of humor to his voice.

"Oh no, he's here, too. Our cook called off also."

"You really need to find more reliable staff. You know, you and Jack can't run a twenty-four hour diner all by yourselves. You need to make time for other things, like, I don't know, *sleep*."

"I'll sleep when I'm dead." She waves her hand dismissively. "So, how's that oldest brother of yours? Is he behaving himself in California?"

"You know Adam." He chuckles. "He's incapable of anything else."

If I had to guess, I'd say I pick up a slight hint of resentment in his voice but his expression shows nothing of the sort. He seems comfortable and happy, exchanging polite conversation with someone who clearly knows him and at least one of his brothers.

"Is he still working on that research project of his? I haven't talked to your mother in what feels like ages."

"As far as I know." Abel's gaze slides to mine, causing the woman to look at me for the first time since approaching our table.

"Oh, how rude of me. Hi love, I'm Claudia, Abel's aunt." She extends her hand to me and I take it, giving it a light shake.

"Finley," I reply, a little taken aback that Abel didn't mention this was a family introduction.

"Finley. Such a pretty name." Her eyes bounce back and forth between the two of us.

"I was telling Finley here how Jack has the best hamburgers in all of Chicago."

"Is it that they're the best or that they're free?" His aunt gives him a knowing look.

"If I say both will you make me pay?" he jokes.

"What do you think?" She crosses her arms in front of herself, giving him a pointed look.

"In that case, we will take two burgers and two fries." He grins up at her.

"And to drink?"

"Water for me," he says before both sets of eyes come to me.

"Water is good for me as well."

"Two waters, burgers, and fries. Coming right up." She quickly turns and walks away without another word.

"You didn't tell me your aunt works here. Does she own the place?" I take a guess based on the information I picked up from their conversation.

"She does. Well, Uncle Jack and her do."

"I don't think I've ever met an owner who actually works the floor," I say.

In my experience, the owners rarely leave the office and are usually the first to leave for the day, if they even show up at all.

"She and Uncle Jack work twelve hours a day, six to seven days a week. Sometimes more. They have for as long as I can remember. My mom used to say it's because they couldn't afford to hire that many people, but if you ask me, I think they love it that much. They were never able to have children so this place became their baby."

"I guess I get that." I stop talking when Claudia reappears with our waters.

"Anything else I can get you in the meantime?" she asks.

"I think we're good." Abel smiles up at his aunt who nods once before making her way back into the kitchen.

"She seems really nice."

"She's the best. On more than one occasion I wish I would have gotten her as a mother instead of her sister."

"That's an awful thing to say," I scold teasingly.

"Maybe so, but Claudia and Jack are like me. The black sheep of the family. While all her other siblings moved on to bigger and better things, Claudia always followed her heart and her heart was with Uncle Jack. They didn't need big houses or expensive cars. They just needed each other and to be doing what they loved. I've always envied them for that."

"Tell me about your parents," I prompt, thinking now is as good of a time as any to broach the subject and hopefully learn more about the man sitting across from me. A man who is still very much a stranger to me, even if I feel like I've known him my whole life.

"Not much to tell, honestly. Mom's an attorney. Dad's a surgeon. They're good people, a little judgmental but overall good hearted. They're the kind of parents that expect perfection, though, and perfect is something I've never been. Not by a long shot."

"I guess their definition of perfect and my definition are something that we look at differently," I say, the words off my lips before I can even think to take them back.

"Are you saying you think I'm perfect?" His smile slides into place causing his dimple to pop. My heart quickly picks up speed at the sight.

"Don't let it go to your head." I lean back in the booth, knotting my hands together on the table in front of me. "I'm just saying, I think they're lucky to have a son like you."

"If only. My brothers have made it pretty difficult in that department."

"Tell me about them."

"Well, Adam is in California. He's a doctor like our father. He's currently working on research that could change the face of medicine as we know it, or at least that's what our father says. Alex is an engineer and about as smart as they come. He's married with his first child on the way. Aaron went to NYU and now works for one of the top computer software firms in the country. And Andrew is in his last semester of law school. Because you know, at least one child had to follow in my mother's footsteps." He sighs. "And then there's me. I'm the only child that didn't go to college. The only one that doesn't have a *real* career. An all-around disappointment."

"Are those your parents' words or yours?" I can't help but ask.

"Trust me, they're not just mine. Attend one family dinner at my parents' house and it will become incredibly clear who the odd man out is."

"I guess being the odd man out isn't the worst thing in the world. Sure beats having no family at all."

"I don't mean to sound ungrateful. I know how lucky I am to have them. Sometimes it just gets to me. I wish they could be happy that I'm happy."

"Maybe they are." I shrug. "Maybe they're just really shitty at showing it."

"Maybe," he agrees on a light chuckle. "What about you? Tell me about your family."

"I kind of already did," I remind him.

"Not really. All I know is you have one sister who shares the same father as you. And that you never met him. What about your mom?"

"What about her?" I try to keep my emotions hidden beneath the surface but it's hard. I have a lot of mixed feelings when it comes to my mom.

"Tell me about her."

"I don't really know what I can tell you." I nibble on my bottom lip, afraid what he'll think of me if I tell him where I came from.

"Tell me the truth."

"Well, the truth is… Complicated." I pause, not sure how to word this so it won't make me sound like complete trash. "My mom's an addict. Heroine mostly. I spent half my life living on friends' couches and in the back of our car. The other half bouncing around from foster home to foster home. I couldn't wait for the day I could get the hell out of South Carolina and never look back. When Claire found me the timing couldn't have been more perfect. A week after my high school graduation I packed up what little I had to my name, which mainly consisted of as many books as I could fit into one duffel, and the bus ticket Claire sent me. I boarded a Greyhound and never looked back. I haven't seen or spoken to my mother in a year and a half. For all I know she's dead."

"Fuck, Finley. I'm so sorry." He reaches across the table and takes my hand. "I had no idea."

"How could you have?" I hate that when I meet his gaze I find pity there. Pity is the last thing I want him to feel when he looks at me. "Don't look at me like that."

"Like what?"

"Like I'm some sort of victim."

"I don't see you as a victim, Finley. I see you as a survivor."

Tears prick the backs of my eyes but I manage to push them down. I haven't shared my story with many people, but usually when I do it's always the same reaction. No one has ever acknowledged what I gained from growing up the way I did. No one except Abel.

"Thank you for saying that."

"I mean it." He runs his thumb along the back of my knuckles, the small, innocent gesture making me feel a hell of lot more than it probably should. "And what about your sister? Tell me about her."

"Claire. She's amazing. Truthfully, I don't know where I'd be without her. She grew up a lot differently than I did. Not in the sense of rich or poor, but more that her mom had her head on straight and always put Claire first. She didn't grow up with much, but she grew up with love. And if you ask me, that's all you really need. To know that while the world may not revolve around you, someone's world does. I spent years wishing I meant anything to anyone." I stop myself from saying more. "I'm sorry, I didn't mean to bring down the mood." I shake my head, having trouble meeting his gaze.

"Don't be sorry. It's part of who you are and I want to know everything I can about you."

"And why is that?"

"Because *just* Finley, you are the most intriguing person I think I've ever met."

"Not how I would describe myself but thanks, I think."

"I may have not known you for that long," he starts.

"Try like five hours." I glance up at the small clock hanging above the bar.

"Okay." He chuckles. "I may have only known you for five hours, but in that five hours I've learned one very important thing."

"And what's that?"

"I've never met someone like you before. You are unapologetically you and I envy that in a way I can't begin to explain."

"Five hours," I remind him.

"Five of the best hours of my life."

Our gazes lock and there's something behind those crisp blue eyes of his that tells me this night is far from over. Something that makes my stomach twist and my heart begin to race inside my chest. Something that makes me certain that, in this moment, we are both thinking the exact same thing but neither of us is willing to voice said thoughts.

"Two cheeseburgers and two fries." We both jump, Abel dropping my hand when Claudia seems to appear out of nowhere, setting a plate in front of each of us. "Anything else I can get you right now?"

Recovering first, I answer, "No, this is perfect. Thank you."

"You two enjoy." She smiles before spinning around and walking away.

"Are you ready?"

"Ready for what?" I ask, the heaviness of our conversation evaporating in an instant when I see the playful expression he's wearing.

"Ready for the best burger of your life of course." He picks up his sandwich before gesturing for me to do the same.

"I should warn you, I'm very picky about my burgers," I tease.

"Just eat." He laughs before he tears off a huge chunk of his sandwich in one big bite.

"Okay," I draw out playfully, picking up my own sandwich before lifting it to my lips. I get one whiff of the delicious smelling burger before I'm sinking my teeth into it.

And damn it if he isn't right. The moment it hits my tongue I'm confident that it's the best thing I've tasted in a very long time, maybe ever.

My eyes dip to his mouth and I can't help but think, *okay, maybe the second best.*

Chapter Seven
Abel

"I'm so full I could burst." Finley relaxes back into the booth, her hands sliding across her slender belly. "Why did you make me eat so much?" she playfully whines.

"Pretty sure the milkshakes were your idea," I remind her.

"Well how could I resist after you raved about how fantastic they were for five minutes solid. Besides, I didn't want to seem rude when Jack offered me one."

My uncle seemed nearly as taken with Finley as I am when he came out halfway through our meal to say hello. Claudia, no doubt, was back in the kitchen giving him all the details the second she saw us walk in. It's not often that I bring anyone here, especially not a girl. This has always been my safe space and as such I try to keep it separate from other aspects of my life. It's the one place I can come when the rest of the world feels like it's falling apart. It's been that way since I was a kid.

"I think that might be a slight over exaggeration," I respond on a grin. "And it wouldn't have been rude to decline. But they lived up to the hype, did they not?"

"Oh my god, and so much more." She groans and I feel myself twitch under the strict confines of my jeans.

This girl is driving me mad and she doesn't even know it. More than once I wanted to pull her into the bathroom at the

House of Blues and have my way with her. I've had the same thought several times as I've sat across from her in this booth as well. How could I not?

But Finley isn't a bathroom sex kind of girl. She's the real thing. The kind of woman that you take home and pray like hell she's still there when you wake up in the morning so you don't have to say goodbye. Finley is the forever type.

Even thinking it sounds crazy. I've known her only a few short hours and already I'm planning our future. I can't help it. When she looks at me I feel at home in a way I've never felt with another person before.

Sure, I've had a couple relationships that I thought could go the distance, but none that ever felt this right, or this intense for that matter. It's like there's an invisible force pushing us together and we're powerless to stop it.

Finley lifts her hand to her mouth to stifle a yawn. "Sorry." She shakes her head. "I just got really tired all of a sudden. I think I'm going into a food coma."

"Jack's burgers will do that to you. If you want I can order a car and we can get you home. It's getting pretty late."

"Are you trying to get rid of me?" She cocks a brow and relief floods through me.

The last thing I want to do is take her home, but I also don't want to selfishly keep her out if she's ready to call it a night.

"Not a chance. Just testing out this whole gentleman thing." I give her a cocky smile. "How am I doing?"

"Eh, you could use a little work. But good on you for trying." She giggles, her shoulders moving up and down as she does.

"In all seriousness, though," I start.

But she cuts me off before I can continue, "I don't want to go home."

"Okay." I try to fight the smile that threatens to spill across my lips but fail miserably. If she didn't already know that I'm completely enamored with her, there's no way she's not picking it up now.

"Okay," she repeats.

"So then where should we go?"

"I thought you were the one with all the great ideas." She crosses her arms in front of her chest.

I think on that for a moment, deciding I know the perfect place. "I may have a place in mind."

"Then what are we waiting for?" she asks, snagging her coat off of the seat before quickly sliding out of the booth. "You coming or what?" she asks when I still haven't moved from my spot.

"Are you in a rush?" I look up at her with amusement on my face.

"Time isn't a guarantee. No need to waste what little we get." Something passes over her face, something that doesn't sit right with me, but before I have time to process it, it's gone, replaced by an easy smile. "You coming or what?"

I chuckle, grabbing my coat as I slide out of the booth.

"So, do I get to know where we're going this time?" she asks, following me out of the diner after we've said our goodbyes to my aunt and uncle.

"Nope."

"But we're walking?" she guesses, looking around.

"It's not far. I promise." I reach out and take her hand, sliding my fingers through hers with such ease you'd think I'd done it a million times before.

I've never been much of a hand holder. Hell, I've never really been one for any kind of PDA that didn't end up with me sneaking off somewhere for a quickie. But it feels different with Finley. I want to touch her as much as I can, anyway I can.

"So, you've lived here your whole life?" Finley inquires after a couple minutes of silence passes between us.

"Born and raised." I nod.

"I bet you were super popular in high school." She looks up at me and I swear my knees fucking wobble.

What the hell is wrong with me tonight?

"I guess you could say that."

"Let me guess." She taps a gloved finger on her chin, pretending to mull it over in her head. "Captain of the football team, prom king, and if I had to place a wager, my bet would be you dated the head cheerleader who walked around school in your letterman jacket."

"In my letterman jacket?" I bark out a laugh. "What era are you living in?"

"What? Those aren't a thing?" She looks amusingly confused.

"Not around here they aren't." I shake my head, not able to brush the smile from my lips.

"Okay, nix the jacket. How did I do with everything else?"

"Well, I didn't play football."

"Really?" She seems surprised. "I thought for sure I had that one pegged."

"I was more of a basketball guy."

"Were you the captain of the basketball team?"

"I don't know that there was a captain. We were just a team. But yes, I'd say I was as close to a captain as you can get."

"Close enough." She nudges me with her shoulder. "Prom king?"

"Homecoming."

"Of course you were." She sighs. "And your high school girlfriend?"

"Which one?"

"I had a suspicion you were a bit of a player but I was trying to be nice."

"I wasn't a player. I just wanted to explore my options."

"Which is kind of what a player is, is it not?"

"Okay, fine. Maybe I had a bit of a reputation. But I'm not that guy anymore," I add, knowing she can probably see right through me.

"Sure you aren't." She smiles.

"I've just been waiting for the right woman to come along."

"Is that so?"

"Maybe I've been waiting for you." The instant the statement leaves my mouth she bursts into a fit of laughter, her breath fogging the cold air around us.

"Please tell me how many women you've gotten to fall for that line."

"I wouldn't know, I've never used it," I tell her truthfully.

"Well put it in your back pocket because that one is definitely a keeper."

"No, I think that's a once in a lifetime line."

"And he keeps going," she says to herself, still laughing.

"You know, laughing at a guy who's trying to tell you he's into you is really kind of tough on the ego."

"You're into me, are you?" She looks down at her feet as she walks.

"I think I've made that pretty apparent, have I not?"

"I suppose." She gives me a shy smile, and once again I'm left trying to get a handle on this girl.

She's reserved and yet clearly adventurous. Outgoing and yet sweetly shy. She's hesitant to say certain things but then has no problem calling me out the very next minute. She's soft but strong. Open but definitely has a guard up. She's like the perfect fucking contradiction in every single way possible.

"So, what about you?" I ask when she falls silent next to me, clearly mulling over my words.

"What about me?" she questions, meeting my gaze.

"What were you like in high school?"

"I'm sure you had kids at your school that always ate alone, walked through the halls with their heads down, and were basically invisible to everyone?"

She waits until I nod before continuing.

"Well, that was me."

"I have a hard time believing that. I mean, look at you. There's no way you didn't have guys tripping over their feet to talk to you."

"Try going to school wearing old, tattered clothes and having everyone know you're the daughter of one of the town druggies. Trust me, the only guys interested in me were the ones that assumed I was easy like my mother."

"That sucks. I'm sorry." I let out a slow breath, not able to envision the picture she paints even a little bit.

"Don't be. It is what it is."

"So you didn't have any boyfriends?" I ask curiously.

"One. Dean. We met senior year when we ended up in the same foster home. He came from a similar background as mine and we bonded over that fact."

"So what happened?" I ask when she stops talking.

"We dated a couple months. I thought I had finally found someone real in a world hidden beneath masks. But alas, his mask was just a better fit."

"That bad, huh?" I ask based on the way her forehead furrows.

"Try, he took my virginity and then a week later I caught him with his penis in another girl's mouth. Turns out he had been seeing us both for weeks. Thankfully, I was back home with my mom by that time, so it was easy to cut ties, but it still…" she pauses. "It stung."

"I can imagine it did."

"It was good that it happened when it did. I learned a very valuable lesson."

"But did he?"

"Did he what?" She seems confused by my question.

"Did he learn his lesson?"

"Why? Are you prepared to go to South Carolina and defend my honor?" she jokes.

"Maybe. I'm sure as shit tempted."

"Well I appreciate that but in all fairness Dean did me a huge favor. Because of him I knew that the only way out was to leave."

"Are you telling me I should be thanking him then?"

"Not sure I'd go that far." She laughs lightly.

"So then there's no one else?"

"Nope. After Dean my sole focus became escaping, not finding a reason to stay."

"And you haven't dated anyone since coming to Chicago?"

"I went out on one date with a guy my sister works with. He was nice enough but there was no chemistry."

"That's it?"

"Not a very impressive dating history, is it?" She smirks.

"I don't know. I think I kind of like it." I shrug. "You don't find that very often in this day and age."

"Find what exactly?"

"People who haven't slept around," I answer truthfully.

"Says the man who admitted to being a player."

"Refer to my previous statement – you don't find people like you very often."

"I'm going to take that as a compliment."

"Good, because it was meant as one."

"So does that mean you won't be inviting me to come home with you later?" She smiles mischievously, narrowing her eyes at me.

"Now I didn't say that." I shake my head, not missing the nervous way she drags her bottom lip between her teeth. "But in the meantime." I stop walking and abruptly pull her against me.

It's only seconds before my lips are pressed to hers. She hums against me, reaching up to wrap her arms around the back of my neck.

I deepen the kiss, not able to suppress the low groan that escapes my throat at the taste of her. Her hands dive into my hair and she pulls me closer, tugging desperately at the unruly strands.

It takes every ounce of will power I have not to back her into a dark alleyway and have my way with her. That's how crazy she drives me. I can't remember a time when I've ever wanted someone as much as I want her. My body literally aches for her.

And when she pulls back, her breathing labored, her cheeks bright pink from the cold, an entirely different part of me aches for her. A part I'm not sure should be aching for her given the short amount of time we've spent together.

But it's there all the same, so prominent I don't think I could deny it even if I tried.

Chapter Eight
Finley

Abel's kiss is electric, surging heat through my half frozen limbs and warming me from the inside out. I don't ever want to stop kissing him.

I've never met someone like Abel. Someone who makes me feel like the world revolves around me rather than the sun. Someone who makes me feel more than I am.

"We should get going." He pulls back, his hooded gaze locked on mine. "It's freezing out here."

"I thought you said this wasn't cold," I remind him, once again taking his hand as he begins leading us back down the sidewalk.

"I take it back, it's cold as hell."

"Why do people say that?"

"Say what?" I feel his eyes on the side of my face but I keep my gaze forward.

"Cold as hell. Hell isn't cold. In fact, last time I checked it's an eternal pit of fire. So why do people always say cold as hell?"

"You know, I have no idea. I hadn't really thought about it before."

"I mean, I guess hell could be cold. How would we actually know?"

"That's true, too." He grins, amused by my rambling.

"Do you believe in Heaven and Hell?" I ask.

"Yes and no."

"Explain."

"I don't know. I mean, isn't that what we're raised to believe?" He pauses. "Do you believe in Heaven and Hell?"

"I don't know." I shrug. "I thought I did. Now I'm not really sure of anything."

"This conversation really took a turn." He laughs.

"I suppose it did," I agree, not really sure why I brought it up in the first place. "So how much further? I'm pretty sure I can no longer feel my toes." I look down at my feet.

"It's right there." He points across the street at the tall, brick building directly in front of us, pulling to a stop when we reach a cross walk. He looks both ways and then tugs my hand, not waiting for the walk sign before pulling me across the street.

"Um, you realize jay walking is a crime, right?"

"Sometimes you just gotta live a little." He flashes me a quick smile before turning his attention forward.

"Where are we?"

"My apartment building," he tells me, stopping at the front door to punch in a code before pushing his way inside, pulling me in behind him.

"Your apartment?" I choke out, a nervous knot forming in my throat.

Truth be told, there's honestly no other place I'd rather be, but that certainly doesn't mean the thought of being alone with Abel in his apartment doesn't terrify me. Because it does.

"Relax, we're not going to my actual apartment." He pulls me down a short hallway to a set of elevators. "At least not yet," he adds, throwing me a wink as he hits the up arrow on the control panel.

"Then why are we here?" I ask, ignoring the last part of his statement.

"You'll see." He guides me into the elevator the instant the doors slide open.

"There you go again." I cross my arms in front of myself as I lean against the back wall of the elevator car.

Abel hits a button labeled RT before we start to climb.

"What's RT?" I ask when he slides up next to me.

"Rooftop."

"We're going on the roof?" I look at him like he has five heads. "Are you forgetting that the goal was to get out of the cold?"

"Relax, it's enclosed."

"What?"

"The rooftop terrace is enclosed. And heated," he quickly adds.

"You have a heated, rooftop terrace? I didn't know such a thing existed."

"There's only a couple buildings in the city that have them. It's one of the main reasons I chose this one. It's nice to be outside without actually being outside. Especially when it's as cold as it is tonight."

"So explain to me how a struggling musician affords to live in a place like this?"

"I never said I was struggling. You assumed." He grins. "I actually do pretty well for myself."

"Sorry," I mumble, feeling slightly embarrassed.

"Don't be. Most people assume I can afford to live here because of my parents, which isn't entirely untrue. My parents set up savings accounts for all of us when we were younger, something to help get us started when we ventured out on our own. That money has definitely helped."

"It's nice that you have parents that care enough to do something like that."

"Yeah, I guess. I just wish it didn't come with so many strings."

The elevator doors slide open and Abel exits onto the terrace, leaving me to follow after him. I immediately scan our surroundings, a bit taken aback by how nice it is up here.

I was expecting to walk out onto an actual rooftop. Instead it's like being on the top floor only the walls and ceiling are all made of glass. There are several comfortable looking outdoor couches and chairs spread throughout the large area. And a few small tables with chairs are lined against the outer walls. Strand lights sweep across the ceiling above us, giving off a soft glow that illuminates the space perfectly.

"This is amazing," I say, more to myself than to Abel.

"Isn't it?" He looks around the space. "In the evenings there are usually quite a few people up here."

"I can see why. I think I'd live up here if I could."

"There's an outdoor space too, so when it's warm you can sit outside." He draws my attention to the door directly in front of us. I look beyond the glass walls to what looks like an oversized balcony that wraps the entire enclosed area.

I don't even notice the view right away, although you would think that would have been the first thing I noticed. We're up high enough that you can see nearly half the city stretched out in front of us.

"Wow," I say under my breath, crossing the space.

"Pretty amazing, huh?" I jump slightly when I feel Abel settle in behind me, his arms wrapping around my middle before his chin settles on my shoulder.

"I've never seen the city from this high up."

"Really?"

"Really," I confirm. "I don't get out much. Work. Home. Repeat."

"That's a shame. It's such a beautiful city and there's so much to see and do."

Sadness fills my chest and I blink slowly, trying to digest the emotion. So much to see, so much to experience, so many things I thought I'd have all the time in the world to do...

When I look at Abel it's so easy to forget, but forgetting doesn't change the truth. I'll still wake up tomorrow morning with cancer. I'll wake up not knowing if tomorrow will be my last day. I'll wake up not knowing if I'll ever see Abel again.

The thought has me turning in his arms. I look up at him – at his messy hair and brilliant blue eyes that remind me so much of the color of the ocean waves that I grew up looking at. I commit every inch of his face to my memory. The cut of his jaw. The dip in his cheek where his dimple peeks through when he smiles. His full lips and the tiny dent in his chin. I soak every inch of him in, my mind taking mental snap shots as my eyes trace his face.

I reach up and slide my hands down his scruffy cheeks, loving the way the hair tickles my palms.

I feel like I've spent my entire life looking for this. For someone like Abel. Someone who makes me feel... Alive.

And I can't help but wonder, what if. What if I wasn't sick? What if what I feel for this man is something I could explore beyond tonight? What if...

Our gazes lock and I suck in a sharp breath, fairly certain that my heart is going to pound out of my chest at any moment.

"Tell me what you're thinking about at this exact moment," I murmur, my hands falling from his face as I continue to stare up at him.

"I'm thinking you're the most beautiful thing I've ever seen." His tongue darts out, sliding along his lower lip in a way that makes me desperate to feel his mouth on mine.

I swallow hard, having to resist the urge to press up on my toes and kiss him. It would be so easy, so effortless, and yet for reasons I'm not sure I fully understand, something stops me from doing it.

Maybe it's because deep down I know that if I start I may never stop and there's still so much I want to know. So many questions I want to ask.

Stepping out of his embrace, I head in the direction of a small two person sofa with a wicker table in front of it. Sliding my coat off, I drape it across the back of the couch before taking a seat, my eyes locked on Abel as he tosses his coat onto the table and takes the spot next to me.

"So this is where you live?" I gesture around the space.

"Well, not up here." He smiles. "But in this building, yes. My apartment is just one floor down."

"That's convenient."

"Yeah, it's nice that I don't have to wait for the elevator if I wanna come up here." He shifts so that he's angled toward me. "What about you? Where do you live?"

"I'm not telling you that. What if you decide to start stalking me?" I tease.

"I can't promise that I won't. However, I don't think you'd mind it too much if I did."

"You're very sure of yourself."

"Some things a man just knows." He grins.

"Is that so?"

"It is." He nods, clearly still waiting for me to answer the question.

"I live over off of Birch."

"That's all I get? That's a pretty residential area. Apartment or house?"

"Apartment."

"Big building or small?"

I shrug, choosing not to answer.

"Come on, you gotta give me more than that."

"Nope, that's all you get." I can't help but smile at the playful frown that slides across his mouth.

"Fine. Don't tell me. I think you'll find I'm a very resourceful person when I need to be. Just wait until I show up on your doorstep. Then you can see for yourself."

"How do you know I'd even want you to show up on my doorstep?" I narrow my gaze at him, sucking my lower lip into my mouth to keep myself from grinning.

"Same way I know that when I do this—" he reaches out and gently slides his fingers down my cheek "—that you'll do that." His gaze goes to my mouth and only then do I realize my lips have parted.

He smiles knowingly and lets his hand fall.

"You're really, really sure of yourself."

"So you've said, a few times actually." He smirks.

"Well, it's true."

"Maybe. Or maybe I just know that there's no way I'm the only one that feels this." He gestures between the two of us.

"Maybe you aren't." I look down to where my hands are knotted in my lap. "So, you got me up here, now what?" I lift my gaze and look around the vacant space.

"I didn't really have a plan. Just figured most places would be closing soon."

"So why bring me here and not to your apartment?"

"Truth?"

"Always."

"I was worried it might freak you out if I suggested it."

"What vibes have I given you tonight that would make you think that?" I arch a brow.

I'm not sure where this Finley has come from, but I got to say I like her. I can't remember a time where I've ever been so upfront with someone, let alone a guy. Maybe it's my situation or maybe it's Abel and how he makes me feel. Whatever it is, it has me wanting to reach out and take exactly what I want. No hesitation. No second guessing.

"Do you want to come to my apartment?"

I think on his question for a long moment, every fiber of my being wanting to scream *yes!*

"Maybe in a little while," I tell him, giving him a sly smile. "First I want to know more about you."

"I feel like I've told you everything there is to know."

"I highly doubt that. I barely know anything about you."

"Okay, then." He looks at me for a long moment. "What is it that you want to know?"

"Tell me about those," I say, pointing to his left arm that is covered in various splatters of ink. "I've always wanted a tattoo but never had the courage to get one."

"I love them. They're therapeutic in a way. My parents despise them." He lifts his arm and looks at it.

"Well, I love them. Though I do have a question."

"What's that?"

"Do you only have them on this arm?" I reach out and gently touch his forearm.

"Yep." He nods.

"Is there a reason for that?"

"Not really." He shrugs. "It started with one." He lifts his arm and points to a shaded guitar that extends the length of his forearm along the back. "After that I had the itch and decided to get another." He lifts his sleeve and runs his hand along the brilliant red, yellow, and orange phoenix on his bicep. "I've always liked the look of a sleeve, the way the pieces all fit together in a perfectly jumbled puzzle, so as I continued to get more I decided to stick with this arm."

"What's that say?" I point to the tattoo directly below it where words are etched in beautiful cursive.

"Dream as if you'll live forever. Live as if you'll die tomorrow." My eyes trace the tattoo long after he's read the quote.

What are the odds that he, of all people, would have a tattoo that can describe exactly what I'm doing here with him?

Dreaming that I'll live forever. That I'll get a million more days with him. Living as if I'll die tomorrow. Because, let's face it, I very well may, and as such I don't want to walk away from this night with one single regret.

After a moment of silence, I muster up the strength to speak. "I like that."

"It's kind of the motto I've always tried to live by. It's easy to forget that our days are not limitless. We tend to act like death has a snooze button and we can prolong it until we're ready to pull the covers away. I don't want to wake up one day and realize that everything has passed me by. I want to enjoy each moment as it comes."

"Because you never know which moment will be your last," I say, more to myself than to him.

"Exactly. That's why I refuse to be pushed into the life that my parents want for me. It's not about what they want. It's about what I want. It's about being able to wake up in the morning and look at myself in the mirror and be happy with the person looking back at me."

"I get that."

"Anyway, that's what it means." He steers us back toward the tattoo.

"And what about this one?" I point to another tattoo, this one a strand of musical notes that wraps around his wrist.

"This is the guitar notes for the chorus of 'Somebody Somewhere' by..."

"Halobridge," I answer before he can finish. "I love that song."

"And so the world keeps spinning. Minute after minute. Hour after hour. Day after day. And yet I stand, stuck in place." He quotes the lyrics.

"Waiting for you," I finish the line, our gazes locking.

Something passes between us. I don't know what it is or how to even begin to explain it. It's a feeling – something that rockets deep into my core. And I know with complete certainty that he feels it to. In fact, I've never been more certain of anything in my life.

"Where did you come from, *just* Finley." A trace of a smile forms on his lips.

"I already told you." I'm barely able to get the words out, the way he's looking at me stunting my ability to speak.

"Because I'm starting to feel like I'm dreaming," he continues, not acknowledging that I spoke.

"Do you want me to pinch you?" I offer, my body moving on its own accord as I press up onto one knee and throw the other over his legs, finding myself straddling his lap moments later.

His hands settle on my hips and he looks up at me in a way I can only describe as pure, carnal need. I know because I imagine I'm wearing a similar expression.

Abel does something to me. And not only to my heart or my mind, but to my body as well. I have been fighting the overwhelming need I feel to be close to him all night and suddenly it feels like the restraints that were keeping me away have snapped free and there's nothing stopping me from taking exactly what I want.

"Or." I lean forward, pausing just shy of his lips. "Perhaps I could do something else." I press a soft kiss to his mouth.

One hand slides into my hair and holds me in place when I move to back away.

"Don't," he breathes, his voice strained.

"Don't what?" I whisper

"Don't stop." He grinds upward. The feel of his hard length pressing into me sends shockwaves of want and need shooting through my body.

"Okay." I resist the urge to moan when his other hand grips my shoulder and he presses me harder against him.

Dropping my mouth back down to his, it's only seconds before the kiss morphs into something else. Something so intense my entire body feels the effects.

I grip his hair and hang on for dear life as his hands explore my body; my face, my back, my stomach, skirting along my skin like he's desperate to feel every inch of it beneath his fingertips.

I grind against him shamelessly, my body filled with a deep ache that is hindering my ability to think or see anything beyond Abel.

I don't care that I barely know this man. I don't care that I have no idea what will happen after tonight. I don't care about one single thing but this. Him. His touch, his breath hot on my neck, his hands warm on my skin. I only see him. I only feel him. I only want him.

Abel is life. And tonight I plan to live life to the absolute fullest.

Chapter Nine
Finley

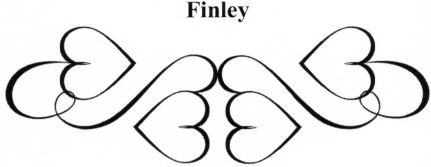

Think about the best dream you've ever had. One where you get absolutely everything you want and life, even in that short period of time, feels perfect. Now multiply that feeling by a hundred and you might have a small idea of how I feel in this moment.

Abel moves above me with skilled perfection, taking my body to new heights with each thrust of his hips. I'm lost to the sensation. To the feeling. To the pleasure that courses through me.

It's as if he's known my body forever…studied it for hours on end and knows exactly what it needs. I am his guitar and he knows exactly how to move along the chords to make me play in perfect key.

We're ravenous for each other. Biting and clawing, crying out in the sweetest kind of agony a person can experience. Over and over again we climb. Over and over again we fall. It's like playing your favorite song on repeat. No matter how many times you hear it, you can't wait for it to start again.

Abel is my new favorite song. The track I will play on repeat in my memories for the rest of the time I have left on this earth and maybe even after.

"Well, if you're goal was to get me in your bed. I guess you could say you succeeded." I snuggle into Abel's chest, loving the way it vibrates with his laughter.

"If memory serves, you were the one who asked me to bring you here," he reminds me, his hand trailing softly up my spine causing my skin to prickle.

"For the record, Dean Presley has nothing on you." I smile when his chest vibrates beneath my cheek again.

"Take that, Dean Presley." He wags his fist in the air playfully.

Silence once again envelops us but there's nothing awkward about it. In fact, it's maybe the most comfortable silence I've ever experienced.

After a few minutes, Abel shifts and I look up to see he's looking down at me. "I'm starving. Are you hungry?" he asks.

I glance at the clock on his bedside table, realizing it's already after three in the morning.

"I could eat," I admit, food being the furthest thing from my mind until he mentioned it. I guess you could say we worked up quite the appetite, despite the fact that three hours ago I was stuffed beyond belief.

"Come on. I'm sure I've got something edible in the kitchen." He sits up, taking me with him.

"I'm going to run to the bathroom. I'll meet you in there in a minute," I tell him, wrapping the sheet around myself before rolling out of the bed.

I pad across the hardwood floor to the large en suite bathroom, flipping on the light before closing the door behind me.

The first thing I do is look in the mirror. I laugh when I catch sight of myself. Tangled, wild hair, bright pink cheeks, and swollen lips. I look exactly how I pictured I would. The thought makes me smile wider.

I reach up and trace my fingers along my bottom lip, the feeling of Abel's mouth on mine burned so deeply into my memory I don't think there's a way I could ever forget it, and I don't want too either.

Tonight has been the best night of my life. In every single way imaginable but one. The lingering thought of what I know comes next is right there, pounding through my mind.

I look away from my reflection, not willing to let myself go there right now. My time with Abel is quickly running out and I don't want to waste a single second of what little we have left worrying over something I can't change or even control.

When I reenter the master bedroom a couple of minutes later, Abel isn't there. The large king sized bed is a scattered mess of pillows, blankets, and sheets. I shake my head, my gaze going to the bedside table where everything but the lamp has been knocked to the floor. I stifle a laugh, remembering the moment when it all went tumbling down.

I hear cabinets opening and closing in the distance and for a brief moment I close my eyes and imagine a world where this is my life. Where hearing something as simple as Abel rustling around in the kitchen makes me feel like I'm floating on a cloud.

Shaking away the thought, I force my eyes open, eventually making my way around the room to gather my clothing that's strewn across the floor. I quickly dress and try to finger brush the tangles out of my hair as I exit the bedroom and head down the hallway into the main living space.

I didn't really get a chance to see Abel's apartment when we came in, as we were a little too preoccupied for him to give me the tour, so I take the opportunity to look around as I head toward the kitchen.

The space is sparse but modernly decorated. While it's definitely masculine in design, I wouldn't call it a bachelor pad. It's much too *grown up* for that term. Dark woods, black leather furniture, and gray accents fill the living room. Floor to ceiling windows line the exterior wall, giving off a beautiful view of the city lights through the sheer curtains that hang in front of them.

I turn toward the kitchen/dining area which sits along the far interior wall and is open to the rest of the room.

The kitchen is gorgeous, far surpassing the one in the apartment I share with my sister. Where ours is more of a shotgun kitchen with run down appliances and peeling tile, Abel's kitchen looks like something from a design magazine. Open concept, dark wood cabinets, gray quartz countertops, stainless steel appliances, and the same dark hardwood floors that run through the rest of the apartment.

When I spot Abel's bare back as he pulls contents from the refrigerator, the rest of the room fades into the background and my eyes lock in on him.

Even though we've spent the last couple of hours in his bed, leaving my body deliciously sore, I still have the overwhelming urge to walk right up to him and ask him to take me again. That's what this man does to me. He makes me feel wild and untamed.

"Hey." He turns, smiling when he catches sight of me leaning against the far side of the kitchen counter. "Hey," I return, eyeing the pack of bacon in his hand.

"How do you feel about bacon?" He quirks an eyebrow, holding up the package of meat.

"Is that even a question?"

"I had suspicions you were the perfect woman but now I know, you really are too good to be true." He drops the bacon onto the counter before leaning down to retrieve a frying pan from one of the lower cabinets.

"I'm the perfect woman because I like bacon?" I laugh.

"Among many other things." He flashes me a knowing look before turning his attention back to the stove as he places the pan on one of the burners.

"So, we're just going to eat an entire pack of bacon and call it a day?" I ask, sliding up next to him.

"Well I was going to make pancakes but I have no batter."

"Do you have flour?"

"Yeah, I think so."

"What about milk and eggs?"

"Yep."

"Then I can make pancakes. Just point me in the direction of where I can find the flour."

"And she cooks." He gives me an impressed look. "Flour is in the pantry." He points to a floor to ceiling cabinet in the corner.

"Yeah, that was kind of a necessity growing up in my house. Otherwise I would have starved to death," I tell him, crossing the room before opening the pantry.

I locate the dry ingredients I need and turn, placing them onto the counter next to me.

"I'm sorry," Abel says, causing my eyes to slide to him.

"Don't be." I shrug. "There are perks to growing up the way I did. For starters, you learn how to make one hell of a pancake," I joke to lighten the suddenly heavy shift in the mood.

"Well I guess there's that." He gives me a soft smile.

"Trust me, you'll be happy I did too once you taste these bad boys. Now, where can I find a mixing bowl?"

"There." He points to the top cabinet directly in front of me.

We spend the next several minutes in easy conversation as we move around the kitchen. Him preparing the eggs and bacon while I work on my epic pancakes, minus the cinnamon and nutmeg I normally add because he didn't have any.

The process of cooking together feels oddly right. Like it's something we've done together a million times before and I take comfort in the feeling. It's not something I've experienced many times in my life – a sense of belonging – and I'm not sure I could have felt it with anyone but the man currently standing feet from me, sliding bacon onto two plates as he hums quietly to himself.

Instead of eating at the table, once our plates are made we decide to curl up on the couch. Abel puts the television on Kids Baking Championship, which immediately makes me giggle.

"What?" He throws me a questioning look as he drops the remote on the couch between us, his plate balanced on his knee.

"Kids Baking Championship?" I question, not pegging him for a Food Network kind of guy.

"Don't look at me like that. These little dudes can bake like you wouldn't believe."

"I've seen the show. I'm just surprised it's something you watch."

"I don't know, I like this channel." He grins, sitting back before shoving an entire piece of bacon into his mouth.

"Okay." I bite back a laugh and mirror his actions, relaxing back into the couch cushions before sliding some eggs onto my fork.

It takes Abel less than five minutes to clear his entire plate – almost all of which he spends moaning over how incredible my pancakes are – which I already knew. When he gets up to take his plate to the kitchen I've barely made a dent in the mountain of food he put on *my* plate.

Feeling like I can't possibly eat it all, I lean forward and set the plate on the ottoman, figuring I'll pick at it in a little while after some of my food has had a chance to settle.

Spying a guitar leaning in a stand against the far wall, I push off the couch and walk toward it, running my hand along the sleek black head of it the instant I reach it.

"That's my very first *real* guitar." I jump at the nearness of Abel's voice. Seconds later he steps up next to me. "My mom bought me a small one when I was younger, but it was cheaply made and didn't last long, so I don't count that one. It was enough to get me started, though." He pulls the guitar out of the stand and looks it over. "This was my thirteenth birthday present. Back when my parents still thought my interest in playing was just a phase. I'd say if they knew I would spend my life chasing music they probably never would have bought this for me."

"Will you play something for me?" I ask, watching him slide the strap over his shoulder and across his bare chest.

"Sure." He turns, heading back toward the couch. I follow him, reclaiming my seat moments later.

He takes a seat in the matching chair that's caddy corner from me, resting the weight of the guitar in his lap. Strumming across the strings, he fiddles with the tuning pegs for a few seconds until it produces the sound he wants.

"Any requests?" He readjusts the guitar and looks up at me.

"Something you wrote." I pull my legs up and hug my knees to my chest.

"Let me see." He strums out a couple of chords. "I know," he announces before his fingers start to move effortlessly along the strings.

It doesn't take me long to figure out he's an extremely talented player. It seems so effortless and natural that I can't help but think that he was spot on when he said he was born to play music.

When his incredible voice fills the space, goose bumps erupt across my skin. His tone is deep and smooth with the perfect hint of rasp. I swear the sound penetrates so deeply inside of me I can feel it vibrating against my bones.

He sings of being lost, of not knowing his place, of fearing he'll forever roam the earth without finding where he belongs. The words cut straight through me, mirroring a lot of how I've always felt. Lost. Alone. Not sure where I fit. It's unsettling and yet oddly comforting at the same time. To feel like we really are kindred spirits, even though our lives are nothing alike.

He grew up with everything. I grew up with nothing. He was popular and liked. I was poor and invisible. He could have any girl he wanted. I was lucky if a guy looked at me with anything other than pity or disgust in his eyes. We come from two separate worlds – polar opposites in every sense of the word, yet when you break it down we are like a mirror image of each other. And in this moment I've never felt more connected to another person in my entire life.

It's like we were put on this earth to find each other. To complete each other. To give each other a place to belong. Unfortunately our timing a cruel twist of fate – finding what you've always been looking for when you know you can't keep it.

No matter how much I pretend. No matter how much I try to ignore it, it's there. The knowledge that when this night ends, I will have to say goodbye to Abel Collins… and when I do it will be goodbye forever.

Chapter Ten
Finley

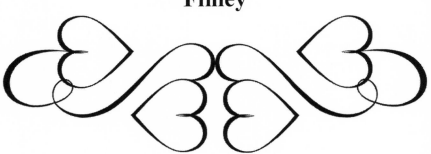

"What's this from?" I trail my fingers across a jagged scar that runs along the front of Abel's shin. We're sitting opposite each other on the couch; his legs stretched out next to me and mine next to him as we both sit propped up against the arm rests facing each other.

"Skiing accident when I was ten." His eyes go to his leg before coming back up to my face.

"Ouch. What happened?"

"My family all loves to ski. Me, not so much. Normally whenever we'd go to the slopes I'd go tubing or hiking. I'm shit on skis." He chuckles to himself. "But on this particular day, Adam was being overly obnoxious, teasing me relentlessly about being the only one in the family who couldn't ski. So, in true brotherly fashion, I set out to prove him wrong. Only problem, wanting to prove him wrong and actually being able to are two very different things. Of course, that thought never crossed my mind until I was already on the hill, by which point it was too late."

"Oh no." I cover my mouth with my hand and try not to laugh.

"I don't even know what happened. One minute I was on my feet, the next I was tumbling down the hill. By the time I reached the bottom, I had a dislocated shoulder, two cracked ribs, and had one healthy gash in my leg." He gestures to the scar.

"How awful."

"Yeah, it was bad. On the plus side, when my parents found out that the reason I was on that hill to begin with was because of Adam, they grounded him for a month. So I guess in the end I came out victorious."

"Not sure I would call that victorious." I shake my head. "Have you suffered any other injuries I should know about?"

"Well, let's see." He taps his chin dramatically. "There was the time when my buddy Chris and I went cliff diving and I got a pretty gnarly gash taken out of my foot." He holds up his left leg to show me the scar that runs the length of the side of his foot.

"Dear god."

"Ended up with quite a few stitches over that one." He drops his leg back down. "Oh, and this one." He lifts up his right arm and points to another scar along his triceps. This one is a straight white line I'd say is no more than three inches in length. "This one I got jumping off a roof into a swimming pool. Snagged my arm on the edge of the ladder as I hit the water."

"Wait, how close to the edge of the pool were you to hit your arm on the ladder."

"Too close," he admits. "Let's just say I never did it again."

"I don't understand why you did it the first time."

"I was a stupid kid." He shrugs.

"Does that mean your days of jumping off cliffs and houses are behind you?"

"Most definitely." A wide smile graces his face, his dimple on full display. I swear my heart leaps in my chest at the sight.

He's gorgeous.

There's no other way to describe it. He's the very definition of good looking, but when that dimple pops out he becomes even more irresistible.

I swallow hard, my throat suddenly dry.

"What about you? Surely you made your fair share of bad choices while growing up."

"I didn't, actually." I reach for the bottle of water on the floor next to the couch, twisting the cap off and taking a long drink before turning my attention back to Abel. "I mean, I made bad choices, but none that ever put me in physical harm."

"Broken bones?"

"None."

"Stitches?"

"Never."

"Wow." He seems genuinely impressed by my lack of injuries.

"I mean, don't get me wrong, I've hurt myself plenty. I've stubbed my poor baby toe so many times it's a wonder the thing hasn't broken off yet." I wiggle the toes on my right foot, which seems to be the foot I'm always kicking things with.

"Poor baby toe." He wraps his hand around the back of my ankle and lifts my foot up, inspecting my toes. Then he does something completely unexpected. He leans forward and kisses my little toe. "There. All better." He smiles, his eyes meeting mine as he lowers my foot back down.

"It's not hurt right now," I tell him, trying to fight the smile that's playing on my lips.

"For next time then." He winks and I swear my insides do a complete one-eighty before everything seems to settle back into place. "So, nothing else?"

"Nope. I was a very careful child. You kind of had to be in the neighborhoods I grew up in. Besides, kind of hard to get hurt when you spend nearly all of your time hidden in your bedroom with your face in a book."

"But didn't you ever want to go out and let loose? Do something completely crazy?"

"Of course I did."

"Then why didn't you?"

"Because I was scared, I guess." I shrug.

"What's the most exciting thing you've ever done?"

"Honestly, this." I gesture between us. "I know it may not seem like much to someone like you, but I've never even come close to doing something like this. It's been quite the adventure."

"Well it's not over yet." He gives me a devilish smile before he shifts his weight forward.

The next thing I know he's on his knees, hovering above me. His fingers latch into the waistband of my leggings as he shimmies them downward, tossing them over the back of the couch the moment they're off.

I watch his eyes darken and his nostrils flare as he slides a hand between my legs, his fingers grazing the thin fabric of my panties. I suck in a sharp inhale, trying to suppress the moan that threatens to spill from my throat.

Another gentle pass over the slinky material before his fingers slide around the midsection of my underwear. He tugs, hard, and I hear the material give way.

I look up just in time to see the tattered remains of my favorite panties dangling from his fingertips. He gives me a wicked smile before pressing them to his face and inhaling deeply.

It's the most erotic thing I've ever seen and while it's not something I thought I'd ever enjoy, I can't deny that watching him do it only makes me crave him that much more.

Letting the torn fabric slip from his fingers, he grabs my arm and gives me a gentle tug forward, managing to get my sweater off in one quick sweep.

"So beautiful," he murmurs as his eyes slide across my bare chest before coming back up to my face. "Come with me." He stands, pulling me to my feet.

I resist the urge to cover my naked body as I allow him to lead me across the living room. I've never been naked in front of anyone like this – out in the open with nothing to hide behind. It's oddly freeing and yet at the same time tremendously unnerving. But like most things tonight, I'm going with it. I'm allowing myself to live outside of my comfort zone for the first time, and maybe the last.

Abel stops in front of the wall of windows and releases my hand. He turns, tucking my hair over my shoulder before his fingers come up to cup my cheek.

"Do you trust me?" He guides my face upward.

"I think so." I give him a questioning look, nervous energy pinging around in my chest like a pin ball machine.

He smiles, leaning forward to lay a soft kiss to my lips before he guides me around so that I'm facing the windows. "Don't move," he mutters against my neck before stepping away.

I watch as he crosses to one side of the windows. In one quick tug, half of the curtains slide open. I instinctively move to cover myself but Abel stops me with one word. "Don't."

I slowly lower my hands back down, my heart beating so violently it feels like it might burst out of my chest at any moment.

Abel crosses to the other side of the window and repeats the process, sliding the other half of the curtains open in one quick pull.

I try to keep my breathing even as he stalks back toward me, his eyes grazing my naked body as he does. He steps around me seconds before his hands slide across my stomach, his hardness pressed to my backside.

"Walk," he orders, guiding me forward until I'm a mere inch from the glass that looks out over the city. "See that building right there?" He points to a building that stands a few floors below his, directly across the street.

I nod.

"That is another apartment building. Now, I'm willing to bet that at any moment someone might look up out of their window or off their balcony and see you, standing here naked." His hot breath on the side of my neck intensifies the deepening ache in my lower belly. "Does that make your heart race?" He nips at my earlobe with his teeth.

"Yes." My voice breaks around the word.

"Does it make you alive with excitement and yet sick with fear?"

"Yes," I croak.

"Good," he hisses, pressing me flat against the window. I jump at the coolness of the glass against my hard nipples. "Because I'm going to fuck you right here." He shifts behind me, followed by the rustle of material. "Right here, against this glass where anyone can look up and see you," he continues.

I hear the tear of a condom wrapper and within seconds, Abel is pressed firmly behind me, his hard length grinding against my backside.

"Life's too short not to feel the rush of living." He kisses his way up one side of my neck. "And you, Finley, you put me on an adrenaline high like I've never felt before." He grips my hips with both of his hands and angles my body so that my butt is sticking out slightly while my upper half is still pressed to the glass.

His hard erection is at my entrance seconds before he thrusts inside. I cry out from the sudden rush of pleasure that floods through me, my palms flattening against the glass as he rears back and slams into me again.

"Keep your eyes open and out the window," he commands through clenched teeth as he establishes a punishing rhythm behind me.

I keep my forehead pressed to the glass, forcing my eyes open. The ground beneath me seems to move, as if the earth is turning on its axis at rapid speed, sending me whirling in every direction.

I clench my hands before flattening them again, the pure pleasure of feeling Abel inside of me combined with the height and exposure of being pressed to the window has my body teetering wildly out of control.   Nothing and no one has ever made me feel the way Abel does. It's like he understands exactly what I need. Things that I want that I'd never be brave enough to vocalize.

But it's not just my body he's taking to new heights. It's my heart, too. Second by second I feel it grow stronger. Like a sound that starts off as a low hum and gradually grows until it's so loud it's deafening.

And as my body trembles and explodes around his touch, I know *it* to the very depths of my soul. I *am* in love with Abel Collins. Madly, deeply, unexpectedly, head over heels. And I know that there isn't one thing I could have done to stop it.

It was inevitable. I knew it from the moment he sat down next to me. The way he looked at me. The way he smiled. Hell, maybe I fell in love with him right then and there.

I look out over the sleeping city below, my body sated, my heart full, and I can't help but think to myself, this must be what people mean when they say they've found their other half. Because with Abel, for the first time in my entire life, I feel whole.

Chapter Eleven
Abel

I'm so exhausted I can barely keep my eyes open but I don't want to close them either. I want to stay here, in this moment, with Finley, and never leave.

"Can I see you tomorrow?" I speak into her hair, the darkness of the room shadowing her face from view.

"It *is* tomorrow," she reminds me, snuggling deeper into my embrace.

"You know what I mean." I kiss the top of her head.

"And if I were to say yes, what would we do?" she asks, trailing slow circles across my abdomen with the tip of her finger.

"Well, for starters we'd get naked." I smile when she laughs. "Then I think a nice dinner would be in order. And afterward, you can come to the Trolley House with me. I'm playing there tomorrow night. Plus, I know the bartender so maybe I can get you hooked up with some of those sugary cocktails you seemed to like so much."

"Another night of debauchery and breaking the law," she teases.

"Rules are meant to be broken, right?"

"But laws are not. You break laws and you end up in jail."

"You're nineteen. I highly doubt someone's gonna haul you to jail for having a drink a couple years before you're technically allowed to."

"Says the man who's old enough to drink, so he doesn't have to worry about it."

"Actually, since I'm the one supplying the beverages, I'm pretty sure I'm the one that gets in trouble if you get caught. So really, it's me taking all the risk."

"My hero," she jokes.

"Drinks or no drinks, I don't care. As long as you're there with me. What do you say?"

"Can I let you know?" Something changes in her voice and a small sliver of panic seeps into my chest.

What if I read this all wrong? What if she has no desire to see me again after tonight? What if this was just a one-time thing for her, the way I'd intended it to be for me when the evening started. What if I never see her again?

The thought of this being all I get is damn near crippling. And that in itself is enough to send another surge of panic straight to my core. The thought of never seeing her again shouldn't bear so much weight, yet it feels like it bears the weight of the world.

"Sure," I answer, sliding my hand up her arm.

"Abel," she whispers against my chest after a couple of silent moments pass between us.

"Yeah?"

"Do you believe in fate?"

"I don't know, I guess. I don't believe that everything that happens is planned out, necessarily, but I do believe the choices we make ultimately guide us to where we're meant to be."

"Explain."

"Take us meeting for example. I spent three hours leading up to meeting my brothers thinking of every excuse in the book to call them and cancel. But then something stopped me from doing it. Had I not gone, I never would have met you."

"Abel." Her voice is softer now, to the point that I have to strain to hear her.

"Yeah?"

"I'm going to fall asleep now." I feel her smile against my chest.

I chuckle, tightening my grip on her.

"Goodnight, *just* Finley." I drop a kiss into her hair.

It's not long before her breathing slows and evens and her body relaxes fully into mine.

I never imagined when this day started that this is where it would end. I woke up dreading that I was meeting my brothers, knowing that I would likely be enduring another round of "don't you think it's about time you grow up and actually do something with your life" speech. Don't get me wrong, I love my family, but this song and dance of theirs grew old a long time ago.

When I offered to get the next round, I did so to give myself a moment of reprieve, not having any idea that in doing so I would be changing the entire course of the night. Maybe even my life.

I close my eyes and remember how she looked sitting at the bar. How in one glance I knew she was the most beautiful woman I had ever seen.

When I decided to go back inside after the guys had left I had no idea what would happen. I thought maybe we'd hit it off, grab a drink, forget about life for a while. And while we did all those things, it was so much more than I could have ever anticipated. Because I wasn't just hanging out with some girl. I was hanging out with *the* girl.

Maybe that sounds crazy. Hell, even thinking it makes me feel mildly mental, but it doesn't change how I feel. It doesn't change that lying here, with Finley in my arms, is about as close to perfect as I think I've ever felt.

Exhaustion starts to seep in and my mind starts to doze. I try to keep my eyes open, to force myself to stay awake, but I can't seem to get them to cooperate.

As I begin to fade, Finley's eyes flash through my mind before sleep finally takes me under.

Chapter Twelve
Finley

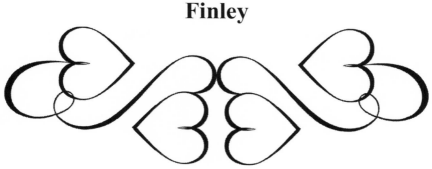

I lay on my side facing Abel, watching the moonlight glitter across his handsome face as it peeks in through the blinds. I can't tear my eyes away, no matter how desperate they are to close.

I pretended to be asleep for the better part of a half an hour before Abel finally dozed off next to me roughly an hour ago. Despite how exhausted I felt, and still feel, I didn't want to lose a single moment of what little time I had left to exist with him.

Last night was the best night of my life. A life I'm not quite ready to let go of yet.

Ten hours, that's how much time had passed from the moment he sat down next to me at the bar until the moment he drifted to sleep with me in his arms.

Ten hours...

Such a small piece of time and yet it feels like those ten hours changed everything. My life went from something I wandered through to something I felt like I was finally living.

I've spent my entire life looking for this type of feeling, this type of connection to another person. I never thought it would happen so fast. That a mere attraction would morph into something as strong as love. But it did.

It sounds insane. Hell, everything about last night and this morning has been insane. But that doesn't make how I feel any less true. It is true. I feel it in every cell and vessel in my body – so strongly that it's a wonder my heart doesn't implode from the weight of it all.

Sadness and dread pool in my stomach.

I've always felt like something was missing in my life. That if I just kept going, kept fighting, eventually I would find the meaning for all of it. And now, now that I feel like I'm finally where I'm meant to be, I can't stay. I can't reach out and take the life I've always wanted because that life is no longer in the cards for me.

I try to picture how Abel will react when he wakes up and finds me gone.

We didn't exchange phone numbers. He doesn't know where I work or where I live. Hell, he doesn't even know my last name. It will be like he spent the night with a ghost, because once I leave that's all I will be to him. A ghost. Some girl he spent one crazy night with.

I hope it meant as much to him as it did to me. I hope he thinks about me often, and when he does that amazing smile of his slides across his face. I may not be alive to see it, but I hope I impacted his life even a fraction of how much he's impacted mine.

I reach out and trail my hand lightly down the side of his face, closing my eyes as the scruff on his cheek tickles my palm. Tears prick the back of my eyelids and before long they are rolling down my face.

I'm on the verge of falling apart as everything I've pushed down over the last few hours comes boiling to the surface, made worse by what I know I have to do next. I have to say goodbye.

I can hate that I'm sick, hate the cancer that threatens to take my life before it's even really begun, but I can't hate what it brought me to.

If I wasn't sick, if dying wasn't something I was facing, I may have never had the courage to explore this with Abel. I wouldn't have been in that bar, and even if I had been, I never would have been brave enough to leave with him. Dying has a way of putting things into perspective and because of this; because I thought there was no possibility of tomorrow, it allowed me to be myself in a way I don't think I've ever been with another person.

I blink rapidly, trying to clear my vision. If I focus on the positive, on what this night gave me, then maybe I can do this. Maybe I can say goodbye and be filled with happiness over what I got to have versus the sadness of what I'm losing.

But this is so much harder than I had anticipated. I knew this night would end. I knew I'd have to say goodbye. I just didn't realize how impossible it would feel when the moment finally arrived.

Letting my hand fall away, I gently push back the covers and roll to the side, carefully sliding out from underneath his arm. The second my feet hit the cool hardwood all I want to do is crawl back into bed with Abel and never leave. The urge is so strong that I have to physically force myself toward the door, collecting my clothing on the way out.

I turn for a brief moment, soaking him in one last time. The curve of his back. The messy way his hair falls against the pillow. The slight part of his lips as he breathes. My heart physically aches at the thought of never seeing him again.

But why can't I?

It's a question I hadn't asked myself until this very moment. Why can't I see him again?

Being sick doesn't mean certain death. There's still a chance I can fight this. Still a chance I can survive. And isn't *this* worth it? Isn't *he* worth it? Yesterday I was ready to lie down and accept my fate. But today... Today is a new day.

It really is a testament to how much can change in the course of only a few hours. Take my surgery for instance. The few hours the procedure will take will determine whether I live or die. So many hours pass by with little to no meaning. And yet others are life altering.

I will see him again.

It's a promise I make to myself. A silent promise I make to him. One day. Maybe a year from now, maybe five, I will find him again. When the cancer is gone. When my life is mine again and doesn't belong to a faceless disease. I have to. This can't be the end.

But right as I allow the thought to settle, doubt finds its way back in. *But what if this* is *the end?* What if this really is the last time I ever lay eyes on Abel Collins?

I blink away the new batch of tears welling behind my eyes and take a deep breath. Letting it out slowly, I take one last long look at the first, and quite possibly the only, man I will ever love. And then I turn and walk away.

I dress in the hallway before making my way out into the living space. I let my eyes travel around the apartment, trying to remember everything down to the smallest detail. Not that I could forget a single thing about this night even if I tried.

Sliding on my boots, I grab my coat off the back of the couch before heading toward the door. I pause with my hand on the knob, my knees trembling beneath my weight.

I can't do this.

It's the only thought I have. I can't walk out of his life like I was never here. I can't leave without any explanation. I can't let him believe that last night was anything short of magical.

Dropping my hand from the knob, I turn, heading into the kitchen. I rummage through a few drawers before finally locating a pad of paper and a pen. Dropping the tablet of paper onto the counter, I turn to the first blank page and scribble his name across the top.

I stare at the one word for what feels like hours, my eyes tracing over his name as I try to figure out what to say. The truth isn't an option. I don't want him to think of me as the sick girl he spent one night with before she died. If tomorrow turns out to be my last day, I want him to remember me like this; healthy, happy, full of life. I want him to remember who I was last night, not who I am this morning.

Taking a deep breath in, I press the pen back to the paper. My hand slides across the page as I say everything I need to say in the span of one simple sentence.

Thank you for the best night of my life.
XO
Finley

I read over the single line, wishing I could say more, wishing that I was better with words, wishing I could find a way to explain to him exactly what last night did for me. Knowing I can't, I slide the tablet of paper to the end of the counter so I know he'll see it as soon as he walks into the kitchen.

With one backward glance, I say goodbye to the future I'll never have. I say goodbye to Abel and all the things we could have been if I wasn't sick. And I say goodbye to a piece of myself. The part I'm leaving behind just for him.

Chapter Thirteen
Finley

"It's about time you got home." Claire looks up from the kitchen table as soon as I enter our apartment. "You never stay out. I spent half the night fearing someone had kidnapped you."

"I texted you," I remind her, hanging my jacket on the coat rack next to the door before sliding off my boots.

"You never mentioned staying out until the morning." She purses her lips, accenting how full and plump they are.

Claire is a knock out. Tall, athletic build. Long blonde hair with a slight wave. Stark green eyes. We look nothing alike, other than our eyes, the one feature we both seem to have gotten from our father.

I look just like my mom from when she was younger, before she became all strung out and started losing her hair and teeth. And I know first-hand how much Claire looks like her mom, Cathy. I've only met her once. She lives in Southern Illinois, a few hours from here. Claire usually goes down a few times a year to visit. She took me with her once, not long after I moved in with her. The second I walked in the door I was taken aback by how much they look alike. It was like looking at an older version of my sister.

But for all our differences, every now and again I see the similarities. Like how we both hold a pencil and how she is the only other person I've ever met who likes cheese on her peanut butter and jelly sandwiches.

"I told you not to wait up," I respond after a long pause.

"Not the same thing and you know it." She swirls her spoon in her cereal bowl before shoveling a bite into her mouth.

"What are you, my mom now?" I wrinkle my nose and stick my tongue out as I slide past her into the kitchen.

"I'm your big sister. That makes me responsible for you."

"You're only six years older than me, Claire, not twenty. And I don't need you to be responsible for me. I can take care of myself."

"Where were you, anyway?" She turns to watch me open the refrigerator.

"I was just out."

"Just out," she repeats. "As in out with a guy?"

"Maybe." I pull the jug of orange juice from the shelf before closing the door.

"Shut up!" she squeals, abandoning her cereal completely. "Tell me everything. Oh my god, is he hot? Look at you, of course he's hot! Holy hell, did you stay the night at his place? Gahhh! You totally slept with him, didn't you?" She hits me with questions, one after another, not giving me a chance to answer a single one.

While I know telling her about what I found out at the doctor's office yesterday is the more pressing matter, I'm desperate to hold onto some sense of normalcy for as long as I can.

I've never had someone to talk to about things like this. And I can't tell you how many times I envisioned this conversation. Meeting someone and coming home to gush about all the details with my best friend or in this case, my sister – who happens to hold both titles. So I hold onto the moment a little longer.

"At least tell me his name!" she pleads when I haven't said a word.

I finish pouring my cup of juice before joining her at the table, sliding into the seat across from her.

"Abel." I smile around the word. "His name is Abel."

"Abel," she tries it out. "I really like that name."

"Me too," I agree, taking a drink of my OJ.

"So, tell me everything."

"He's twenty-five. A musician. And I swear he's probably the closest thing to a fictional character *I've* ever met in real life. Until last night I didn't realize people like him actually existed."

"That good, huh?" She snorts out a laugh.

"Better." I sigh, letting my mind wander back to the events that took place hours prior. I think about his face, his smile, those eyes, that damn dimple, and I swear my heart does this little flip flop inside my chest.

But as quickly as the feeling hits me, it dies just as fast. Because reality always has a way of finding its way back in, even when you try not to let it.

"Are you going to see him again?"

Am I? Will I live long enough to see him again? It's the question I've spent all morning asking myself.

"I don't know." I shrug.

"Why don't you know?" Claire eyes me warily, clearly sensing the shift in my demeanor.

"Well, that's the thing." I have trouble holding her gaze as I prepare to say the words out loud for the first time. "You know how I had a doctor's appointment yesterday to discuss the results of my MRI and blood work?"

"I tried calling to find out what they said but someone sent me to voicemail." She gives me a knowing look. "What did they say? Did they figure out what's going on?"

"They did." I nod slowly, swallowing past the sudden lump in my throat.

"Well, what is it?" I can tell by her voice that she's growing impatient.

I force myself to look her in the eyes as I utter the three words I never dreamt in a million years I'd be saying to someone. "I have cancer."

All the color drains from her face as she processes what I admitted.

"A malignant brain tumor to be exact." Even as I say it out loud, it still doesn't seem real.

"A brain tumor," she manages after several long seconds. "But how?" She shakes her head, disbelief written all over her face.

"No idea." I shrug. "How does anyone end up with a brain tumor? It's just something that happens."

"But they can treat it, right? You'll be okay."

"They're going to try. But it's not promising." I choose to give it to her straight. She's going to find out come tomorrow, anyway. The very least I can do is prepare her for the most likely outcome. Which is that I won't make it.

"What do you mean?"

"The position and size of the tumor makes surgery very difficult. So difficult that the success rate is less than thirty percent."

"Surely there are other ways to treat it," she cuts me off.

"Unfortunately, we're way past any other option. The doctor said if they don't operate, I only have months left."

"But..." Tears well behind her eyes and she immediately reaches for my hand across the table. "You can't die," she croaks. "You can't. And you won't." She quickly composes herself, big sister mode switching on. "You will fight this. *We* will fight this. They say you have to have surgery, then surgery it is, and you'll kick that surgery's ass. Just like you'll kick this cancer's ass. How soon are they wanting to operate?"

"Tomorrow."

"Tomorrow?" She draws back as if she's been physically struck. "And you didn't think to tell me this yesterday when you found out?"

"I wanted to. I just didn't know how. And then I met Abel and he was funny and handsome and for a while he made me forget. And I wanted to forget."

"Tomorrow," she repeats, leaning back in her chair before her eyes go up to the ceiling. Something I've learned she does when she's trying to compartmentalize her emotions. "You must be terrified." When her gaze comes back to mine her expression is softer, pity taking the place of confusion and anger. "What time?"

"I have to be at the hospital at seven in the morning."

"Okay." She nods slowly. "I'll take off work. There's no way I'm not going with you." She doesn't give me a choice in the matter, which is fine because I don't think I could even walk into that hospital without her at my side. "What about your mom?"

"What about her?"

"Are you going to tell her?"

"No." I shake my head. "Even if I wanted to, I have no idea how to get a hold of her. It's not like I can pick up the phone and call her."

"Fin, she's your mom. We should find a way to let her know."

"She's the woman who gave birth to me. That doesn't make her a real mom. I doubt she cares one way or the other, anyway. She probably hasn't even noticed that I left and it's been over a year."

"I doubt that's the case. I know she's not your favorite person, but she's still your mom whether you like it or not."

"I'm not doing this with you." I let out a loud sigh. "Monica is the farthest thing from what I need right now."

This isn't the first time Claire has tried to push me to mend fences with my mom. She has some unrealistic notions about what it means to be a drug addict. She thinks that my mom still cares – and maybe she does – but she cares about getting her next fix more.

"What about your friends at the restaurant? Have you told any of them?"

"No."

"Finley, you have to tell people."

"I don't want anyone to know."

"You still can't accept that there are people here who care about you, can you? You can't shut out the world. You need a support system behind you."

"I have one. I have you."

"And you know I'll be here for you every single step of the way. But sis, that doesn't mean you shouldn't tell your friends what's going on. They'll want to know."

"I highly doubt any of them care that much."

"What about Heather?"

Heather is the only real friend I have outside of Claire. We've been working together for almost a year now and have become pretty close over that time.

"I'll tell her if I survive the surgery."

"When," she corrects. "*When* you survive the surgery."

"When," I repeat unconvincingly.

"Hey." Claire leans forward, once again taking my hand. "I don't mean to push. I can't imagine how overwhelmed you must feel. I just think there are people in your life that deserve to know what's going on with you. People who love you and care what happens to you. People who will want to help you through this."

"You just want the best for me, I know that. But I can't. This is something I need to handle on my own."

"Okay," she concedes. "If that's what you want."

"It is."

"We're going to beat this, you know?" she reassures me. "Whatever it takes."

"Whatever it takes," I repeat her words, wishing like hell it were that simple.

"What do you say we spend the day in? We can rent some movies, eat anything we want, and lounge in our pajamas all day?"

"I'd like that," I admit, knowing there's no one else I'd rather spend my final day with.

Just as the thought takes hold, Abel's face flashes through my mind. It still doesn't seem real – everything that happened last night. I spent the entire walk home replaying things in my head, trying to convince myself that the feelings I have for him are born out of my fear of the future. Of dying having never loved a man. But no matter how much I tried, I couldn't make myself believe it.

Nineteen years I've been searching for something to make me feel even a fraction of what I felt last night. It doesn't matter that I've only known him for a few hours. It doesn't matter that I may never see him again. Because he gave me one perfect night. Ten perfect hours. And because of him I feel like I have something to fight for.

And so I will fight. I will fight with everything I have because all I want are more hours, more days, more time… More him.

Chapter Fourteen
Abel

Thank you for the best night of my life.

My eyes scan the note Finley left in the kitchen for what feels like the hundredth time before dropping the notepad back onto the counter.

I have to be at Trolley House in less than an hour and I still haven't even taken a shower. I need to snap my ass into gear and get a move on, but I find my motivation lacking today.

I don't know if it's because I didn't get that much sleep or because I'm too busy obsessing over being ghosted for the first time in my life.

I've done it to people before – snuck out after a wild night to avoid the awkward next morning. But those were always one night. I knew it. She knew it. There was never any reason to delay the inevitable. But Finley? I don't know. I guess I thought she was more.

Clearly she didn't agree. If she did she wouldn't have snuck out while I slept with nothing more than this fucking note. If she had left her phone number at least then I would know that she wanted to see me again. But this? This feels like the ultimate blow off.

Thanks for the best night of my life, but I never want to see you again. Hence why I intentionally didn't tell you where I live, where I work, and made no attempt to exchange phone numbers with you. Oh, and let's really add insult to injury and not tell you my last name either, so there's no way in hell you can track me down.

"Fuck," I grumble, running a hand through my hair as I stare down at the note.

I've never met anyone like Finley before. I've also never read a situation quite so wrong, either. Usually I have a pretty good grasp on where people stand, but with her? It was like trying to piece together a puzzle with several missing pieces.

But even still, I didn't expect this. I didn't expect to wake up to an empty apartment and a heavy feeling in the pit of my stomach that I can't seem to shake.

My phone buzzes to life on the counter, offering me a much needed distraction. I look down to see my buddy, Nick's number flash across the screen.

"Hey. What's up?" I answer the phone the way I always do.

"Hey. What do you have going on tonight? Me and some of the guys were thinking about heading down to Sven's for the evening. You interested?"

Sven is a mutual friend of ours. He comes from a very wealthy family and spends most of his days lounging by the indoor pool or hosting extravagant parties at his parents' lake house a few miles outside of the city. He's an okay guy – a little arrogant, but okay. He attended college with my brother, Alex which is how we all met.

"Wish I could, but I've got a gig tonight at Trolley House. Gotta make a living somehow."

"Lame."

"Yeah, well, not all of us can be lucky enough to develop some stupid app, then sit back and watch the money roll in."

"I worked on that stupid app for four years. I deserve to enjoy the fruits of my labor."

"Not saying you don't." I chuckle. "Tell Sven and the guys I said hi, would ya?"

"You got it."

"Hey, Nick." I stop him right before he hangs up; having a sudden thought hit me seemingly out of nowhere.

"Yeah?"

"You still have that friend that does PI work?"

"Chuck. Yeah, why?"

"How much do you think he'd charge me to find someone? A girl I met."

"Decided to take up stalking as a hobby?"

"She stayed the night last night, but when I woke up this morning she was gone. I didn't get her number before she left," I continue without acknowledging his stalker comment.

"Just look her up on Facebook or something."

"I don't have Facebook and you know that. I also don't know her last name."

"Wait, let me get this straight. You want *me* to help *you* track down some chick you slept with, but you don't even know her last name?"

"How many women have you slept with and didn't know their *first* name?" I turn it around on him.

"Very true, but I'm not trying to track them down the next day. She must be some girl."

"You have no idea," I say, deciding not to elaborate beyond that.

"So then tell me how it is that you didn't think to get her last name."

"I asked when we first met but she evaded the question. I didn't think it was worth pushing. Then again I didn't expect her to ghost me either."

"Abel Collins ghosted by a chick. Never thought I'd see the day."

"Are you going to be a dick about this or can you call Chuck and see if he can help me?"

"Relax. You know I'm just messing with you. I think it's good that you want to find this girl. She must be special if she's got you, the man who chases no woman, chasing after her."

"Are you done now?" I let out an audible sigh.

"Okay. Okay. Tell me what information you *do* know."

"Well, I know she lives in an apartment with her sister off of Birch Street. She moved here from South Carolina a year and a half ago, and I'm pretty sure she's a waitress somewhere."

"Pretty sure?" He laughs.

"She said she waitressed so I'm just assuming here."

"Why not wait and see if she comes back around? I mean, she only left this morning. Don't you think it's a bit early to call out the Calvary?"

"Trust me, she's not coming back. Her note made that pretty clear."

"Oh shit, she left a note?"

"Thanking me for the best night of her life."

"Yep. You're right. There's no way she's coming back." Sarcasm drips from every word.

"You know what, never mind." I'm preparing to hang up the phone before he stops me.

"Wait. I'm sorry. You know I'm only busting your balls. Damn, you're in a mood today."

"Her name is Finley."

"Finley," he repeats. "Well, good news is I doubt there are that many Finley's. I can't say I've ever met anyone with that name so there's a start. Now if her name was Ashley or Stephanie, I would have told you to throw in the towel, because there's no way in hell we would find her. But Finley. Finley we can work with. I'll pass the info along to Chuck and have him do a little digging. See what he can come up with."

"Thanks, Nick."

"You know, Sven's party will go on until morning so if you feel up to it, head out after your gig."

"I'll think about. I gotta go or I'm gonna be late."

"Alright, talk later."

I drop my cell onto the counter before rubbing my eyes with the backs of my hands.

Maybe I'm crazy for asking him to have Chuck look into Finley. I mean, Nick's right, she just left this morning. But I can't shake the feeling that if I don't do this, if I don't try to find her, I may never see her again.

Chicago is a huge city and it's not like we run in the same crowd or anything. From what I gathered she doesn't do much outside of work and spending time with her sister.

I silently curse myself for not asking more questions. For not insisting that she tell me her last name or even thinking to ask where she works.

Now here I am, like some creepy stalker trying to find all this information about her that she would have told me if she wanted me to know.

Normally I wouldn't think twice about a situation like this. I'd take the experience and log it with all the others and move on. But for some reason I can't do that with Finley. She's not just another one-nighter.

I can't erase her from my mind like she never happened. Not when I still crave her touch, her taste, the sound of her laughter. Not when she's been the only thing I have been able to think about since I opened my eyes this morning.

It's so fucking strange. I can't remember a time when I've ever been so knotted up over a girl. And deep down I know it's because she's so much more than just *another* girl.

The Trolley House is pretty slow tonight, not that I'm surprised. Most bars are through the middle of the week. I make it through three of my four set playlists without an issue, but by the fourth set I'm starting to wear down, both mentally and physically. All I want to do is go home, down a few beers, and sleep for the next two days.

Adjusting my guitar strap, I strum out the opening chords for *Stuck* by Imagine Dragons. It fits the mood for how I'm feeling tonight. It's what I do. I use my music as an outlet. If I'm feeling particularly angry or upset about something I tend to go for music that expresses that emotion. Same thing if I'm sad or happy or whatever I happen to be feeling at the time.

Tonight I think the theme is pretty easy to guess. Outside of my regular fan favorites and requests, I've played nothing but sappy ass love songs as I stare at the front door, hoping that Finley will walk through at any minute and flash me that beautiful smile of hers.

In a way I wish I wouldn't have told her that I was playing here tonight. Maybe then I could focus on getting through the night without constantly scanning the crowd for her face.

I never thought I'd be *that* guy. The guy that obsesses over a girl. The guy that sings about a girl. The guy that waits for a girl. I have been so far from that guy my entire life. Now, after only one night with Finley, I feel like I'm doing everything I always swore I'd never do. I guess that's what happens when you meet *the one*. Your entire perspective changes.

Chapter Fifteen
Finley

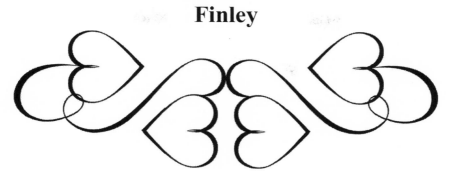

I'm hidden in the shadows, my back pressed against the wall as I watch Abel on stage. He's electric, pure undeniable magic, and try as I may I can't tear my eyes away from him.

I've been here less than ten minutes and already it's killing me not to go to him. Not to tell him that I'm here. But I promised myself I wouldn't. But I had to see him one last time.

He didn't see me come in and I've made sure to stay as far out of sight as possible, which is easier than I thought it would be considering the layout of the bar as well as the dim lighting.

Claire doesn't know I'm here. I didn't want to wake her to tell her I was leaving. I doubt she'd approve of me taking off at one in the morning when I have to be at the hospital in less than six hours.

Even though I told myself I wouldn't, I knew there was no way I couldn't come tonight. I tried not to. I said goodnight to my sister, showered, and got in bed, trying to mentally prepare myself for tomorrow's procedure. But as exhausted as I was, I couldn't sleep. I napped for a few hours this afternoon, but it wasn't enough to take away the tired, burning feeling behind my eyes.

And yet still, I laid there for hours, tossing and turning, trying to talk myself out of coming. But knowing where he was, knowing that with a quick drive across town I could be looking at his handsome face again, made it impossible to resist. So instead of trying to force myself to sleep, I snagged Claire's car keys from her purse and headed to the one place I knew I needed to be.

Abel starts a new song, one that I recognize immediately. It's a song off of the new Imagine Dragons album and one of my absolute favorites. I close my eyes and focus on his voice, letting it take me away and hold me in place at the same time.

Abel is even more talented than I realized. It seems effortless to him. The way his fingers move across the guitar. The way he croons out the words to the song. His voice is so incredible I swear I can feel the vibration of it pouring from the speakers and radiating through my entire body.

I'm transfixed, drawn to the way his lips curve, to the way his eyes sweep the crowd, *and* to the way they keep finding their way to the door like he's waiting for something, or someone.

Could he be waiting for me?

Abel doesn't strike me as a man who waits for anyone, let alone some girl he just met.

His gaze darts in my direction and I slink further into the shadows, not wanting to risk being seen. Luckily the lighting that shines toward the stage seems to obstruct his view and he doesn't see me.

Abel plays twelve songs from the moment I walked into the bar until the moment I leave. I count each one in my head, like a countdown to the moment when I know I will have to turn around and walk out that door, not knowing if I'll ever see him again.

Leaving is probably one of the hardest things I've done, which makes little sense considering I met him yesterday. I've dealt with some pretty tough situations in my past, too, but somehow none of it compares to this. There was nothing that made me feel like my heart was being physically ripped from my chest like it does at this very moment.

As I left Abel's apartment this morning, for the first time since my diagnosis, I allowed myself to believe that there was a chance. A chance that I would live. A chance that I would heal and one day get the life back I was so sure I'd lost. Talking with Claire only further solidified my will to fight, to not roll over and say 'okay, this is it.' Because for the first time in a very long time, maybe *ever*, I feel like I have things to fight for.

My sister. My future. The life that I deserve. Abel...

It's crazy how in the span of only a few short hours he was able to completely shift my outlook from one that was so bleak I couldn't bear to look forward, to one that shines bright with the possibility of hope.

I know the odds are stacked against me. I know that even if I survive the surgery I still have a long fight ahead of me. I know that. But I also know that if anyone can do it, I can.

I have been through hell and back over again, and even though life has thrown every rock it could at me, I've never given up. Even when I couldn't find the strength to go on, I still managed to power through. I didn't overcome all of the obstacles I've faced to give up now.

I turn and look at Abel for one more long moment, my eyes tracing his face from a distance. And then I do what I came here to do. I whisper a silent thank you and turn and walk away.

I may never see Abel again and he may never know how much he changed my life, but I hope somehow he still knows that he did. Because even if this is it – even if there's nothing left – he gave me a reason to fight. And for that I'll forever be grateful.

Chapter Sixteen
Abel

Nick: Chuck thinks he may have tracked down your mystery girl.

I reread the text message ten times before my fingers move across the screen.

Me: He did? Where?

I have to retype the last word three times because my hands are shaking so bad I keep hitting the wrong letters.

I watch as dots begin to blink across the screen, indicating that he's texting back, but the dots disappear and my anxiousness goes from a five to a ten, instantly.

It's been two weeks since the night I spent with Finley. Two weeks since I let her walk out of my life. When Chuck never reached out I assumed he came up empty, much like I have.

I've looked everywhere for her. Hell, I've even gone as far as to ask if a Finley works *here* at every restaurant I've eaten at between then and now. It's pathetic, really. My inability to let this girl go. But try as I may, I can't.

Dots pop back up along the screen and I hold my breath, waiting to see what his response will be.

Nick: There's a Finley that worked at Mitchell's up until two weeks ago.

Me: Two weeks ago?

Nick: Chuck called and confirmed with one of the managers. He wouldn't tell him anything other than she no longer works there.

My heart begins to pound erratically as I type out a response.

Me: Did he happen to get a last name?

Nick: Roberts.

Roberts... I have to stop myself from leaping out of my chair in excitement.

Me: Anything else?

Nick: Not yet.

Me: So what's next?

Nick: Chuck said he'll run her name through the state database and see if anything pops up, but it'll probably take some time.

Another line of dots fill the screen as he immediately starts typing another message.

Nick: I gave Chuck your number so he can contact you directly if he finds anything. He's also going to expect to be compensated.

Me: I don't care what it cost.

Nick: Must be some girl.

I smile.

Me: She is.

I drop my phone onto the table and run through everything I just learned.

"Finley Roberts," I try the name out on my lips.

I know it's not much, but this is the first real lead I've gotten. Now that we have her name, it's only a matter of time before we track her down.

And what if she doesn't want to be tracked down? It's the very question that has plagued me since I asked Nick to have Chuck look into her.

What if I go through all this trouble to find her only to have her turn me away again?

I guess at least then I'll know. At least then I can say I did everything I could and it wasn't meant to be. But this, this waiting around wondering where she is and what she's doing, if she's thinking about me as much as I am thinking about her – it's driving me insane.

I'd rather have answers that I don't want then spend the rest of my life wondering *what if.*

I pick my phone back up when another text message comes through.

Nick: Keep me posted. And let me know if Chuck hasn't messaged by the end of today.

Me: Will do. Thanks again.

Chapter Seventeen
Finley

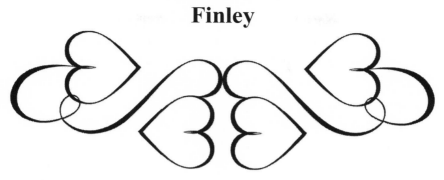

"Finley. Finley, can you hear me?"

I blink, once then twice, having trouble keeping my eyes open.

"Finley." I gravitate toward the sound. My sister's voice.

"Claire," I say, my voice broken and hoarse.

"I'm right here." Emotion is thick in her voice but I still can't get my eyes to focus enough to look at her.

"My head." I groan when a sudden and stomach curdling pain rolls through me. "My head hurts." I try to open my eyes again, my eyelids feeling like they are weighted down.

"Can you give her something for the pain?" Claire asks.

"I'm starting a drip to help manage her pain now that we've got her back awake," an unfamiliar female voice responds.

"She's giving you something now, Fin. Just hang in there." I can tell Claire's hovering close to me but her face is blurred and distorted.

"I can't see." I try to push past the disorientation I feel.

"That's to be expected," a man replies, and even though I don't instantly recognize it, I also know I've heard it before. "Good morning, Miss Roberts, it's Dr. Newton. Can you hear me okay?" I sense movement and then catch the faint scent of cologne before cool hands are on my neck.

"Yes." I continue to blink, my vision finally starting to clear.

His fingers slide gently from one side of my throat to the other, though I'm not sure what he's checking for.

"I'm going to shine a light into your eyes. Can you try to keep them open for me?"

I do as he asks, drawing back slightly when the light hits my eyes. He waves it from one eye to the other and back again before finally clicking it off.

"Can you tell me how you're feeling?"

"I don't know. My head hurts," I repeat for a second time.

"The pain medication should take effect soon." He turns his attention to a monitor next to me and observes it for a brief moment. "Your vitals look good."

"Where am I?" I click my tongue against the roof of my mouth. My mouth is so dry it sticks there for a moment.

"You're in the hospital. There were some complications during surgery and we had to place you into a medically induced coma," he explains. "But don't worry, the worst is behind you."

"Surgery?" I look around the room, my vision still not completely clear. It's like there's a film over my eyes. I can see, but it's all a little hazy. "Claire." I choke when my gaze lands on my sister who's standing on my left side.

"Hey, Fin." Tears swim behind her big green eyes but her emotion only serves to confuse me more.

"I need something to drink," I tell her.

"Here." I look to my right to see Dr. Newton hand my sister a plastic cup. "Drink slowly. You may feel a bit nauseous from the medication," he says, pressing a button on my bed to elevate me enough that Claire can lift the cup to my lips.

I take a tentative sip, immediately going back for more when the cool liquid hits my tongue.

"Easy." Claire smiles, pulling the cup away once I've drank nearly half of it.

"Why am I here?" I ask, the water making it easier to speak. "Why did I have surgery?"

"You don't remember?" She eyes me curiously before her gaze goes to the doctor.

"Temporary confusion and disorientation is expected," he says to her before his attention comes to me. "You came in two weeks ago to have a malignant brain tumor removed. We were able to get the tumor out but there was some unexpected swelling on your brain. We were forced to place you under a medically induced coma until we could get the swelling under control. But as I said, the worst is behind you now." He offers me a reassuring smile. "I'll let you rest. I'll be back in a couple of hours to check in on you. In the meantime, Theresa here will help you with anything you need." He gestures to the middle aged nurse to his right. She offers me a warm smile and a nod.

"Okay," I say, still not entirely clear on what is going on.

It's the strangest feeling. Not knowing where you are or why you're there, yet sensing that you do at the same time. It's like my brain knows exactly what's going on but is too blanketed by fog to cipher through the information.

I watch both the doctor and nurse exit the room before Claire's hand slips into mine, pulling my attention back to her.

"I knew you'd be okay," she tells me, fighting back a sob. "I just knew it."

"I'm so tired." I sigh, my eyelids growing heavy again.

"Rest. I'll be here when you wake up." It's the last words I hear before sleep takes me under once more.

"Stop looking at it." Claire crosses the room and takes the mirror from my hand, placing it face down on the bedside table in front of me. "I leave you alone for less than an hour and you managed to con someone else into giving you another mirror."

"I can't help it. It looks so weird." I run my fingers along my prickly scalp, careful to avoid the incision that stretches from my right temple to about an inch past my ear.

Words can't begin to describe how strange it was to wake up in the hospital four days ago with no real recollection as to how I got there. Thankfully, it was only a few hours before things started to come back to me. Not that it really helped. I still feel a bit off. It's kind of like waking up from a dream and not knowing if you're actually awake or not.

"It doesn't look weird. When your hair is down you can't even see it."

"You have to say that because you're my sister." I crinkle my nose at her. "It looks horrible."

"It does not. Stop obsessing."

"That's easy for *you* to say. You're not the one who has no hair."

"You have hair." She reaches out and grabs a chunk, letting the strands slide through her fingers. "You just don't have quite as much on one side." She grins.

"That's one way to put it." I give her a knowing look which causes her to chuckle.

"So, I brought you these." She slides her backpack off her shoulder and drops it onto the chair next to the bed. Unzipping it, she digs inside before pulling out three books. "I wasn't sure which ones to get. Has anyone ever told you that you have way too many books?"

"There is no such thing as having too many books," I inform her, taking the old, tattered paperbacks that she extends to me.

Growing up I didn't have enough money to buy new books, so I'd save every cent I could find and buy them used at the old book store in town. That place was my saving grace. I went in there so often that the owners started putting books that were in too rough of shape to sell in a box and giving them to me for free. As such, I grew quite the collection over the years.

Of course I lost a lot of them along the way. Some were destroyed by my mom or one of her druggie friends. Some were lost in the shuffle of moving countless times. And some I left behind because I didn't have a big enough bag to bring them all with me when I moved to Chicago.

"If you say so." Claire smiles, shaking her head at me. "I also brought you some clothes." She gestures to the bag. "Just some underwear and pajamas so you don't have to lay around in that gown anymore." She gestures to my hospital attire. "Don't worry," she quickly continues before I can object. "I already checked with the nurse and she said you can wear them as long as they are loose fitting and don't obstruct your I.V." She points to the port in my arm.

"Last time I checked, I don't own pajamas. Or did you forget that I sleep in old tees?"

"I didn't forget." She grins. "I brought you some of mine."

"You're too good to me."

"No, I'm your sister. This is what sisters do."

"I still think you're too good to me."

"And I think you need to start accepting that this is what people do for the people they love." She reaches out and takes the books out of my hands before I have a chance to see what she's brought, setting them on the table in front of me. "Come on. I'll help you get changed before they come get you for chemo."

"Yay," I groan sarcastically. "Something to take away the rest of my hair."

"The doctor said there's a chance your hair won't fall out since you only have six weeks of treatments," she reminds me.

"That's what they tell everyone. Just watch, it'll happen. It's completely my luck."

Claire gives me a sympathetic look but chooses not to comment. She knows I'll just argue with her anyway.

I'm terrified of chemo. Just the mention of it makes me want to vomit. The plan was to insert a chemo wafer into my brain during surgery, but with the complications that arose they were unable to do so. Now I have to endure sitting in a room for an hour every two weeks while they pump it into my chest port.

I guess I should count myself lucky. There are some patients that have to have several weeks of treatment and some that last far longer than mine do for one session.

I try to focus on the positive and not the negative, but sometimes it's hard not to give in to self-pity. Sometimes I want to throw my hands up and scream *'why me'*?

But then I remember how differently this could have turned out. I know how extremely lucky I am to not only have survived a surgery that had less than a thirty percent survival rate, but that they were also able to get ninety percent of the tumor. Unfortunately, that doesn't mean I'm out of the woods yet.

That's where the chemotherapy comes into play. To kill off any cancer cells that might still be there, and to ensure the tumor doesn't continue to grow.

Until the chemo is complete and the doctors are satisfied with my scans, this hospital will be my second home. I've already been warned to prepare to be here at least another week or two, and even then I'll still have to come back multiple times to finish my treatments. While I wish I could go home, I'm grateful to at least be out of the ICU and in a normal room now.

Claire helps me change into a pair of the pajamas she brought for me. While I'm able to get around more easily now, my legs are still pretty weak so I usually need help doing anything that requires me to stand for more than a few seconds.

I guess the plan is to start having me walk the hallway soon, though I still have no idea how I'm going to do it. I guess like everything else I've had to endure, one step at a time.

Once I'm changed, Claire helps me back into bed, fluffing the pillows behind me before pulling the blanket back up over my legs.

"There." She smiles as she eyes the shirt – a soft pink long sleeve top with a unicorn on it. Total Claire. "Much better."

"I don't know. Now I look like a ten year old," I tell her, looking down.

"Oh shut up. Unicorns are magical and right now, little sis, you could use a little magic." She winks. "I gotta get back to work. My lunch break is only an hour and I've already been gone that long. You'll be okay?"

"I'll be fine," I reassure her, leaning forward to read the title of the top book on the table. "Chemo will be much easier to endure with Charlie Hampton to keep me company," I say, picking up *Where the Tide Breaks* and holding it to my chest.

"You and your book boyfriends." She laughs.

"Better than dealing with a real boyfriend," I counter.

"That's not what you said when you were telling me about Abel."

Just the mention of his name causes my heart to pick up speed. I've thought of him so many times over the last couple of days, yet each time I do the memory of him feels more distant. Like he was only part of some wild and crazy dream that will continue to fade into the background until I forget about him all together.

I think that's what scares me the most. The fear that one day I won't remember the sound of his laugh or the way he looks when he smiles. That I won't be able to close my eyes and remember his smell or the way it sounds when he says my name.

I don't know what the future holds or if I'll ever see him again. But the memory of him, that's something I never want to forget.

"Earth to Finley." I jump, realizing my sister is still talking to me.

"What?"

"Where did you go?" She arches a brow. "Off in Abel *la la land*?" she teases.

"Don't you have somewhere to be?" I counter.

"Way to avoid the subject." She gives me a knowing look. "We'll pick this up later." She leans in and lays a light kiss to the side of my head. "Love you, Fin."

"Love you too."

"I'll be back sometime after dinner," she tells me, slinging her purse over her shoulder as she heads toward the door.

"When you come back, bring me a candy bar, would ya? I'm dying for some chocolate."

"Only if the nurse says you're allowed." She gives me a toothy grin before disappearing into the hallway.

I laugh, cringing slightly when a sharp pain shoots through my head.

I think that's the worst thing out of all of this. The headaches. The doctor has assured me that they will pass, that they're just a byproduct of surgery, but at this rate I feel like they'll never go away.

Relaxing back into bed, I close my eyes for a brief moment, knowing the nurse will be in to take me to chemo before too long.

I let my mind drift back to Abel. I wonder where he is and what he's doing. I wonder if he ever thinks about me. I wonder if I'll ever have the courage to find him again when this is all over.

I think about what our lives could be like. How happy we could be together. It's something that has carried me through some very rough days. And even if nothing ever comes of it, even if I never see him again, I know that he's one of the reasons I'm alive today. And for now, that's enough.

Chapter Eighteen
Abel

I knock on the door, my heart beating a million miles a minute. It took Chuck a few days to track down Finley's apartment, but eventually he was able to locate the address where her driver's license is registered. An apartment off Birch, just like Finley had said.

I have no idea what I'm going to say to her when I see her. How I'm going to explain how I found her, but right now all that matters is that I do. And as soon as I see her face, I know the rest will come to me.

I wait in agonizing silence for several long moments before knocking again. That's when I hear it, light footsteps padding toward the door.

When the lock clicks and the door begins to open, I can't remember how to breathe. Unfortunately, when a face comes into view, it's not the face I've waited weeks to see.

"Hi." I'm greeted by a young woman with blonde hair and big green eyes. Finley's eyes.

"Claire?" I take a wild guess.

"Yeah." She nods. "Do I know you?" She glances down the hallway in both directions to see if I'm alone.

"No, you don't. But I know your sister, Finley."

She takes one long look at me, a slow smile forming on her lips.

"You're Abel."

I don't pretend that the fact she knows who I am comes as a surprise because it does. If she knows who I am, that means Finley told her about me. This knowledge makes me feel like a fucking giddy teenager.

"I am," I confirm after a long pause. "I'm sorry to show up like this, but I was hoping I could speak to Finley."

She gives me a sympathetic look.

"She's not here."

"Do you know when she's coming home?"

"She's, um, away for a while." She stumbles over her words.

"Okay," I draw out. "How long is she going to be gone?"

"A few weeks, maybe longer."

My heart sinks into my stomach.

"Oh." I try to mask my disappointment with an easy smile, but I'm pretty sure she sees right through it.

"I'm sure she'll be happy to hear you stopped by though."

"Is there any way I can get her number from you? I'd really like the chance to speak to her."

"I'm sorry, but I don't want to give out her number without speaking to her first." She shakes her head slowly. "But if you want to leave your number with me I'd be happy to pass it along."

"Yeah, okay. That would be great."

She pulls her phone out of her pocket and slides her finger across the screen.

"Go ahead." She waits for me to ramble off the number, typing it into her phone as I do. "There. Got it." She locks her phone and shoves it back into her pocket.

"You'll make sure she gets it?"

"I will." She smiles. "It was really nice to meet you, Abel."

"It was nice to meet you as well, Claire." I step back, watching the door close in front of me moments later.

While a part of me can't help but feel disappointed, I also feel relieved. As long as Claire gives her my number then I've done what I can. The ball is now in her court. At least now I know that she has a way to reach me if she wants to.

I know our connection wasn't something I imagined. I know she felt it. But I also know there was a lot she purposely avoided telling me. It was like she knew that she was going to sneak out and she didn't want me to come looking for her after she did.

But I'm not so easily swayed. I've never been one to take things lying down. I fight for what I want. I always have. And right now I want Finley Roberts. I want her in a way I've never wanted a woman before. It's both terrifying and exhilarating.

As I exit the apartment building and cross the lot toward my car, I can't help but wonder where she is. Claire said she'd be gone a few weeks but she never mentioned she was going anywhere. Then again, there's a lot she didn't mention. I'm starting to realize that even though I feel like I've known Finley my whole life, I really don't know that much about her.

And now learning that she quit her job and has apparently left town for a few weeks leaves me even more baffled. I'm not sure if this ties into why she ghosted me after our night together, but I'm guessing it does. I highly doubt it's just some random coincidence.

My phone buzzes to life seconds after I drop it in the passenger seat of my car. Glancing over, I let out a loud sigh when I see my mother's number flash across the screen.

I love my mom, don't get me wrong, but over the last couple of years our relationship has been more about how I've disappointed her and my father than anything else. Truthfully, it's pretty fucking exhausting.

Deciding to let it go to voicemail, I start the car and slowly pull out of the parking lot, glancing in my rearview mirror several times as Finley's building fades from view.

I've only made it a few blocks when my phone starts ringing again. This time it's my brother, Aaron. Tapping the phone button on my steering wheel, it's only seconds before the call connects through the speakers.

"Hey, Aaron." I flip on my turn signal as I come to a stop at a red light.

"You need to head over to mom and dad's." There's something off in his voice and I can tell something's wrong.

"Why, what's going on?"

"I'm not sure but Mom called me. Said she needed to see all of us and that it's important."

"She didn't say anything else?" I question, a nervous knot forming in the pit of my stomach.

"No, just that her and dad need to talk to us. I could tell something was wrong but she didn't want to discuss it over the phone. Andrew is already there and Alex and I are heading over now."

"Okay, yeah, I'll head that way. Give me about twenty minutes," I say, turning when the light turns green.

"Okay, see you then." He disconnects the call without waiting for a response.

"Somebody needs to start talking." Adam's voice rings out from my mother's tablet that's propped in the middle of the table where she has him on Facetime. Considering he's all the way in California it's not like he could pop over.

The rest of us are all circled around the table facing our parents. Mom is sitting in the chair at the head of the table and my father is standing behind her, one hand resting on her shoulder. "We haven't had a family meeting since Roger died nearly ten years ago," Adam continues, referring to the old golden retriever that we had as kids.

"Seriously, Mom, you're starting to freak us out," Aaron chimes in next to me.

"A few weeks ago I found a lump in my right breast." As soon as she starts speaking I know exactly where this conversation is going. "I went in for some blood work and scans a few days ago and had a follow up appointment with my doctor this morning." She pauses, looking up at my father who gives her an encouraging smile.

Fuck, this is bad...

"He confirmed that I have breast cancer." She nearly chokes on the words. "It's stage two and the doctors seem confident that we caught it early enough. I have surgery scheduled for next week to remove the mass and then we will discuss chemotherapy."

"Mom," Adam's voice rings out from the tablet.

"Now, before anyone says anything I want you to know that I have no intentions of going anywhere. It's not a matter of *if* I beat this, it's when." She forces a smile but I can tell it's more for our benefit than anything else.

Mom has always been the strong one of the family. I can count how many times I've seen her cry on one hand over the course of my entire life. She's the only one that seems to have it all together, even when the rest of the world is falling to shambles around her.

"What can we do?" Adam is the first to ask.

"Nothing for now," she answers simply. "I don't expect you to come home," she says directly to Adam before her gaze slides to the rest of us. "And I don't need anyone to do anything for me. But these next few months will be difficult, so I want everyone to prepare themselves. Just in case."

"In case what?" Alex leans forward, his elbows resting on the table in front of him.

"In case she dies." The words tumble from my lips unintentionally and every set of eyes in the room fall on me.

"Abel," my father scolds, his forehead creasing.

"It's all right, honey." She reaches up and pats the hand he has resting on her shoulder. "Abel's just saying what no one else wants to." Her gaze comes back to me. "Yes, in case I die," she confirms.

"I'll fly in for your surgery." Adam breaks the awkward silence that follows.

"You'll do no such thing." My mother shakes her head at the tablet. "I don't want everyone fussing over me. Let's see how the surgery goes. Then we will go from there."

"I have the time available to take off work. I'd feel a lot better if I was there."

"It's really not necessary."

"Mom," Aaron interrupts. "We love you and we're *all* going to be there for you."

I can tell by the way her eyes glass over that she's trying really hard to hold it together, though I'm not sure why. We're her family. She should be able to tell us how she's really feeling. But that's not Mom. Even though we're all grown, she's still trying to protect us like we're still kids.

"Okay then," she concedes.

We spend the next several minutes listening to her tell us exactly what the game plan is and what to expect in the days to come. I listen to it all in a haze, not sure how to process what I'm hearing.

Mom has always seemed invincible to all of us. Andrew and I used to joke that she'd outlive us all. Finding out that she's sick is hitting me a lot harder than I expected it to.

I sit in silence for most of the conversation, trying to digest everything I'm learning.

Aaron and Alex are the first to leave, followed shortly after by Andrew. I hang back for a few minutes, hoping to get some alone time with my mom.

While my parents are hard on me, it doesn't change how much they mean to me. I know they do it because they want what's best for me. I just wish I could convince them that what's best for me is doing what makes me happy. I don't measure success on the amount of money I make or the fancy title I have at work. In my family I'm in the minority with that way of thinking.

But despite our difference in opinions, I know my parents, especially my mom, would do anything for me. And I would do the same for them.

"Hey, Mom." I step into the living room where she's sitting on the couch with a book in her lap.

Despite everything that's happening, the first person I think of is Finley. I've never met anyone who talks about books the way Finley does. When she talked about them, her whole face lit up and it's like she floated away to another existence.

I smile despite myself.

"Hi, hon." My mom sets the book on the end table and pats the seat next to her.

"How are you feeling?" I ask, crossing the room toward her.

"I'm okay." She smiles but it doesn't quite reach her eyes. "I thought you left with your brothers." Her gaze follows me as I claim the seat next to her.

"I have the night off. Thought I'd hang out here with you if that's okay." I settle back into the couch and reach for the remote. "Anything good on?" I ask, powering on the television.

"Jeopardy starts in five minutes."

I smile, remembering all the times we'd sit around and watch Jeopardy when I was younger. We made somewhat of a competition out of it. Then again, with five boys in the house everything became a competition in some way, shape, or form.

"What's the wager?" I ask, giving her a knowing look.

"How about the loser has to treat the other to dinner?"

"Oh you're on." I wink, selecting the channel I need before dropping the remote next to me.

Chapter Nineteen
Finley

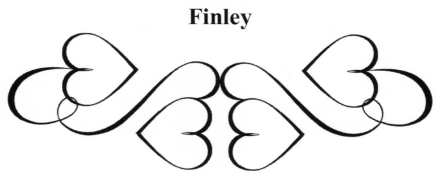

"Knock, knock." I look up from my book to see Heather slip into my room, two whipped cream covered drinks in her hand.

"Hey." I smile, laying my book face down on the bedside table. "I didn't know you were coming by today."

"I can't stay long. I'm picking up the evening shift tonight for Tracy. I just wanted to stop by and see how you're feeling."

"Better now." I smile, taking the drink she extends to me.

"Mocha frap, extra whip." She smiles.

Considering Heather is my closest friend outside of my sister, and she had no idea what was going on with me until three days ago, she's handled the news of my cancer and surgery pretty well. If the roles were reversed I'd probably be upset if she'd left me in the dark. But not Heather. She wasn't even a little mad. Just happy that I was doing okay.

She's stopped in to see me the day before yesterday after she talked to Claire, which was a welcome distraction from how awful I felt after my first round of chemo.

"You're the best," I tell her, taking the straw from her hand before opening the wrapper and dropping it into my drink.

"Yeah, I know." She laughs, plopping down in the lounge chair to my right. "Where's Claire? I expected her to be here by now."

"She should be here soon. She usually goes home after work and changes before coming over."

"So how are you doing? Really?"

"I'm hanging in there. The nausea medication is helping, thank god. I swear I've never vomited so much in my life." I giggle when she curls her nose in disgust. "How's work?"

"Boring without you." She pouts out her bottom lip. "Henry was pissed when you stopped showing up but he's forgiven you now that he knows why. I dare say he'd even give you your job back once you bust out of this popsicle stand."

"I think it will be some time before I'm able to go back to work. But I'll definitely keep that in mind."

"You should have told him, you know? You should have told all of us. I get why you didn't but I still think you should have."

"I know. Truthfully it just all happened so fast. And honestly I didn't think I'd survive the surgery. Now that I have, I'm realizing there are a lot of things I should have handled differently."

"Like that mystery man of yours?" She arches a brow at me. "Claire told me," she adds when she catches my surprised expression.

"And what exactly did that big mouth sister of mine tell you?"

"Only that you met some guy that you were all starry eyed over."

"I guess that's one way to put it." I slide the straw between my lips and take a long drink of the sweet, icy goodness. "God, I forgot how good these things are."

"Right?" she agrees, taking a drink of hers as well. "So, tell me."

"Tell you what?"

"About this mystery man of yours."

"Abel." Just saying his name out loud makes my skin prickle. "And there's not really much to tell. We met at a bar, spent an incredible night together, and then I left."

"God, don't give me too many details or anything," she grumbles sarcastically.

"I don't know what to say," I admit. "I met him the day I found out about the cancer and surgery and my chances of survival. I thought my life was over."

"So you're saying it wouldn't have happened if you weren't sick?"

"I'm saying, I don't how much of it was *because* I was sick. It brought out something in me, courage, and a boldness I wouldn't have otherwise possessed."

"So you took a chance." She shrugs. "What's so wrong with that?"

"Nothing. It was the best night of my life."

"Then why haven't you contacted him?"

"Well for one, I don't have his number," I start. "And two, what would I say? Hey, sorry I disappeared on you but I thought I would be dead by now."

"For starters. Yeah." She laughs.

"Well again, I don't have his number so it doesn't matter."

"But you know where he lives, do you not?"

"How much did Claire tell you?" I set my drink on the table, pinning my gaze on her.

"Enough." She gives me a toothy smile.

"Well, going to see him isn't really an option now is it?" I gesture around my hospital room.

"No, but calling him is," Claire announces as she appears in the doorway.

"I don't have his number," I repeat what I just said to Heather.

"You don't. But *I* do." She holds her phone up as she crosses the room toward me.

"What do you mean you do?" I don't try to hide my confusion.

"Someone came by to see you today."

"What? Who?" My heart begins to thump violently against my ribs.

"Who do you think?"

"I have no idea. Who?" My voice shoots up an octave.

"Abel," she practically squeals. "And oh my god, Fin, he's even hotter than you described."

"Wait? What?" I force out, pushing past the cloud of confusion and surprise that has settled over me.

"He stopped by shortly after I got home from work."

"Wait, how did he know where we live?"

"Your guess is as good as mine. You sure you didn't tell him?"

"I *know* I didn't."

"Well somehow he found out." She reaches for the Frappuccino on my table, lifting it up to inspect the contents. "Did you make sure you're allowed to have this?"

"Oh relax. It's fine. Now tell me what he said." I snatch the cup from her hand.

"He asked if you were home. I told him you weren't."

"You didn't tell him…" I start.

"I didn't tell him anything," she reassures me. "I told him you were gone for a few weeks and that I'd be happy to pass along his number if he wanted to give it to me."

"And that's it?"

"That's it." She nods. "I don't know what kind of spell you put on that man but he seemed very eager to speak with you."

"He did?" My heart leaps.

"Oh my god." Heather draws my attention back to her. "You weren't lying, Claire." She gives me a knowing smirk.

"Told ya. Stars in her eyes." Claire giggles.

"Shut up, the both of you. I feel like I'm about to have an anxiety attack," I say, suddenly having difficulty breathing.

"That's what love will do to you," Claire tells me, her and Heather having a good laugh at my expense.

"I do not love him. I don't even know him," I object, not for one second buying into my own lie.

I know what I felt that night and what I feel every time I think about Abel. If it isn't love then I don't know what is.

"So then you don't want his number?" Claire holds her phone out to me, a wicked smile on her lips.

I stare at the device for a few seconds, making no attempt to take it from her.

"No," I answer, shaking my head.

"What?" Heather erupts, jumping from her seat. "Why the hell not?"

"Because look at me." I gesture to myself.

"I *am* looking at you." She cocks a brow at me. "It's his phone number, Finley. What's the harm in talking to him?"

"She's right," Claire chimes in. "All he knows is your away for a few weeks. Call him. Text him. Just talk to him. He doesn't have to know where you are or why you disappeared until you're ready to tell him."

"You guys ever hear of peer pressure?" I tease, my gaze bouncing back and forth between the two of them.

Don't get me wrong, there's nothing more that I want than to pick up the phone and hear Abel's voice. To get some kind of reassurance that I'm not crazy and that he really is everything I thought he was that night. But the other part of me is terrified.

What if I'm not who he thought I was? Not to mention that I still have a long road ahead of me. How selfish would it be of me to drag him into my life when everything is still so up in the air? That wouldn't be fair to him or me.

"Here." Claire unlocks her phone and taps the screen. "I'm texting you his number. I told him I'd give it to you and that's what I'm going to do. What you do with it from there is on you." She taps the screen one last time before locking it, my phone signaling an incoming text moments later.

"Well, as much as I want to hang around and see how all this unfolds, I gotta get to work." Heather stands, turning toward me. "You want my opinion? Don't let that number go to waste."

"Yeah. Yeah." I swipe at her. "Get out of here or you'll be late."

"I'll come back by later this week. Any requests when I do?"

"Strawberry milkshake?" I give her a pretty please face.

"Strawberry milkshake it is." She laughs. "Love you, girl."

"Love you, too," I call after her, watching her exit the room moments later.

"So, what are you going to do?" Claire starts in on me the instant Heather disappears into the hallway.

"I don't know," I tell her truthfully.

"Something tells me he's not going to let this go. The man tracked down where you live for goodness sake. I don't know whether I should feel worried or impressed."

"It's not like it's that hard to find out where someone lives," I point out.

"Perhaps not. But even still, he came looking for you. That has to tell you something."

"How did he look?" I can't help but ask, wishing I had been there to open the door so I could lay eyes on him again.

"Gorgeous." She sighs. "I thought you were over exaggerating about those eyes, but holy crap."

"Incredible, right?"

"I swear the minute he said your name I knew exactly who he was because of the color of his eyes. The way you described them, like the sun reflecting off the ocean."

"Breathtaking." I smile, remembering how I felt when those eyes met mine for the very first time.

"Exactly." She nods in agreement.

"What else did he say? Anything?"

"No. When he found out you weren't home he asked if he could have your number and I told him I didn't want to give it to him without asking you first."

"You did?" I snort.

"I figure it isn't my place. So, instead I offered to give you his number. Figured this way you would be able to decide for yourself rather than have someone decide for you."

"You really are amazing." I smile up at her.

"And you really should call him." She taps me on the tip of my nose.

"I don't know. I want to. It's killing me knowing his number is sitting in a text message on my phone and with one quick dial I could hear his voice. On the other hand, the timing isn't good."

"You met him on the day you found out you had cancer. To be fair, your timing up to this point hasn't been stellar. And yet it still worked out okay for you, didn't it?"

"I guess," I admit, weighing the pros and cons in my head.

"Look, you have his number, just think about it. Yeah?"

"Yeah." I nod.

"If nothing else maybe you two can just text. It will give you an opportunity to feel out the situation while still keeping your distance."

"I guess." I knead my bottom lip between my teeth. "Now tell me it all again."

My sister laughs, claiming the seat Heather occupied a few minutes earlier.

"Okay, but only one more time." She wags her finger at me. "I heard a knock at the door," she starts off like she's reading me a story. I smile, closing my eyes as I picture it all in my mind.

His eyes. His smile. The way he says my name. Just thinking about it sends a flutter of excitement through me. I've never met someone who makes me feel like Abel. Just the mere mention of his name sends my heart into a frenzy. I can only imagine what it will do if I actually lay eyes on him again.

And while I know the timing isn't right, just the knowledge that he came to my house, that he's out there looking for me, confirms all the things I already knew. I'm not ready to give up Abel Collins just yet. And clearly he's not ready to give up on me either.

Chapter Twenty
Finley

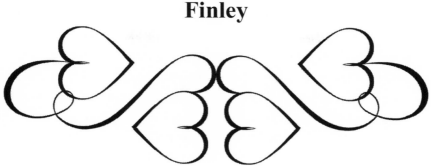

I hold my phone in my hand, my fingers hovering over the screen for several long moments as I talk myself in and out of texting Abel for the millionth time since Claire gave me his number yesterday.

It's so stupid really. I mean, clearly I'm into him and his actions would suggest he feels the same about me. So why can't I do something as simple as text him?

I just survived a very risky brain surgery. I'm battling cancer, for goodness sake. And yet I can't pick up the phone and text a guy?

Because you're afraid... a small voice in my head says. And it's right. I am afraid. I'm just not sure what it is that I'm afraid of.

Taking a deep breath, I begin to type out a message, deleting it several times before leaving it at *Hey, it's Finley.* Seems innocent enough, right?

Only, I know as soon as I send this message there's no taking it back.

Before I can talk myself out of it – again – I press the send button, squeezing my eyes tightly shut the instant I hear the swooshing sound that indicates the message was sent.

A small moment of panic washes over me but then it quickly morphs into excitement.

How many times did I wish for this? Pray for this? That I would live and find Abel again? The night leading up to surgery, it's all I could think about.

And now here I am. I'm alive.

I'm not ready to tell him everything and that's okay. I just want the opportunity to speak to him, to know how he's doing, to be a part of his life, even if it's from a distance.

My heart leaps into my throat when I hear my phone ping a response. I peel one eye open and then the other, smiling the instant I read the message displayed across the screen.

Abel: Just Finley… Or should I say Finley Roberts. Did you know that you're the only Finley over the age of eighteen registered in the entire Chicago area. Guess I'm lucky your name isn't Sara.

I cover my mouth to suppress a laugh. One text message and already I'm smiling like a damn idiot.

Me: Guess so. Maybe I should have given you an alias. LOL.

I chew nervously on my bottom lip as I wait for his response.

Abel: Well for the record, I'm glad you didn't. How are you?

Me: I'm doing okay. How are you?

Abel: Shitty, actually. Wishing you were around so I could see you. Where are you anyway?

Me: Why shitty? What's going on?

Abel: Family stuff. I'd rather not get into it right now. Where are you?

I try to come up with something to tell him. Claire told him I was away for a few weeks. I want to play into that. I don't want him knowing that I'm still in Chicago or that I'm sick. At least not yet.

Me: Dealing with some personal stuff. Don't wanna get into it right now.

I turn his words around on him.

Abel: Fair enough.

Me: So how are you? Other than the family stuff?

Abel: Right now I'm doing amazing. You have no idea how good it is to hear from you. I didn't think I could miss someone that I just met so much.

I'm not sure if I want to laugh or cry at his words.

Me: I know the feeling.

"Good afternoon, Miss Roberts. I'm here to take you down for your scan." Laura, one of the nurses steps into my room with a wheelchair in tow.

"Give me just one sec," I say, turning my attention back to my phone.

Me: I gotta go. Text later?

I drop my phone on the bedside table before swinging my legs over the bed and allowing Laura to help me into the wheelchair. Even though I can get around a lot better now, they still insist on wheeling me for any tests or treatment.

"Only a little bit longer and I hear you'll be free," Laura comments as she slides down the footholds on the chair.

"Thank goodness." I sigh, feeling more run down than I think I've ever felt before.

I've heard horror stories about chemotherapy, but nothing can prepare you for what it's like to actually go through it. I shudder to think how much worse it will get. At least I'll get to go home soon where I can recover in my own space, and with all my books.

"All set?"

"One sec." I lean forward and grab my phone, seeing Abel's reply message displayed on the screen.

Abel: As long as you promise not to ghost me again.

I laugh, garnering myself a curious look from Laura as I drop my phone back on the table, knowing I can't take it with me.

"Boyfriend?" she guesses, as she leads me out of the room toward the elevator.

"Something like that." I smile, watching the doors slide open in front of me.

Abel: Please tell me your day is going better than mine.

I read Abel's message, wishing I could tell him it was. Truthfully his message is about the only good thing that's happened to me today.

The anti-nausea medication has lost its effectiveness and as such I've spent the last day and a half sick to my stomach, unable to hold anything down.

Chemotherapy is no joke. And I've only been through one session. I wonder how people deal with these symptoms because I feel like death.

Me: Sorry, nothing good here to report.

Abel and I have been texting on and off for the last two days. Nothing of any real significance, but even still, it feels so good to talk to him.

Abel: Well, that's unfortunate. What's going on with you?

Me: Stomach thing. What about you?

Abel: Mom thing.

Me: Wanna talk about it?

The dotted line dances across my screen for several moments before disappearing altogether.

Me: Or not?

The dots instantly reappear.

Abel: Sorry, Adam just flew in from California so things are kind of crazy here right now.

Me: I'm guessing this has something to do with your mom?

I take a wild guess.

Abel: Yeah.

Me: Still don't wanna talk about it, I see.

Abel: I do. I would just rather talk about it face to face. When can I see you?

Me: I still have some things to take care of. It's going to be at least a few more weeks.

Abel: I wish you were here.

Me: Me too.

Abel: Can I call you later?

I hesitate with my fingers over the screen. Can he call me? Is that a good idea?

I weigh the pros and cons. While I may look like hell, the cancer hasn't affected my voice. As long as it's just talking, I can't see the harm in it. Then again, there are so many people in and out of my room, not to mention the monitors that seem to go off without warning or explanation, usually scaring the crap out of me.

Deciding it's probably better to keep it to texting until I get to go home, I try to figure out an excuse that doesn't seem like complete and total garbage.

Me: Not sure if I'll be able to talk. It's easier just to text right now.

I bite the inside of my cheek as I wait for his response, which comes after two very long minutes.

Abel: Why won't you tell me where you are?

Me: It's too much to get into. I promise when I get back I'll explain everything.

Abel: I'm going to hold you to that. I gotta go. My mom is threatening to take my phone away.

Me: Well we don't want that now, do we?

I laugh.

Me: Just text me later when you can.

"Uh oh, I know that smile." I look up right as Claire enters my room. "What's our *perfect* Abel up to today?"

"He's with his family right now. I guess his oldest brother is in from California."

"How fun."

"I don't think it's a regular visit. I guess there's something up with his mom but he hasn't said what."

"Have you asked him?" She sets a white paper bag on the table in front of me.

"Yeah. He said he'd rather talk about it face to face."

"Sounds like maybe he's trying to make an excuse to see you." She gives me a knowing grin.

"You think so?"

"Oh, I know so." She nods, peeling open the paper bag.

"Is that McNally's?" I ask, recognizing the emblem on the bag.

"I know you haven't had much of an appetite recently, so I thought I'd try one of your favs."

"You didn't?" I smile when she digs into the bag and pulls out a white takeout box.

"Oh, I did." She sets it on the table and flips open the lid, revealing a huge helping of Chicken Alfredo. She chuckles when she catches my expression. "But that's not all." She reaches back into the bag. "Tada." She pulls out a stack of breadsticks and drops them next to the container of pasta.

"I could kiss you right now," I tell her, my mouth already watering.

"I thought this might cheer you up." She pulls out another container of Alfredo for herself before she tips the bag upside down, spilling plastic silverware and napkins onto the table.

Crumbling the bag into a ball, she turns, dropping it into the trash before plopping down into the chair next to my bed.

"Hand me a breadstick, will ya?" She peels the lid off her pasta.

"Here." I slide one out of the pack and hand it to her before dragging one out for myself.

Tearing off the tip, I pop it into my mouth, moaning around the bite.

"Good?" she asks, even though she already knows the answer.

"So good." I wait until I swallow to answer. "Now let's see if I can keep it down."

"You look good today," she observes, forking some pasta into her mouth.

"I feel okay. Well, when I'm not throwing up anyway."

"I've noticed your spirits have been up over the last few days. I'm guessing I have a certain hot guy to thank for that." She smirks.

"Maybe." I shrug sheepishly. "He asked if he could call me later."

"And what did you say?"

"I said it's better just to text right now."

"Why?" She gives me a questioning look.

"I don't want to risk him hearing something that gives away where I am."

"And would it be such a bad thing if he did know?"

"Yes," I blurt.

"Why?"

"Because look at me." I gesture to myself.

"I *am* looking at you."

"I look horrible."

"You do not look horrible. Considering everything you've been through over the past few weeks you actually look really good."

"I beg to differ." I snort, shoving a bite of pasta into my mouth. "I'm just not ready for him to know," I say around a mouthful of food.

"I can't pretend to understand what you're going through, but from where I'm sitting, I can't see where him knowing would be anything but a good thing. If he can make you smile the way you were smiling when I walked in this room with nothing more than a few little text messages, imagine what he could do for you if he was here with you."

"That's just it, though. Once he finds out it won't be the same. Once he finds out I become the patient. Weak. Sick. Something for him to pity. I get that from everyone else. I don't want that from him, too." I pause. "When I see him again I want to do it on my terms. I want to wait until I'm better. Until I know I have a future to explore with him. I can't bring him back into my life just to lose him all over again."

"Honey, I hate to break it to you but you've already let him back in."

"You know what I mean. I can't be the sick girl with him. I want him to remember me exactly as I was until I can be that girl again."

"And you're willing to wait months until that happens?"

"If that's what it takes." I nod, not sure if I'm trying to convince her or myself.

"What happens if you don't get better? Are you really ready to give up what time you could have with him because of your pride?"

"It's not about being prideful." I don't try to mask the aggravation in my tone. "I'm trying to protect him."

"You're trying to protect him or you're trying to protect yourself?"

"Both." I blow out a defeated breath. "Can we please not do this? I don't want to argue with you."

"We're not arguing." A small smile pulls at the side of her mouth.

"You're such a brat." I wave my fork at her.

"Look," she leans forward slightly, balancing the container of pasta on her knee, "I don't mean to press. I just hate to see you push away someone who clearly means a lot to you. But at the end of the day it's your choice and I'll stand behind you no matter what."

"Thank you." I let out a deep sigh. "Now can we please talk about something else?"

"Sure," she agrees. "What would you like to talk about?"

"Well, for starters, you can tell me how your date with Michael went last night."

"Work meeting," she corrects.

"Right. A work meeting at eight o'clock on a Tuesday night at one of the nicest restaurants in the city."

"Spinning Fork is hardly one of the nicest restaurants in Chicago." She avoids the point.

"Nicer than any place I can afford to eat."

"It was company paid," she interjects.

"They supply the wine, too?" I tease.

"For your information, I drank water."

"Sure you did." I roll my eyes, forking another bite of pasta into my mouth.

"Michael's good looking enough but I can't handle his arrogance. I swear I want to stab him with my pen every time he sits next to me in a meeting."

"Pent up sexual frustrations?" I continue to poke fun at her.

"Hardly." She snorts. "Besides, I'm pretty sure he's sleeping with Sharon."

"Ah, the inner drama of the office." I smile.

Claire is a personal assistant for a business executive. It's not the most glamorous job in the world – her words not mine –

but she makes pretty decent money and it gives her an excuse to stock her closet with cute pencil skirts and girly blouses that cost more than three of my outfits combined.

"Yeah, because food service is any better," she points out. "You forget, I waitressed through school. I know the kind of shenanigans that go on behind the scenes."

"I wouldn't know anything about that. You know me. I tend to mind my own business and keep to myself."

"I know." She shakes her head at me. "You're the only nineteen year old I've ever met that would rather sit in the break room with her nose in a book than catch up on all the gossip going around."

"And that's a bad thing?"

"No. But it also wouldn't hurt you to get out and live a little."

"And partaking in work gossip is living?" I counter.

"Not what I meant and you know it. I'm just saying, you act way too old for your age most days. Well, now that I think about it, you have for as long as I've known you."

"Guess that's what happens when you're forced to become the parent before you've hit puberty." I give her a sad smile.

"I'm sorry," she starts.

"Don't be. It's not your fault."

"I just wish I would have known about you sooner. Maybe then I could have done something…"

"Claire." I stop her from saying more. "Don't do that to yourself."

"I just can't help but think…"

"Stop," I cut her off again. "You found me. You saved me. In more ways than one. You took me in when you barely knew me. You clothed me and fed me until I found a job. You put a roof over my head. You gave me a chance at a normal life. I don't know where I would be without you."

"You're family."

"And that's what family does for each other," I repeat the words that she's said to me more times than I could ever possibly count.

"Exactly." She smiles. "I'm sorry if sometimes I stick my nose where I shouldn't or if it feels like I'm pushing you. I just want to see you put yourself out there. I want you to have a chance to be happy."

"I am happy. Despite everything I think I'm happier than I've ever been. And yes, a large part of that has to do with Abel," I say what I already know she's thinking. "But it also has to do with you. And Heather. It has to do with realizing just how lucky I am to have people like you in my life. It has to do with all of this." I gesture around the room. "Because I'm alive when a few weeks ago I didn't know if I would be."

"I'd do anything for you. I hope you know that."

"I do." I smile. "And I hope you know that goes both ways."

"Even when I'm acting like a pushy big sister."

"Even then." I pop a big chunk of breadstick into my mouth seconds before giving her a toothy grin.

Chapter Twenty-one
Abel

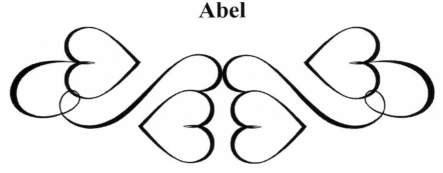

I watch my dad make his way out of post-op, his gaze going to his five sons all lined against the far wall of the waiting room.

"How is she?" Aaron is the first to ask the moment he enters the room.

"She's doing okay. Surgery went well and she's awake now."

"When can we see her?" Adam asks, standing.

"In a little bit. She's still pretty groggy from the anesthesia. They're going to move her up to her own room and then you can visit her."

I sit silently, bent over with my elbows on my knees and my head in my hands. I don't think I've been so scared before in my entire life, and while I know it's not over yet, the relief I feel is so overwhelming I'm not quite sure how to compartmentalize it.

I give my parents hell but at the end of the day they are two of the most important people in my life. I don't know what I'd do if I lost either one of them, especially my mom.

"She's going to be okay, son." My dad's hand settles on my shoulder and I look up to see him towering over me.

There's so much emotion on his face it nearly breaks me. My dad has always been emotionally disconnected. We always knew he loved us, but he was never one to show any real feelings or emotion. Seeing it written so clearly on his face now is almost like I'm seeing him for the first time. And not just as my dad, but as a man. A man who is facing the very real possibility of losing the woman he's loved over half his life.

I can't imagine what he must be feeling. And yet here he is, comforting me. Reassuring me that she's okay.

"I know," I mutter, reaching up to pat the hand resting on my shoulder.

"It's going to be a little while before she's in her room. Why don't you all run down to the cafeteria and grab a bite to eat or get some coffee. I'll call as soon as she's ready for visitors."

"I could use a bite to eat." Aaron nods, standing. "Abel?" He turns toward me.

"Yeah, that sounds good," I agree, knowing I'd rather be anywhere than sitting in this tiny room for a second longer.

"We haven't really had that much time to catch up since I've been home," Adam says, sliding down into the chair next to me while my other brothers are still browsing the vending machines. "How is everything going?"

"Pretty good." I nod, picking at the label of my water bottle. "What about you? Any closer to saving the world?"

"It's times like this I wish I were." He blows out a hard breath, popping off the lid of his coffee cup before emptying a couple sweetener packets into it.

"Yeah, no shit," I agree.

"How's the music biz treating you? Aaron said you've been playing a lot."

"It's been good. I've got a few regular weekly gigs lined up which is good."

"You still go down to Plymouth and play?"

"Sometimes." I smile, thinking about the many times they found me there when I was younger. If my parents couldn't get a hold of me they'd send one of my brothers out looking for me. They always knew where to find me. Sitting on the corner of Plymouth Street with my guitar case open as I played for anyone who cared enough to stop and listen.

"God, I remember the first time I found you there. You couldn't have been more than fourteen but the way you played made it sound like you'd been playing for twenty years. I've always envied your talent."

I'm not sure what to say to that. I think it's the first time any of my siblings has actually complemented me when it comes to my music.

"That means a lot, Adam." It's all I'm able to get out before Aaron, Alex, and Andrew join us. Andrew and Alex are loudly debating the difference between baked chips and regular.

"I'm only saying, just because it says baked does not mean it's healthy." Andrew rips the bag of chips out of Alex's hand and starts to read the back.

"You two will find anything to argue over." Adam shakes his head. "You sound like two teenage girls."

"Because I care about what I put into my body I'm a teenage girl?" Andrew sneers.

I shake my head, my gaze locking on a blonde that enters the cafeteria to my right. Recognition is instant and I find myself standing, completely oblivious to the conversation taking place around me.

"I'll be right back," I mutter, not sticking around to hear what, if anything, my brothers have to say.

Crossing the cafeteria in record speed, I close in on her right as she reaches the coffee machines.

"Claire?"

She whips her gaze in my direction, surprise the first thing that registers across her pretty face.

"Abel." She quickly recovers, an easy smile falling into place. "What are you doing here?"

"My mom had to have a procedure done. What about you?"

"I'm just visiting a friend." She looks away and reaches for a coffee cup and proceeds to fill it. "Everything okay with your mom?"

"Yeah, I think so. Your friend?"

"I think so." She adds some creamer to her cup.

"That's good."

"It is." She pops the lid on her coffee and turns to face me. "Well, it was good seeing you again, Abel." She smiles, shuffling her weight from one foot to the other. "I really should get back upstairs."

"Yeah, you too," I say, taking a step back so she can pass. "Have you talked to Finley recently?" I call after her before she's taken more than a handful of steps.

She turns slowly, meeting my gaze.

"Yeah, why?"

"Is she doing okay? It's hard to tell through text messages and since she pretty much refuses to talk to me on the phone." I sigh.

"Don't take it personally." She smiles. I wouldn't say Finley and Claire look alike – both are beautiful but in very different ways – but when she smiles it's impossible not to see Finley's smile. And her eyes. She has the same stark, green eyes as her sister. "She's going through some stuff right now. But trust me, when she gets back you'll be the first person she calls."

"Is that so?" I can't help the slow grin that falls into place.

"It is." She gives me a knowing look. "I really need to get going." She gestures toward the door. "It was good seeing you, Abel," she says again.

"You too." I nod, keeping my eyes locked on her until she exits the cafeteria and disappears moments later.

Chapter Twenty-two
Finley

"Abel's here." Claire bursts into my room, causing me to jump.

"What?" I stutter out, sure I heard her wrong.

"Abel is here," she repeats slower. "I ran into him downstairs in the cafeteria. Something about his mom having a procedure done."

"You didn't tell him I was here, did you?" Panic rises in my chest.

"Of course not." She crosses the room, placing her coffee on the bedside table. "I told him I was here visiting a friend."

"What's wrong with his mom?"

"He didn't say. Sounded like she'll be okay." She shrugs.

"He's here," I say more to myself than to Claire. After over three hellish weeks we're existing in the same space again. Even if we aren't physically together, it's something I wasn't sure would ever happen again.

The urge to see him becomes almost too much to bear. Knowing that he's here, in this very hospital. That with a quick trip to the cafeteria I could be standing face to face with him all over again. The realization sends both fear and excitement coursing through me.

I jump again when my phone signals a text. I already know who it is before I lift my phone from the table.

Abel: So funny thing. I just ran into your sister at the hospital.

I take a deep breath, trying to calm my shaking hands.

"Is that him?" Claire leans forward and looks down at my phone. "Well that didn't take him long." She laughs to herself.

Me: Oh yeah. Why are you at the hospital?

"I already told you why."

"But he doesn't know that."

"Oh right."

"What was he doing when you went down there? Who was he with?"

"Honestly, I have no idea. I didn't see him until he was standing next to me."

"How did he look?" I ask, suddenly so envious of my sister I could curl up into a ball and cry like a two year old.

"Is that man capable of looking anything outside of incredible?" She gives me a knowing smirk.

"Good point," I agree right as my phone pings again.

Abel: My mom had to have a procedure done. Nothing to worry about.

Me: Is she doing okay?

Abel: I think so. It's been a long day.

I look up at Claire who's standing next to my bed, reading over my shoulder.

"Do you mind?" I flatten my phone against my chest.

"I wanna know what he's saying." She pouts out her bottom lip.

"You're ridiculous." I playfully push her away. "Don't you have somewhere to be?"

"Is that your way of telling me to get lost?" She arches a brow at me.

"I would never tell you that."

"Sure you wouldn't." She laughs, grabbing her coffee off the table. "I have a phone call to make anyway." She heads toward the door. "But I expect a full report when I get back."

"Yes, ma'am." I stick my tongue out at her seconds before she disappears into the hall.

Holding my phone back up, I reread Abel's last message before finally responding.

Me: Anything I can do?

Abel: Hearing your voice would help.

I think about it for a long moment before deciding against it. It would be too tempting to talk to him, knowing that he's here, in this very building. I'd probably lose my damn mind and tell him I'm here too.

Me: Sorry, I can't right now. Anything else I can do?

Abel: You can't or you don't want to?

Me: Trust me, I want to.

Abel: Everything is so crazy right now. I wish we could go back to that night. I wish I could disappear in that space with you and lose myself all over again.

Me: I wish that, too.

Abel: I've gotta get back. Talk soon?

Me: I'll be here.

Abel: As will I.

I smile, locking my phone before dropping it into my lap.

Never in a million years did I think I could feel so strongly about a man I barely knew. But ten hours with him felt like ten lifetimes. Every moment more incredible than the one that came before it.

But then there's that little voice in the back of my head that wonders if I didn't make it all up. If it wasn't my way of coping with what I knew was to come. That maybe I was so desperate to hang onto this life that I grabbed the first person I could and entangled myself so deep into them that I would have something to hold onto when the time came.

It's easy to justify it that way. Easy to brush it off. But deep down I know what I felt for Abel – what I *feel* for Abel – is more than just real. It's engrained into every fiber of my being. I can't explain it or make sense of it. He's there – like he's a part of me. Like he's been there all along.

I've just dozed off when my cell phone springs to life next to me, jolting me from my sleep. I sit up, frantically searching for it on my night stand before I'm able to locate it.

Pulling the charging cord from the bottom, I slide my finger across the screen without registering who's calling.

"Hello," I grumble into the phone.

"Finley." The instant his smooth voice hits my ears I'm wide awake.

"Abel?" My heart drums loudly in my ears.

"Did I wake you?"

"Yes. I mean no. I'm awake," I stutter out.

"I'm sorry to call so late. I guess I just really needed to hear your voice. I honestly didn't think you'd answer."

"Is everything okay?" I immediately sense that something is off.

"Yes." He blows out a hard breath. "No."

"What's wrong?" I push up further in bed.

"I told you last week that my mom had a procedure done at the hospital."

"The day you ran into Claire, I remember."

"It wasn't just *some* procedure. It was to have a mass removed from her breast."

My stomach instantly twists.

"Breast cancer?" I guess, my voice breaking.

"Yeah." He blows out another hard breath.

"Abel," I start, but immediately stop, not really sure what to say. We've been texting every day for over a week and while I knew something was going on with his mom, I never imagined it was cancer.

"When did she find out?"

"A week or so ago."

"I'm so sorry. Are you doing okay?"

"Yeah, I'm okay. Worried. But okay." He pauses. "They removed the mass but there's indication that it's spread to outer lying tissue. She starts chemo this week."

"Is that why your brother is in town?"

"Yeah. He flew in for the procedure but he couldn't stay. I dropped him off at the airport earlier today." He pauses. "Let's talk about something else. Tell me what's going on with you."

"Nothing much. You know me, I'm pretty boring."

"I don't remember you being boring." I can hear the smile in his voice and a warm sensation passes through my chest. "Read any good books lately?"

"A ton actually," I admit, knowing that's really all I've had to do – not that I much mind. I could spend my entire life reading books and be perfectly happy.

"I bought you something the other day."

"You did?" I question, surprise apparent in my voice.

"I was at a book store with Andrew and I saw something. You probably have it already, but on the off chance that you don't, I went ahead and picked it up."

"Wait, you were at a book store?" I question, finding this picture hard to imagine.

"Andrew had to pick up some books for school on our way home from visiting Mom last week. Normally I would have waited in the car, but this time I decided to go in."

"And do I get to know what it is that you bought for me?" I pull my bottom lip into my mouth to try to suppress the ginormous smile creeping across my lips.

"Yeah, when I give it to you."

"That's not very nice." I huff.

"What isn't?"

"That you tell me you got me something but I have to wait to find out what it is."

"Well, you could always tell me where you are and I could bring it to you."

"Nice try." I laugh.

"You're seriously not going to tell me where you are?"

"Nope."

"You have to be the most secretive person I've ever met before, you know that?"

"How so?" I play coy.

"Because we spent an entire night together and somehow you managed to avoid telling me your last name, where you work, and where you live. And now, apparently you're off somewhere doing who knows what and you refuse to tell me where you are."

"Makes things fun, doesn't it?" I tease.

"It's maddening." He chuckles. "My Finley, so full of mystery."

My heart flips in my chest. *My* Finley. He's staking his claim and I'd be lying if I said it didn't make me outrageously happy.

"What are you doing right now?" he asks.

"At this very moment?" I question, not waiting for his response before answering. "Lying in bed. What are you doing?"

"The same." He sighs loudly. "It's impossible not to think of you. I swear I can still smell you everywhere."

My stomach twists.

"What do you mean you can smell me?"

"I'm sure it's all in my mind, but if I close my eyes I can imagine you here, next to me. Your scent dancing around me.

It's impossible not to think of you. Your hair spread out on my pillow, lips parted, cheeks pink."

Heat spreads across my face.

"I want you here again."

"I want to be there again."

"Then why did you bolt on me?"

"I wouldn't say I bolted."

"You bolted."

"Whatever." I huff, my smile firmly intact.

"Why?"

"It's complicated."

"I'm sure I could keep up."

"It's not something I can easily explain. Just know I wanted to go back the instant I left."

"Then why didn't you leave your number?"

"Because I thought it'd be easier that way. Things are… complicated right now."

"There's that word again… *Complicated*."

"It's true. I didn't want to drag you into what I have going on. We spent an incredible night together. I wanted to remember it that way and not have it be tainted by *other* things."

"Other things," he repeats slowly.

"I came to your show," I blurt, not sure why I feel the need to tell him that.

"What show?"

"The one at Trolley House?"

"Wait? You were there? And you didn't say anything?"

"I didn't want you to know I was there. I knew I was leaving the next day and that seeing you wouldn't have changed anything. But I wanted to be there."

"And what did you think?"

"You were incredible, just like I knew you would be."

"I can't believe you were there."

"I wanted to hear you play at least once. And not in your living room, but up on stage."

"You say that like you're never going to get the chance to see me play again."

"At the time I wasn't sure I would."

"Okay, now I'm really fucking curious. What the hell is going on with you? Where are you… Really?"

"I can't tell you that."

"Why not?" he groans.

"Because then you would come looking for me?"

"And that would be such a bad thing, why?"

"Because I need to take care of some things first." I sink my head further into the pillows and look up at the dark ceiling. "How did you find me anyway? When you showed up at my sister's apartment. How did you find out where I live?"

"This is going to sound really bad." He laughs nervously. "A buddy of mine knows a PI. I paid him to do a little digging."

"Wait, you hired a private investigator to track me down?" I sit straight up in bed.

"It's not like you gave me much of a choice."

"So what else did you find out about me?" Nervous energy pumps through my veins.

"Nothing really. He found out where you worked and was able to track your address through the DMV. Once I had that I really didn't need to know anything else. I wasn't trying to invade your privacy, I just wanted to be able to see you again. God, even saying it out loud makes me sound completely fucking mental."

"I don't think you're mental." I smile, relaxing back into the bed. "I think it's kinda sweet. That you went through so much trouble."

"Trouble that I could have avoided had you just left me your number."

"I couldn't make it that easy on you," I joke, knowing that my intention was never to play games with him. I thought leaving the way I did would be easier. For everyone.

"Your sister seems nice."

"She is. She's the best."

"How's her friend?"

"What friend?" I ask, confused.

"The one in the hospital? The one she was visiting the day I ran into her."

"Oh, that friend." I try to cover the nervous jitter in my voice. "Yeah, she's doing okay."

"What was going on there?"

"Not sure exactly," I lie. "I guess she had a bit of a health scare, but from what I understand she's on the upswing."

"Well that's good."

"Yeah, it is." I nod even though he can't see me.

"Finley." He says my name so softly it causes the little hairs on the back of my neck to stand.

"Yeah?"

"Would you think I was completely crazy if I told you that you're all I can think about?"

It takes everything I have to keep my voice calm.

"If I did then I guess I'd be crazy too, because you're all I can think about."

"It's insane, isn't it? To feel this drawn to someone after one night?"

"It really does." I let out a nervous laugh.

"But I can't fucking help it."

"Neither can I." I smile, feeling like I might burst open at the seams at any moment.

"I *need* to see you." The urgency in his voice is damn near crippling.

"Soon," I promise.

"How soon?"

"Soon," I say, hoping that I can will it to be.

It's all I want. To be better. To get a chance to see where this thing between us can go. All my life I feel like I've been searching for a place to belong and now that I think maybe I have, I want nothing more than to reach out and take it.

We spend the next hour talking about everything and yet nothing at the same time. I'm content listening to his voice. Something I swear I could do for hours on end and never tire of.

And even though I was hesitant to talk to him on the phone, now that I have I can't imagine going a day without hearing his voice. It's like the more I get of him the more I crave him and I don't think I'll ever get enough of the way he makes me feel.

Chapter Twenty-three
Finley

"So the doc said you can go home tomorrow?" Claire asks into the phone, sounding even more excited than I feel.

"He said the initial scans look good, and as long as I don't respond too negatively to the chemo treatment this afternoon, he sees no reason why I can't be released as early as tomorrow morning."

"Oh my gosh, Fin! That's amazing!" her voice singsong.

"It is," I agree.

"Then why don't you sound more excited?"

"Because it means I have to get through chemo first." I exhale loudly.

"You'll be fine. I know the first round was rough, but look at it this way, it can't get any worse."

"You say that now and then it will," I scold.

"Don't be so superstitious. Me saying something doesn't mean the opposite will happen."

"How do you know?"

"I tell you what, how about I come sit with you during your session today?"

"I thought you had to work."

"I do, but I have some sick time saved up. It will make me feel better knowing you don't have to sit there alone."

"I did just fine the first time on my own. You don't have to come."

"I want to," she insists. "What time are they coming to get you?"

"Three o'clock, I think."

"Perfect. I'll be there before then."

"Okay," I agree, honestly feeling a million times better knowing Claire will be there with me.

"See you then."

"Okay. See you then."

"I do not get the fascination with this dude. He's not even that good looking," Claire says, looking down at the magazine in her lap.

"Who?" I ask, looking over to see who she's talking about.

"Jason Momoa." She holds the article up.

"Have you lost your ever loving mind?" I look at her like she has five heads. "Jason Momoa is gorgeous."

"I beg to differ." She curls her nose.

"Watch an episode of Game of Thrones with him in it and then tell me he's not the most mouthwatering thing you've ever seen."

"Overrated." She shrugs.

"I think you've officially lost it," I tell her, shaking my head, laughing.

"You feeling okay?" Her gaze goes to my chest port before finding my face.

"Yeah. So far so good." I give her an encouraging smile. "You being here helps. I'm sure I don't have to tell you this, but this room is depressing." I gesture around to the handful of other people also here for treatment.

"I won't disagree with you there. They really should consider brightening this room up. Maybe it wouldn't be so bad if it didn't feel so sterile in here."

"I highly doubt the color of the walls has anything to do with it."

"You'd be surprised how much things like that can affect a person's mood."

"Says the person who's *not* having an array of chemicals injected into her body."

"Fair enough. At least you won't have to do this for much longer."

"Four more sessions."

"That's not so bad."

"No? Maybe you should give it a try."

"I'm just saying, it could be worse." She holds her hands up in surrender.

"I'll give you that. I'll be glad when this part is over. I can't wait to get back to some semblance of a normal life."

"You'll get there." She reaches over and pats my leg.

"How are we doing over here, ladies?" One of the nurses comes over to check my drip.

"We're hanging in there," I say, dropping my head back on the head rest of the chair.

"Looks like you're just about finished."

"Thank goodness." I let out a deep sigh of relief.

"Let me go grab a few things and we will get you unhooked and on your way."

"Thank you," Claire replies, folding her magazine before dropping it onto the small table next to her.

Within ten minutes I'm cleared to be released back to my room where the doctor will come in and check on me. Claire helps me into the wheelchair before wheeling me out into the hallway.

I feel utterly exhausted, even though I haven't really done anything. I can't wait to get back upstairs and close my eyes for a little bit.

We stop at the elevator and wait less than a minute before the doors slide open in front of us.

"Oh, excuse us," Claire says, rolling my wheelchair backward as two people step off the elevator.

I'm so tired I don't even bother looking up, but after several seconds have passed and Claire hasn't moved I finally do.

The second my eyes lock with his everything slows down. I feel like I've been transported into an alternate universe where nothing feels real, yet I know that it is.

"Finley," he whispers after what feels like an eternity, confusion peppering his handsome face. "What are you…" His gaze slides up to Claire and then back down to me.

I sit in stunned silence, a thick knot forming at the base of my throat.

I look to Abel's left, spotting an attractive middle aged woman holding onto his arm.

His mom…

God, how could I have been so stupid. I knew she was starting chemo today. How did I not put two and two together? If she had surgery at this hospital it would only make sense that her chemo would be here, too.

"Claire." My voice quivering with a riddled sob, needing to get out of here before I completely melt down. My stomach twists but I don't know if it's from the chemo or because I find myself face to face with Abel under the worst conditions possible.

"We have to go." Claire makes a bee line for the elevator, which has started pinging because it's been open for so long. Without another word she wheels me inside, Abel's clouded blue eyes the last thing I see before the elevator doors close between us.

"Oh my god. Oh my god. Oh my god," I chant to myself as the car starts to climb upward. "Oh my god," I say again, on the verge of having a panic attack.

"It's okay, Fin. It's okay." Claire kneels down in front of me, taking both of my hands in hers.

"Look at me," I scream in her face. "Nothing about this is okay."

"Honey, you're sick. It's nothing to be ashamed of."

"Nothing to be ashamed of?" I draw back, catching sight of my reflection in the mirrored elevator doors. "Look at me." I point to myself.

I look even worse than I thought. Dressed in light blue, plaid pajamas, my hair in a knot on top of my head which does little to hide the large bald area that stretches down the side. I have no make-up on, my cheeks are sunken in, and there are deep, dark circles lining both of my eyes. I look like death.

"Take a deep breath. He's just a guy."

"He's not *just* a guy," I sob. "And now he's never going to want to see me again." Tears prick the back of my eyes.

I know I'm probably overreacting, but I can't stop myself. It's like every emotion I've bottled up over the last few days comes spewing to the surface and I can't hold it back any longer.

"You know that's not true. You're just upset and tired. Once we get back to your room and you've had a chance to rest, you'll feel differently. You'll see."

"Why am I so unlucky?" I croak, sniffing when Claire reaches out to wipe my cheeks with her thumbs.

"You're not unlucky. You've just had a rough go of things as of late."

"By, as of late, you mean my entire life."

"Hey." She tips my chin up and forces me to meet her gaze. "I promise this isn't as bad as it seems. Who knows, maybe this will be a good thing."

"How could this possibly be a good thing?"

"Because now you can tell him the truth and let the chips fall where they may." She gives me a sympathetic smile, standing when the elevator stops climbing and the doors slide open.

My phone pings in my lap as she wheels me out into the hall, and even though I'm scared to look, I can't stop myself at the same time.

Abel: You're the friend Claire was visiting?

I feel horribly nauseous and have to swallow down the sudden urge I feel to vomit.

Me: Yes.

Abel: Explain. Now.

Me: Can you come to my house tomorrow? I should be home sometime in the afternoon. I'll explain everything then.

Abel: Tell me what is going on, Finley.

Me: Tomorrow. I promise. I'll text you what time.

I lock my phone and drop it back into my lap, letting out a slow and shaky breath. The moment I've been avoiding is here and now that he's seen me, there's nothing I can do to hide the truth.

Maybe Claire's right. Maybe this is a good thing. Maybe this is our jumping off point. I made it through surgery and I'm nearly half way through chemo. Maybe now is as good of a time as any.

I had convinced myself that I could wait until I was better, until I knew I was cancer free. But the truth is it was only a matter of time before I finally caved. I hate that it happened this way. I hate that he had to see me like this. But now that he knows I've been lying, I think it's time he knows why. No matter how hard it will be to face him, I have to.

Like Claire said, maybe this will be a good thing. I don't relish the idea of him seeing me, but if he wants to be in my life, this is my reality. I'm sick. Surgery didn't magically fix me; it just gave me a fighting chance. Now it's up to him to decide if I'm worth it. And maybe he'll decide that I'm not. Not that I could blame him. He's already dealing with a sick mom. A sick girlfriend might be too much for him. And that's okay. I mean, I'll be devastated but at the end of the day I'll understand.

How much can I really ask from a man I only spent ten hours with?

Sure, we shared an undeniable connection. And yes, it was hands down the best night of my life. But it was only one night. *One* night. We're talking about something so far beyond what he should have to deal with at this point in our relationship, if that's even what you would call it.

Then again, nothing about *us* has been normal so why would this be any different? Maybe it's because we're not normal. Maybe the reason we've been so drawn toward each other is because we both know it's right.

We don't need weeks, or even months, or years to get to know each other. Or at least I don't. I knew that very first night that I'd love him for the rest of my life. Granted, I expected my life to be a lot shorter at the time. But it still doesn't change how I felt that night or how I've felt since then.

Abel is everything I want. I guess it's time to see if I'm everything he wants... Sickness and all.

Chapter Twenty-four
Abel

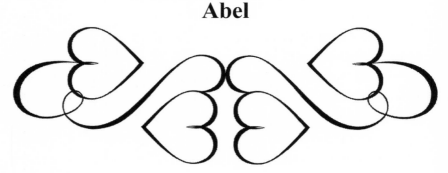

I can't get the image of Finley sitting in that wheelchair out of my head. She looked so frail, so weak, and yet every bit the beautiful woman I fell hard and fast for weeks ago.

I knew she was hiding something from me. She's been hiding things from me since the moment we met, but I never dreamed this was it.

Hell, I still don't even know what *this* is.

I keep running over the details in my head. The incision down the side of her head. The port in her chest. The paleness of her flesh. The way her eyes seemed to have lost some of their luster. Like the light was being snuffed out.

Considering she was being wheeled out of the cancer ward, it doesn't take a genius to figure out what all this means. And yet at the same time I can't make sense of it.

Cancer?

She seemed perfectly fine the night we spent together. Happy. Healthy. Full of life. I would have never guessed there was something wrong with her.

Clearly she had her reasons for leaving me the way she did, with no way of contacting her, but only now am I starting to realize why.

I need answers. I need to know what the hell is going on. It's been impossible to focus on anything but Finley since I saw her yesterday.

My poor mom had no idea what was going on, and even though I insisted everything was fine, I know she could tell something was up. But I was there for her and I didn't want to make it about me. She's having a hard enough time as it is and I'm trying to be there for her in a way I haven't been in the past.

I stop outside of Finley's apartment door, remembering how anxious I was the first time I came here. I think I might be even more so now.

Raising my fist, I knock it against the door a couple of times before taking a step back. It's only seconds before the door swings open and Claire is staring back at me.

"Hi." She smiles softly.

"Hey."

"We really have to stop meeting like this," she jokes, clearly trying to lighten the mood.

"She here?" I cut straight to the chase.

"She is." She nods slowly, opening the door further so that I can step inside.

I slide past her, hearing the door snap closed behind me seconds later.

"She's only been home a few minutes so she's still getting settled. You'll need to wash your hands before you go back there." She gestures down the hallway. "And you're not sick or anything, right?"

"Not that I'm aware of."

"Okay, good. You can use the sink in the kitchen." She points to my right.

My eyes do a quick sweep of the apartment. It's your standard, run of the mill apartment. A living room, dining area, and kitchen all crammed together into a small space – a tiny wall separating the kitchen from the other two rooms.

Sliding into the small galley style kitchen, I make quick work of washing my hands with the antibacterial soap Claire instructs me to use.

When I finish, Claire is standing at the mouth of the hallway waiting for me.

"She's the last door on the left. She knows you're here so there's no need to knock. There are a couple things I need you to know before you go in there." She waits until I nod before continuing, "She's going to try to put on a brave face for you and pretend everything is okay when in reality she is very sick. Don't let her down play it. You deserve to know what you're getting into before you decide."

"Decide what?"

"Whether or not this is something you want to continue."

"Is that even a question?" I arch a brow, not missing the way the side of her mouth hitches as she tries to fight off a smile.

"Go. She's waiting for you."

I nod, heading down the hallway toward Finley's room. I'm so nervous. The only thing I can hear is my heart hammering inside my chest.

Pushing open the door, I immediately spot Finley propped up against the worn headboard of her bed, a big, thick comforter pulled up to her waist.

Her hair is down, and while she still looks tired, she looks much more herself today than she did yesterday. Some of the color has returned to her cheeks and she smiles when she sees me enter.

"Hey." I shut the door behind me, slowly crossing the dimly lit room.

"Hi." She pats the bed next to her. "I'm not contagious," she tells me when she senses my hesitance.

"I wouldn't care if you were." I grin, taking a seat on the side of the mattress before angling myself toward her. "How are you feeling?"

"I'm good." She smiles, sending an assortment of feelings swarming through me.

"So…" I look around the room that's sparsely decorated, not missing the piles of books stacked in the corner. "This is where you live."

"It's not much." She shrugs. "But it's home."

"I see you weren't kidding about the books." I gesture to the corner.

"That's just what I've purchased over the last year, plus what I brought with me. If I could have brought all the books I've had in my life they'd likely be piled to the ceiling." She laughs.

"Speaking of books." I reach inside my jacket and pull out the gift I bought her when I visited the book store with Andrew. Extending the book to her, I watch an array of emotions pass over her face as she looks at it.

"Tam Thompson." She smiles, running her finger over the author's name. "You remembered."

"Of course I did." I lean forward. "I know you probably already have this book, and that it's not in the best shape, but look." I flip open the cover to reveal the author's autograph. "I'm guessing your copy doesn't have that in it."

"Abel." Her hand goes over her mouth and I'm not sure if she's about to laugh or cry. "This is incredible. I don't know how to thank you."

"You don't have to thank me. I practically walked out of the store with it for free. Clearly whoever it belonged to didn't treasure it the way I knew you would."

"I seriously don't know what to say." She looks up, her glassy eyes meeting my gaze.

"You can start by telling me what's wrong with you." I take the book from her hand and set it on the bedside table.

"Abel."

"Just be honest with me, Finley. Whatever it is, I promise I can handle it."

"Brain cancer," she blurts so quickly it takes me a moment to process what she actually said.

"Brain cancer?" I draw back slightly.

"They think they got it all but we won't be sure until a few weeks after I finish chemo."

"Okay." I blow out a breath. "How about you start from the beginning?"

"I can do that." She nods. "I actually found out the day I met you." She looks down to where her hands are knotted in her lap. I reach over and grab one of them, wrapping my fingers tightly around hers, urging her to continue. "That's why I was in that bar. I'm obviously not old enough to drink, and it's not like I was meeting friends there. I don't know. I had been walking for hours and I saw that bar and something came over me. I knew I had to go inside. And that's where you found me." She finally meets my gaze, a sad smile tugging at her lips. "I should have told you right away. I should have been up front with you. But when you looked at me, I don't know, I just couldn't do it. You smiled at me and I forgot. And it was so easy to pretend with you."

"Tell me what led up to you being in the bar. How long have you been sick?"

"That's just it. I *wasn't* sick. Or at least I didn't know I was. I had been having some headaches, a few dizzy spells, nothing major. I went in for some testing the week before never dreaming that the outcome would be cancer."

"But you had surgery?" I gesture to her head where her incision is now covered by her hair.

"I did. They removed ninety percent of the four centimeter malignant tumor two days after I met you. They didn't think I'd survive the surgery, let alone that they could remove so much of the tumor without complications."

"But they did?" I question, my chest tightening.

"There were some minor complications, but yes, they did." She nods.

"So that's why you ghosted me, because you thought..."

"Because I thought in the matter of a day I would be dead."

"You should have told me."

"What good would it have done? Besides, had you known you wouldn't have looked at me the same."

"That's not true," I argue.

"That's easy for you to say now, but we both know it's true. I would have become the *sick* girl and everything would have been different. I needed to not be sick for just one more night. I needed to let myself live in a way I never have before. And you gave me that. One perfect night."

"So then what? You thought you'd just sneak off and die and that would be it?"

"Yes," she admits apologetically. "I never meant to deceive you. I just really liked the way you made me feel and I wanted to feel it for as long as I possibly could."

"Why didn't you tell me? After you survived the surgery."

"I didn't want to bring you into all of this." She gestures around the room. "They got most of the tumor but that doesn't mean I'm not sick anymore. There could still be more cancer. The tumor could regrow. So many things can still go wrong."

"But that's what the chemo is for, right?"

"Yes, but even still, chemo is no guarantee."

"So how do we know that you're cured?"

"I have four more rounds of chemo before I go in for my next scan. We will know more then. I might end up cancer free at the end of this. But if they find something else or the tumor has grown..." She trails off. "It's very possible I may not survive. And I didn't think that was fair to you. I wanted to wait until I knew I was out of the woods before I told you any of this. I didn't want to put this on you, especially after learning about your mom."

"But don't you think that should have been my choice to make? Do you know how confused I was to see you at the hospital the way I did? To have to find out that way…"

"I'm sorry. But I did what I felt was right."

"So now what?"

"Now the choice is yours. And listen," she leans forward, wrapping her fingers around the back of my hand that's still holding her other hand, "I'll totally understand if you need to back away. This is a lot, I know that. And it's going to get a lot worse before it gets better."

"You really think so little of me? That I would abandon you because you're sick?"

"You barely know me, Abel. How could I expect anything else?"

"We may not have known each other for a very long period of time, but I've shared more with you in one night than I've ever shared with another woman. And I only fell harder in the weeks that have followed. Talking to you, laughing with you, you make me feel things I've never felt before. You make me feel…"

"Free," she finishes for me and I'm not even a little surprised that she does. Our connection really does run that deep.

"Exactly. I don't feel like I have to hide from you. You see me more clearly than anyone I've ever known. Because you see *me*. Not what you want to see, not what I want you to see, but me. The real me."

"I feel like I've waited for you my entire life. Why did I have to find you now? Like this." Her eyes glaze over.

"Maybe you found me when you needed me the most." I smile, tightening my grip on her hand. "Nothing about this has been normal, Finley. From the moment I sat down next to you at the bar everything has happened in hyper speed. Sometimes it's

184

hard to wrap my head around, but when I look at you." I reach up and tuck a strand of hair away from her face. "When I look at you everything feels right."

"I feel the same."

"So then it's settled."

"What is?" She grins, and when she does it's hard to remember what I was going to say next.

"You and me."

"You and me?" She cocks her head to the side, the cutest fucking expression on her face.

"It's you and me now. No more secrets. No more lies. And no more disappearing. Think you can handle that?"

"I think I'll manage." She crinkles her nose. "Does this mean I'm your girlfriend now?" she teases, shoving at my shoulder playfully.

"You got a problem with that?" I challenge.

"Does it look like I have a problem with that?" She gives me a knowing look. "I'm going to lose my hair, you know that, right?"

"And so what if you do? I don't have anything against bald chicks." I smile when she shakes her head at me.

"You just can't help yourself, can you?"

"What do you mean?"

"You always have to say the right thing."

"It's a gift." I lift her hand and gently kiss the back of it.

"Okay, maybe not always." She giggles and I swear it's the sweetest sound I've ever heard.

There's a soft knock on the door and both of our gazes swing toward the door right as it opens.

"Fin." Claire peeks her head in hesitantly, her gaze going to me before sliding to her sister. "Hey, sorry to interrupt but it's time for your medication." She steps into the room carrying a glass of orange juice and a medicine cup.

"Thank you." Finley takes them from Claire, emptying the cup of pills into her mouth before drinking them down with the juice.

"You two need anything?" Claire asks, taking the cups back from Finley.

"We're good." Finley relaxes back against the pillows.

Claire gives me one more sweeping glance before she turns and quickly exits the room.

Chapter Twenty-five
Finley

He's saying all the right things. And the way he looks at me, the way he touches me, I swear I couldn't make this up if I tried.

If I could pick a perfect moment out of one of my books, one that feels like it's crafted by the heavens, this would be it. Only it's not a book. I used to think fiction was better than real life, but Abel makes me see things differently.

Maybe real life isn't so bad after all.

Abel is propped up in bed next to me, holding my hand. We've been like this for hours and even though I'm so tired I can barely keep my eyes open, there's not a chance in hell I'm going to close them.

We've talked about everything from our childhoods, to our favorite movies, and even had a pretty interesting conversation about politics, though I'm still not sure how we got on the subject.

"How's your mom doing?" I finally broach the subject.

"She's hanging in there. I talked to her earlier and so far she seems to be handling the chemo pretty well."

"It didn't bother me too bad right away. It was the second and third days that were the roughest for me. But everyone handles it differently. Maybe she'll be one of the lucky ones."

"Maybe." He thinks on that for a moment. "Is it painful?"

"Chemo?" I ask, not continuing until he nods. "I wouldn't say it's painful, per se. It's kind of like getting sick. You feel it coming on slowly and then all of a sudden you feel like you've been hit by a truck. The nausea is the worst. I go from feeling perfectly fine to deathly ill in the blink of an eye."

"You seem okay today."

"Check in with me tomorrow. If this time is anything like the last then you may want to stay away for a couple days."

"A little puke doesn't bother me."

"You say that now." I give him a knowing look.

"Guess I'll just have to prove it to you." He shifts, reaching over to lift a section of my hair, revealing the incision site from surgery.

I flinch, ready to pull away.

"Does it hurt?" he asks, pressing up to get a better look.

"Not as much anymore. In the beginning the pain was excruciating. I spent days after I finally woke up feeling like my head was going to explode from the inside out." I force myself to stay still, allowing him to look.

"That had to have been hard." He releases my hair and relaxes back.

"It was. But it sure beat the alternative."

"Which was?"

"Being dead." I shrug.

"Definitely better than the alternative," he agrees. "I wish I could have been there for you."

"I'm glad you weren't," I admit. "Trust me, it wasn't pretty."

"You must think I scare easily." He smirks.

"Give it time. I might frighten you off," I tease, leaning into him so that our shoulders touch.

"Not gonna happen." He turns his face inward and presses a light kiss to the top of my head. "But I probably should go. I have a gig at nine and you need your rest."

"I wish I could come watch you play."

"Soon," he promises, kissing my head again before shifting off the bed.

"Guess you'll have to bring your guitar over and give me a private show."

"I think that can be arranged," he tells me, crossing around to my side of the bed. "Call me if you need anything." He leans forward, supporting his weight by pressing his hands into the mattress next to me.

"I think Claire has me covered, but yes, I'll call if I need anything."

"Promise you won't disappear on me again." He leans in further so that his face is hovering inches from mine.

"I promise. I'll be right here."

He closes the distance between us, laying a soft kiss to my lips.

It's the lightest touch – a brush of his mouth against mine, but it's enough to ignite an inferno through my veins.

"Goodnight, Finley." He smiles, pushing up into a full stand.

"Goodnight, Abel." I offer him a small wave as he backs slowly out of the room.

Pausing at the door, he stares at me for a long moment.

"I thought you were leaving," I say after several seconds of silence have stretched between us.

"I'm finding it hard to make myself," he admits, causing a full blown smile to slide across my face.

He smiles and damn it if that dimple doesn't pop out making my heart flutter against my ribs.

"Go. I'll be fine."

"Maybe it's not you I'm worried about."

I pull my bottom lip into my mouth to keep myself from professing my love for him right here on the spot. Things between Abel and I have progressed at rapid speed, but that doesn't mean I'm ready to start throwing out the L word just yet. Even if I feel it, I'm not ready to say it. Some things need time and this is one of them.

"You're going to be late." Glancing at the clock on my bedside table, I see it's already after eight o'clock which seems impossible.

We've been in my room talking for nearly four hours and yet it feels like only minutes have passed since he got here.

"Okay." He lets out an exhale. "I'm going," he says, still not moving.

"I'm waiting." I laugh, crossing my arms in front of myself.

"Fuck." He chuckles. "Okay, I really am going." He peels open the door and steps into the hallway before once again turning back toward me. "What do you want for breakfast tomorrow?"

"Abel!" I laugh, pointing in the vicinity of the front door.

"Fine. I'll surprise you." He grins. "Goodnight, Finley."

"Goodnight." The ridiculous smile on my lips only gets bigger when he walks away.

I feel so happy I swear I could get out of this bed and run laps, screaming it to the world.

I don't know how he does it. I don't know how he makes me feel like everything is perfect when in reality it's far from it.

I want to bottle up this feeling so that whenever I'm feeling weak or down I can open it up and remember how I feel right now in this very moment. Beautiful. Loved. Wanted.

It's everything I've always desired. The perfect man. The epic love story. A life that amounts to more than just surviving. And Abel is giving that to me. Piece by piece. Minute by minute.

Word by word. He's writing our story. And what a perfect story it's turning out to be.

"Hey." Claire startles me when she suddenly appears in my doorway. "Someone looks happy."

"Who?" I look around the room, laughing when my eyes swing back to her.

"I hate to be *that* person, but…" she pauses for dramatic effect. "I told you so," she sings in a high pitched voice.

"No one likes a gloater." I laugh. "But in this case I'll let you get away with it."

"You look like you're about to float away." She leans against the door frame.

"I feel like I'm about to float away," I admit.

"He looked pretty happy, too." She gestures down the hall. "You should have seen the smile on his face as he left."

"God. How is it possible that he makes me so insanely happy and I barely even know him?" I pick up a spare pillow and cover my face with it.

"Sometimes people we know the shortest amounts of time have the biggest impact."

"Are you getting all philosophical on me?" I drop the pillow onto my lap.

"I'm just saying, stop focusing on how short of a time you've known each other. In the grand scheme of things it really doesn't matter. What matters is how you feel, and by the looks of things, I'd say you're mad about this guy."

"Mad about him." I shake my head. "Claire, I love him."

"I know." She smiles.

"Am I that transparent?"

"Um, yeah." She chuckles. "Now what do you say, love bird, how about I warm you up a little something to eat? You haven't had anything since you left the hospital."

"I'm not hungry." I shake my head. "But thank you anyway." I push out past a yawn.

"Okay, well then how about you try to get some sleep."

"I'm so tired but I feel so wired I'm not sure I could fall asleep if I tried."

"Love is the perfect drug," she says knowingly.

"It really is." I sigh, feeling so happy I swear I could burst wide open.

Chapter Twenty-six
Finley

"You came back," I say, looking up from my book when Abel steps into my bedroom.

"I told you I would."

"I know, but I thought maybe after you had a chance to process everything you might have changed your mind."

"That's not gonna happen, so you might as well get that out of your head." He drops his jacket at the foot of my bed before climbing in next to me. "What are you reading?" He settles back against the headboard and looks down at the book.

"Little Women," I tell him, closing the book so he can see the cover.

"And how many times have you read this book?"

"Only like ten times."

"*Only*." He chuckles. "I'm lucky to get through a book once." He takes the paperback from my hand and turns it over. I watch as he reads the description on the back, not able to tear my eyes away from him.

Last night, after he left, after the high of seeing him again after so many weeks had worn off, I started to question how sincere he was about sticking around.

Not that he gave me any reason to doubt him. It's just, how much can I really ask of someone who's still getting to know me?

Yes, we've been texting and talking for a couple weeks, but that was before he knew I was sick. Which, no matter how much he wants to act like it doesn't change things, we both know it does. How could it not?

"Sounds interesting." Abel hands me the book back.

"It is. Hence why I've read it multiple times." I turn, setting the book on my nightstand before looking back at Abel. "What are you doing here?"

"I wanted to see you. Should I have called first?"

"No, I'm glad you're here. Just surprised is all."

"Well you better get used to it because I'm not going anywhere." He takes my hand, entwining our fingers together. "How are you feeling today?"

"Not great," I admit.

"Your stomach?"

"Among other things." I nod. "I just feel really run down."

"Want me to go so you can get some sleep?"

"No." I shake my head.

"Claire's out there making a feast for ten it looks like." He gestures toward the door.

"She's decided if she makes all my favorite foods it will increase the odds that I'll eat something."

"Sounds like one hell of sister." He leans his shoulder into mine. "You're lucky to have her."

"I really am. I may have gotten the short stick in the mom department, but I hit the jackpot when it comes to sisters."

"Speaking of your mom, does she know?" he asks, not having to elaborate on what he's talking about.

"No." I shake my head.

"Are you going to tell her?"

"No." I shake my head again.

"I'm sorry if this is out of line, but don't you think she should know? I mean, she is your mom after all."

"She's the woman who gave birth to me. She's *not* my mom. Never has been. Besides, I wouldn't know how to find her even if I wanted to. Which I don't. If I had to guess she's either dead or living on the streets with a needle permanently attached to her arm. Either way, I don't want to know. I shut the door on that part of my life a year and a half ago and I don't ever plan to open it again. If she wanted to be my mom, she would have done it when I was a child. It's too late now."

"I'm sorry. I didn't mean to pry," he says, clearly seeing that he's struck a nerve.

"Don't be. I just don't want to add her to the list of things I have to worry about. If I allow myself to think on it for too long then I will. I act like I hate her and maybe a part of me does, but the other part of me…"

"Loves her," he finishes my sentence. "Despite everything she's done, she's still your mom."

"God, I can only imagine how this must all seem to you. My life has always been a bit of a hot mess express."

"Well you're the prettiest damn hot mess I've ever seen," he tells me, giving my hand a squeeze.

"You know, it's still not too late to make a run for it." I turn toward him, resting the side of my head against the headboard of the bed.

"I don't want to go anywhere." Reaching out, he trails the tips of his fingers down my cheek. "I'm exactly where I want to be."

"Good. Because I don't want you to go anywhere," I whisper.

Abel leans in so close that our noses are almost touching, his gaze holding mine.

"I'm going to kiss you now," he tells me but makes no attempt to move any closer.

"Okay." I push past the nervous lump in my throat.

I can't see his lips but I feel the smile on them as they brush gently against mine. It's a tentative kiss, slow and unsure at first, but it doesn't take long before it quickly intensifies.

"Hey, Fin." Claire's voice causes us to jump apart and I look up right in time to see her step through the door.

Her eyes go to me and then to Abel before moving back to me. Realizing she walked in on something, she quickly starts to apologize while backing out of the room.

"Claire, wait." I laugh, having never seen my sister quite so flustered before.

"I'm so sorry," she tells us, pausing in the doorway. Her cheeks are pink with embarrassment. I'm not sure what the hell she has to be embarrassed about. I was the one in here practically swallowing Abel's face. "I just wanted to tell you that the food's ready."

"You hungry?" I turn toward Abel who seems completely unphased by the intrusion.

"I could eat." He smiles.

"Great." Claire nods. "I'll just go set the table then."

"Don't." I throw my legs over the side of the bed. "Let's eat in the living room. I don't feel like sitting in those hard chairs," I tell her, slowly pushing to a stand.

I wobble slightly, my legs still pretty weak. Within seconds, Abel appears at my side and Claire is moving toward me.

"I'm okay," I reassure them both, holding my hands up. "My legs are just a little weak."

"Let me help you," Abel insists, linking his arm through mine despite the fact that I'm perfectly capable of walking on my own.

"That's really not necessary." I look up at him.

"Maybe I just want an excuse to be close to you. Did you ever think of that?" He leans down and rubs his nose against mine. My knees wobble again, only for a completely different reason this time.

"Okay, on that note." Claire reminds us of her presence. I look up just in time to see her spin and disappear into the hallway.

I can't help the small laugh that escapes my lips.

"Come on." Abel nudges my hip with his before guiding me out of the bedroom and down the hall to where Claire is carrying various plates and saucers of food into the living room.

Abel helps me onto the couch before going to the kitchen to help Claire with the food. When they reappear moments later, they are both smiling about something and the sight warms me from the inside out.

As crazy as this seems – as much of a whirlwind this whole situation has been, I have to say that nothing has ever felt quite so right.

"There she is." Abel steps into the apartment balancing two large paper grocery bags in his arms. He hits me with the smile he reserves only for me, kicking the door closed behind him. "How are you feeling today?" he asks, dropping the bags on the dining room table.

It's been three weeks since he found out about my cancer and while he's been here nearly every day since, I still can't get used to him standing in my living room. I want to pinch myself each and every time.

"I'm okay." I shrug, tugging at the beanie on my head.

"You sure?" He crosses the room toward me, sliding down next to me on the couch. "What's with the hat? You cold?" He reaches out and tugs on the side of the stitched material.

"Don't." I jerk away from him.

"Hey." He slides in closer. "What's going on?"

I have trouble looking at him. I knew I was probably going to lose my hair, but I didn't realize how much it would bother me when I finally did. It's been falling out for the last couple of weeks and today I finally reached a breaking point and shaved it down to stubble.

Then I proceeded to call Claire at work and have a complete and total meltdown. I swear my poor sister deserves an award for all the crap I've put her through these past few months.

Of course she handled it beautifully, the way she does with most things. She promised to take me wig shopping this weekend. I wasn't really keen on the idea at first, but Claire reminded me that I can get multiple wigs in different colors and I got to thinking that this might be fun.

But even still, nothing compares to having real hair. I don't regret shaving it off. It needed to be done. But I'm so scared to show Abel. Deep down I know he won't care, but I care.

"Finley." He reaches out and slides a hand along my cheek, guiding my gaze back to him. "What's up?"

"It's gone," I croak, not sure why I feel so emotional over something as superficial as hair.

"What's gone?" He gives me a curious look before his eyes shift up to the beanie.

"I shaved it off," I tell him, crossing my arms in front of myself like a protective barrier.

"Well then, let me see." He smiles like it's just an everyday haircut.

"I can't. It looks awful."

"Hey." He slides down onto his knees in front of me, giving me no choice but to look at him. "You are the most beautiful woman in the world. Nothing, and I mean *nothing*, is going to change that." He reaches up and slides the hat off, his eyes giving my new hairstyle a quick once over.

"Stop staring. I know how bad it looks," I say after several long moments have passed.

"Actually, I was thinking how incredibly cute you look." He grins and I'm not sure if I want to punch him or hug the hell out of him.

"Don't patronize me."

"I'm not. Finley, you couldn't look bad if you tried. Do you hear me? This is just part of the process. We knew it was going to happen. You're lucky you kept your hair as long as you did. My mom started losing hers after two treatments. And look at it this way, it's only hair."

"Says the person who has a headful of it." I pout childishly.

"You want me to shave mine?" He rocks back, challenge in his eyes.

"You wouldn't." I shake my head.

"Oh, but I would." He smiles, moving to stand.

"Don't you dare!" I grab his forearm to keep him in place. "I love your hair." Reaching out, I run my fingers through it.

"I love everything about you." He leans in, laying a soft kiss to my lips.

"Why do you have to be so perfect?" I grumble against his mouth. He pulls back, a soft chuckle escaping past his lips. "You always know exactly what to say, what to do, how to make the worst situation seem okay. It's infuriating. Sometimes I just want you to get mad with me."

"I hate to break it to you, love, but I am far from perfect. And sometimes I do get mad. I get so angry that you're having to go through this that I don't know what to do with myself. But then I look at you and I don't know. I can't help but feel so fucking lucky to be here with you that the anger just kinda fades away."

"You're doing it again," I point out, rolling my eyes.

"Then tell me what to say. What can I say to make you feel better?"

"You can tell me I look like a boy and you hate it."

"I won't lie to you, Finley. Because I do not hate it." He grins, kissing me again. "And you certainly don't look like a boy." He deepens the kiss, sliding his tongue between my lips.

"You heard the doctor," I remind him, pulling back before the kiss gets too heated.

"I know. I know. No sex. But that doesn't mean I can't kiss you as much as I want." He slides his tongue into my mouth again, his hand wrapping around the back of my neck to hold me in place.

Heat creeps down my cheeks and quickly spreads through the rest of my body. We've been skirting this line for two weeks, ever since the doctor told me I should refrain from having sex until at least two weeks after I've finished chemo.

I didn't even know that was a thing, but apparently it is, depending on the situation. In any normal circumstance I probably wouldn't want to have sex. I have no hair, I've lost fifteen pounds off of my already slender frame, and my energy level is at an all-time low, but every time Abel kisses me all I can think about is how incredible it is to have his weight on top of me. How it feels to have him drive into me over and over again. The sounds he makes when he comes apart.

It's maddening.

"Abel," I pant against his mouth, managing to break free.

"Okay. I'm stopping." He pulls back, a grin etched onto his perfect face. "I gotta get the groceries put away anyway. I don't want the ice cream to melt."

"You got me ice cream?" I immediately perk up as I watch him stand. He crosses the room, throwing me a smile over his shoulder as he grabs the bags off the table and heads into the kitchen.

Ice cream is about the only thing that sounds good to me anymore and as such, I eat it just about every day. Well, I was eating it every day until I ran out two days ago. I haven't had the energy to go out and get more and I didn't want to ask Claire because she's already doing so much for me.

"Not only did I get you ice cream. I got you four different kinds. Thought maybe you'd like a little variety," he says from the kitchen, seconds before I hear the refrigerator door open.

"You really are the best." I slide my beanie back on and stand, my legs wobbling slightly under my weight.

"Just remember that the next time when you're mad at me for saying the right thing." He smiles at me when I step into the kitchen.

"Shush." I reach for him and he stops what he's doing to pull me into his arms.

"What are you doing?" he asks, burying his face into my neck.

"Thanking you." I wrap my arms around his middle and squeeze tightly.

"Well then by all means, thank away." He presses his lips to the soft spot where my pulse thrums.

I don't know what I did to deserve someone like Abel in my life. It's one thing to meet a good looking guy and share one hot night together. It's quite another for that guy to step in and care for you when things are at their worst. And not because he has to but because he wants to.

Pulling back, I slide my hands up to his cheeks and pull his face down to mine.

"I love you, Abel Collins." I let the words I've been holding in fall from my lips so effortlessly you'd think I had said them a million times before.

He sucks in a sharp breath, his gaze holding mine.

"You have no idea how long I've waited to hear you say that." He drops his forehead to mine. "I love you, Finley Roberts. More than I ever thought possible to love another person."

"There you go again." I pull back, not able to fight the smile on my lips.

"What?" He cocks his head to the side.

"For saying the perfect thing."

"Guess it must be a gift." He laughs. "Come here." He pulls me closer, sliding the beanie from my head before tossing it somewhere behind me. "I love you," he says again, his lips finding mine seconds later.

Chapter Twenty-seven
Finley

The next seven weeks pass by in a blur. And while they are hard weeks to get through, they are also the happiest I've ever had.

Abel has a way of making everything feel okay even when things aren't okay. Even on days when I'm too weak to get out of bed or too sick to pull myself out of the bathroom, he still finds ways to make me smile.

I finished my last round of chemo this past week, and while the last session definitely took its toll, I'm feeling stronger than I have in a very long time.

The doctors still aren't giving me any guarantees but they all seem pretty optimistic about how I'm progressing. It will be a few more weeks before we know for sure if the cancer is completely gone, but unlike before, I feel good about my chances.

I'm done allowing cancer to define me. Whether I live another fifty years or only a few more months, I'm determined to make every single day count.

"You nervous?" Abel reaches across the console and grabs my hand, giving it a firm squeeze.

"A little," I admit.

"Don't worry. They're going to love you." He winks, turning his gaze back out to the road.

When Abel had first brought up me meeting his family, I was hesitant. We've existed in this little bubble for so long I didn't want to let anyone or anything in. I had to remind myself that this is a good thing. That this is how a real relationship progresses. If anything I should have met his family already, but given my health I wanted to wait until I was feeling a little more like myself.

I tug nervously at the shoulder length brunette wig I chose for the occasion. It's the closest I have to my natural hair – before it all fell out – and I wanted to present myself in a way that felt like me.

"Stop messing with it." Abel catches me out of the corner of his eye. "It looks good."

"You can't tell it's a wig?" I ask for the hundredth time.

"You really can't. Besides, they all know you've just finished chemo. No one is going to care if you're wearing a wig. Or do I need to remind you that my mom will be wearing one as well."

"You're right. I know it's such a silly thing to worry about. I just really want to make a good impression."

"And you will. Trust me, compared to me you're going to be a breath of fresh air."

"Compared to you?" I arch a brow.

"It's no secret that I haven't always fit in with my family."

"The black sheep," I tease, having a hard time envisioning any world where Abel doesn't fit in.

"Just wait. You'll see what I mean." He squeezes my hand again before releasing it.

"As if I need a reason to be more nervous." I sigh. "Besides, if you're a black sheep what does that make me? I didn't exactly grow up on the right side of the tracks, if you know what I mean."

"It'll be fine. I promise. Things have actually gotten a little better between me and my parents since my mom's diagnosis. Maybe because it's softened my mom a little or because now, I appreciate her a little more. Either way, things have been good recently. And they are so excited to meet you. You know you're the first girl I've ever brought home?"

"I am?" I draw back, surprised by this news.

"I've never had anyone I cared enough about to introduce them to my family."

My heart does that little flutter thing again. I wonder if I'll ever get used to the way this man makes me feel.

"So remind me again who all is going to be at dinner."

"All of my brothers, besides Adam. Andrew is bringing his longtime girlfriend, Sam, and Alex's wife, Tanya will be there. She's out to here, pregnant." He gestures in front of himself with his hand. "And of course, my mom and dad."

"Any chance Claudia and Jack will be there?" I ask, hopeful. At least then I will know more than just Abel, and even though I don't know them well, the thought makes me feel a tiny bit better.

I've only seen them a couple of times; once the night Abel and I met and again a couple weeks ago when he took me to their diner when I had a craving for one of Jack's famous burgers.

"I wish. Claudia hasn't come to a family dinner since I was a teenager. She says it's because they can't take the time away from the diner, but I know it's really because they've always felt out of place. Not that I can blame them. My mom and Claudia have never been close and that was only further solidified when my mom married my dad."

I suck in a shaky breath and let it out slowly, my earlier nervousness returning tenfold.

"It's going to be fine," he reassures me again.

"I know. It's just… Well, this is the first time *I'm* meeting someone's family. Someone I happen to be crazy about. I really want them to like me."

"And they will."

"And if they don't?"

"Well then you can join me in the ranks of the disapproved." He grins, slowing before turning right down a long curvy driveway.

When a beautiful two story brick home comes into view I sway slightly in my seat. It just reaffirms how differently Abel and I grew up.

The house is quite large, set on a gorgeous plot of land that is not visible from the road because of the trees that seem to cage it in like a hidden oasis.

He pulls the car to the far end of the driveway where it circles in front of the house before killing the engine.

"Looks like everyone is already here," he observes, causing my gaze to slide to the handful of cars already parked.

"Awesome," I say under my breath.

"Well, let's get this over with, shall we?" He chuckles at my expression.

"I think I'm going to be sick," I say, releasing my seatbelt before pushing the door open.

"You and me both." He laughs again, joining me next to the car. "Listen, we don't have to stay long if you're not comfortable. I'm sure my family will understand if we need to call it a night a little early given your health."

"How much do they know?" I ask, not sure why I hadn't thought to ask this question before now.

"Just the basics. They know about the cancer, the surgery, and the chemo. I left out the part about you ghosting me after the first night we met because you thought you were going to die." He drops an arm over my shoulder and gives me a knowing smile.

"So then what did you tell them? About us, I mean," I ask as we make our way toward the house.

"The truth. I just left out the details of how it all went down in the beginning."

"Probably for the best," I admit, my feet feeling like they weigh a hundred pounds each as we climb the steps leading up to the front porch.

"Well, here we go." He gives me one more encouraging smile, dropping his arm from my shoulder as he pushes his way through the front door, turning to make sure I follow in directly behind him.

"Wow." It's the first word that leaves my lips as I take in the grand staircase and high ceilings. "This place is like a mansion." I shake my head, allowing Abel to slide my coat off my shoulders before hanging it on a hook next to the door.

"I wouldn't go that far." His gaze follows mine. "But it's home."

"If you saw some of the places I lived growing up you wouldn't be saying that. This place is incredible."

"There you two are." I look to my left just in time to see Abel's mother step around the corner. I recognize her from the time I ran into her and Abel as I was leaving chemo, though I was so thrown from seeing Abel I didn't get that good of a look at her at the time.

She's a very attractive woman, though that comes as no surprise. She looks a great deal like her sister, but unlike her sister there's a very intimidating quality about her. Maybe because she looks so put together or simply because she's Abel's mom. Either way my knees shake slightly at the sight of her.

"Finley. It's so good to see you again." She reaches for my hand, reminding me that we've already kind of met.

"Hi, Mrs. Collins." I take her hand, giving it a shake. "Thank you so much for having me." I let my eyes travel to her blonde wig, thinking if I didn't know it was a wig I would have never guessed it wasn't her real hair.

I doubt mine is quite as believable. Then again she probably had hers custom made, whereas mine is from a cheap wig shop at the mall.

"Please, call me Gail. And we're so glad you could join us." She releases my hand and takes a step back. "I never thought I'd see the day when Abel would bring a girl home." She gives her son a knowing smile. "Come on, everyone is in the back."

Abel takes my hand, entwining his fingers with mine as we follow his mom through a formal living room, then down a wide hallway that opens up to another living room at the back of the house. The entire back wall is made of floor to ceiling windows which gives off a beautiful view of the grounds outside.

The room looks to have been professionally decorated. I'd say the couch alone costs more than every piece of furniture in mine and Claire's apartment combined. I shrink a little into Abel's side, feeling more out of place by the second.

To our left I see a formal dining room and to our right is a huge brick fireplace that acts as the focal point of the room. I purposely focus on the décor to avoid the stirring queasiness in my stomach as I feel every set of eyes in the room hone in on me.

"Finley, I'd like you to meet my husband, Adam," Gail says when a man who looks remarkably like an older version of Abel steps up in front of us.

I swear I have to do a double take. It's like I'm looking at Abel thirty years from now. Same eyes. Same nose. Same small dip in his chin. Even their hair is the exact same color other than the gray that peppers his temples.

"Adam." I force myself to smile, taking the hand he extends to me.

"So nice to meet you, Finley." He smiles and I realize that's the one thing he and Abel do not share. Where Abel's smile is full and genuine, his father's seems more rehearsed. I'm sure that stems from his profession. I've seen countless doctors smile at me the way he's smiling at me right now.

"And you as well." I release his hand and look up at Abel. "Your brother's name is Adam, too," I state the obvious.

"He's Adam Junior," Gail speaks before Abel has a chance to, pulling my gaze back to her. "Come; let me introduce you to everyone." She sweeps her arm through mine and pulls me away from Abel.

For the next ten minutes she bounces me around the room introducing me to all of Abel's brothers and a couple of their significant others. With each introduction she tells me at least one personal thing about each of them before moving on to the next.

I smile at all the appropriate times and tell each person how nice it is to meet them, but all I can think about is getting back to Abel and the comfort his presence provides.

I've felt so completely out of my element since the moment I stepped through the front door and when we all gather around the dining room table for dinner that feeling only intensifies.

I think it's safe to say I've never been in a house this nice or sat down for dinner with people quite like this before. I have definitely never had lamb served to me by someone who was hired to cook for the evening. I mean, who does that? I was lucky if my mom would throw a T.V. dinner in the microwave for me and here Abel's parents hire people to come in and cook for family dinners.

Two different worlds is starting to become the understatement of the century.

I find myself watching Gail more than anyone else. Maybe because I know she has cancer. Or maybe it's because I'm floored by how unaffected she seems by it. She still smiles and laughs like everything is perfect. I can't help but wonder if she truly feels that carefree or if it's an act she puts on for the rest of her family. If I had to guess I'd say it's the latter.

Abel's family isn't what I expected, yet at the same time exactly as I pictured. His brothers are all handsome, all successful, and all clearly thrive on the praise and acceptance from their parents. They all clamor over each other to talk about what exciting thing they are doing at work or school, in Andrew's case. From what I gather he's only got a few weeks left before he can take the Bar Exam. I can't imagine being in school for as long as he has been.

Sam, Andrew's girlfriend, reminds me of one of the really popular girls I went to school with. She's wearing a dark blue dress that looks like something a forty year old might wear to the office even though she's only in her mid-twenties. No doubt she's trying to make herself seem more mature. She also seems quite content talking about herself.

She's gorgeous, too. Like, tall, slender, blonde model gorgeous. If I didn't already feel like the ugly duckling, she sure would have driven the feeling home. At least I traded in my normal comfy attire for dark jeans and a black top, but even then she still makes me feel underdressed. I mean, she seems nice enough, but it's hard not to feel like every word spewed from her mouth isn't a jab at everyone else. She seems to be trying to prove that she and Andrew are above the others. I don't get that vibe so much from Andrew, but if he's been with her this long then what does that say about him?

Alex is probably the most full of himself out of all the brothers. He has this arrogance about him that rubs me the wrong way. However, his wife, Tanya is shy and seems very sweet. She's also very pretty. She too is dressed like she's about to go to some fancy office job, but there's something very down to earth about her at the same time. She has her long brown hair tied off to the side and given how swollen her pregnant belly is I'd guess she's only a couple months away from giving birth.

And then there's Aaron, who I think is probably my favorite out of the three brothers in attendance. He has the same easy smile as Abel which oddly makes me feel more at ease. He's also the only one who hasn't made me feel like a complete outcast for most of the night.

I don't think anyone is doing it on purpose, or perhaps they're not doing it at all and it's my mind seeing what it wants to see. All I know is that every time the conversation turns to me I feel like they're all judging every word that comes out of my mouth.

I don't think they're bad people, I just think they're not *my* kind of people. The longer I sit here the more I see what he meant when he said he didn't fit in with his family.

His brothers are all wearing khakis and button downs while Abel is sporting faded jeans and a plain white t-shirt, his tattoos on full display. They all boast about their awesome, high paying jobs, while Abel is perfectly content playing gigs at the most run down of places. Material things don't matter to him while that seems to be the one thing the rest of the family values.

I'm starting to think I would have been better off suggesting we have dinner with Claudia and Jack instead of agreeing to come here tonight. At least then I wouldn't feel so uncomfortable.

At the same time I'm happy to see where Abel comes from, and it's not all bad. His dad has the same full belly laugh as him and I love how his mom is always finding excuses to reach out and hold her husband's hand or touch his arm. It's clear the two love each other very much.

We may not fit in their world, but we're a part of it just the same. So I'm trying my best to not let my insecurities hinder my chances of getting to know everything I can about Abel – which includes his family.

It's just after seven-thirty when everyone retires to the living room, by which point I feel physically drained, even though I've done nothing but sit for the better part of an hour. I still haven't gotten all my strength back and as such I find myself tiring a lot more easily than I normally would.

Abel must sense this because he grabs my hand and hauls me backward right as I'm following his mom out of the dining room.

"You okay?" He smiles, running the back of his hand down my cheek. "You've been awfully quiet the last few minutes."

"Yeah. Just tired." I shrug.

"We should go."

"No, we can stay. I don't want to seem rude."

"Fin, you're sick." I don't miss that this is the first time he's shortened my name. Probably a product of being around Claire who calls me Fin more than she calls me Finley.

"I feel fine."

"Not what I meant and you know it. If you're tired then we should call it a night. Everyone will understand."

I think on that for a moment.

"Only if you're sure." I knead my bottom lip between my teeth.

"Any excuse I can use to get out of here as quickly as possible I will use." He grins, dropping a kiss to my forehead. "Why don't you go grab your coat and I'll meet you in the foyer."

"Shouldn't I say goodbye to everyone first?" I ask.

"Not if you wanna make a swift exit." He chuckles. "Go. I'll say goodbye for you."

"Okay." I nod, heading toward the foyer while Abel takes off in the opposite direction toward the living area.

I've just slipped my coat on when I hear a throat clear behind me. Turning, I spot Aaron leaning in the large arched doorway that leads into what looks like a den.

"Making a run for it I see," he jokes with a smirk.

"I'm feeling a bit run down," I admit, buttoning the front of my coat.

"It was brave of you to come here tonight. Not always the easiest crowd." He gestures toward the back of the house.

"It wasn't so bad." I smile.

"You're being polite. You forget, I've had to live with these people my whole life." He chuckles.

"I enjoyed myself. Maybe next time I'll feel like staying longer."

"Maybe if you're lucky, next time you'll have another excuse to leave early," he teases. "I'm trying to come up with an excuse myself, as we speak."

"So that's what you're doing up here? Hiding out until you can think of a reason to duck out."

"Something like that." His smile broadens and for the first time I notice that he too has a solitary dimple on one cheek.

"Well I wish I could help you out but I'm awful at stuff like that."

"Guess it's lucky you can play the cancer card then, huh." He stops, realizing what he just said. "Shit, sorry. That sounded wrong."

"No, it's fine." I laugh it off. "You have to find the positives somewhere."

"That you do." He nods in agreement. "I just want you to know that I've never seen my brother this happy before. He's always been kind of a brooding asshole, but with you, I don't know. He seems different. A good different. So, do us all a favor and get yourself better, yeah?"

"That's the goal." I rock back on my heels, not sure what else to say.

I knew there was a reason I was drawn to Aaron more than the others. Because out of everyone here he's the most like Abel. I think maybe he's just better at pretending to fit in than actually fitting in.

"Well, I should probably get back in there. Oddly enough, I'm feeling a little queasy." He rubs his stomach and winks. "It was nice meeting you, Finley. Try not to be a stranger."

"It was nice meeting you too," I say, my gaze darting to Abel who pops around the opposite corner.

"You ready?" he asks, turning just as Aaron disappears down the hallway.

"Yeah."

"What was Aaron doing up here?" He hitches his finger in the direction his brother just went.

"Hatching a plan to make an early escape." I giggle.

"Is that so?" He chuckles, sliding into his jacket. "He likes you. I can tell."

"Well, the feeling is mutual. I think he's my favorite," I whisper the last part.

"That makes two of us." He gives me a knowing smile before pulling the door open and leading us outside.

Spring is upon us but unfortunately the temperatures are still stuck somewhere back in January. It's been so cold the last few days I've barely been able to stand to go outside.

"Come here." Abel pulls me to his side as we make our way toward the car.

"Was anyone upset that we were leaving so quickly after dinner?" I ask.

"Not at all. They're all too self-absorbed to really care about anything but themselves." He stops and pulls the passenger door of his car open for me.

"That's not a very nice thing to say."

"But still true." He laughs, closing the door once I'm settled inside.

He crosses around the front of the car and slips into the driver's seat next to me moments later.

"Well, we did it." He lays his head back on the headrest and turns his face toward me.

"And we made it out alive." I mirror his action, dropping my head back onto the headrest.

"Not only did we make it out alive, but I think my family thoroughly enjoyed having you."

"I thought they were too self-absorbed to care," I mock, reminding him of his earlier statement.

"Well, a couple of them are. But I know it meant a lot to my mom. So, thank you."

"You don't have to thank me. I wanted to meet your family. They are a part of you." I pause. "I just wish I had a family I could introduce you to."

"You have Claire."

"True. But getting to meet one sister versus an entire family is very different."

"It is. But I don't care that you don't have some big family. Families are overrated." He winks. "I just need you."

"And I just need you." I can't contain the love swept smile as it slides across my face.

That smile only widens further when Abel leans forward and brushes his nose against mine.

"I love you," he whispers, his gaze hard to lock onto with his close proximity and the dimness of the car.

"I love you too." And I mean it down to my very core.

"What do you say we go home, snuggle in bed, and watch one of those rom-coms you love so much?"

"Abel Collins, did you just offer to watch a romance movie with me?" I pull back in mock surprise.

"As long as you're in my arms I don't care what we watch."

"You may live to regret that," I warn playfully.

"Do your worst." He drops a quick kiss to my mouth before pulling back, the engine of the car firing to life moments later.

I snap my seatbelt in place and look back toward Abel, not able to wipe the ridiculously happy smile off my face. I can't help it. He makes me feel… everything. I love every second of every minute I get to spend with him and that feeling only intensifies with each day that passes.

I've spent my entire life looking for something, never actually knowing what I was searching for. Now I know. All this time I was looking for him. And now that I've found him, I'm never letting him go.

Chapter Twenty-eight
Abel

"Good morning." I roll into Finley, kissing her shoulder as my hand slides around her middle, caging her against me.

"Morning," she grumbles, her voice heavy with sleep.

"Do you know what today is?" I ask, trailing my lips up her neck to the soft spot right below her ear.

"Day fourteen." I hear the smile in her voice.

"One more day." I slide my hand down her side, squeezing her hip gently.

"You better have something really romantic planned." She laughs, rolling toward me.

"Is that so?" I look down at my beautiful girl who I swear gets more breathtaking with each day that passes.

Now that she's two weeks out from her last chemo session she's starting to feel and act more like herself. The color has come back to her face and her eyes are brighter than they've been in weeks. It feels so good to see her getting better, stronger.

Two weeks also lifts the doctor's restrictions on sex. While it's not an expectation, it's something we've talked about several times. I think she's been counting down the days more than I have – if that's even possible.

Then again, there's something to be said about waiting. About the anticipation of it all. I'd be lying if I said I haven't been enjoying this little game we've been playing the last few days.

"You know, we could always just say it's been two weeks and call it good?" She gives me a sly smile.

"You know I'd love nothing more but doctors' orders," I tisk.

"Doctors don't know everything." She rolls her eyes.

"They know enough." I tap her on the tip of her nose.

"Fine, then midnight tonight." She slides a leg over my hip and presses her body against mine. I immediately tighten under the contact. "Then technically we won't be breaking any rules."

I think on that for a moment.

"Okay, then." I dip my mouth down to hers and press a deep kiss to her lips. "Midnight." I groan, pulling back before all that goes out the window and I take her right here and now. "Although it might be more like one-ish because I have a gig until midnight."

"I guess I can wait until you get off work." She sighs playfully.

"What do you say we catch dinner before my show and then you come with me? Considering you're going back to work in a couple of days it might be your last chance to see me play for a while."

"As long as you'll have me back here and naked directly afterward, I'm up for whatever." She smiles, grinding into me again.

"It's a date." I kiss her forehead before abruptly rolling out of bed.

"Where are you going?" she whines, reaching for me.

"I've got a few errands to run before tonight," I tell her, grabbing my shirt off the floor before slipping it over my head.

"Are you sure they can't wait?" She props up on her elbow and gives me *the look*.

"We said after midnight." I chuckle. "Stop looking at me like that." I step into my jeans and slide them up over my hips.

"You're so easy to work up." She smiles.

"Glad you think so." I grin, leaning down to lay a quick kiss to her mouth before standing back up. "I'll pick you up around five. Does that work?"

"I'll be ready." She flops onto her back and watches me cross the room toward the door. "I love you," she calls after me right as I pull the door open.

"And I love you," I tell her, giving her one last long look before forcing myself to leave; knowing if I stay a second longer I may never make it out of this room.

Finley consumes me in the best fucking way possible. But sometimes it's hard to make myself do anything when all I want to do is be with her.

I jump slightly as I enter the living room, having not expected Claire to be up yet.

"You're up awfully early," she observes, lifting her cup of coffee to her lips.

"I've got some things to take care of for my mom today. What are you up to? Lazy day?" I take in the way she's curled up on the couch, her legs covered in a throw blanket.

"Until I have to get ready for work it is." She sips her coffee. "I don't function until I absolutely have to."

"You sound like your sister," I point out.

"Speaking of, how is our girl this morning?"

"She seems good. Getting stronger every day."

"Thanks to you."

"To me?" I question.

"Before you came back into her life it was like she was trying to find a reason to care. Now all she wants is to be better so that she can be with you. She really loves you, I hope you know that."

"I really love her." I grab my jacket off the back of the chair and slide it on before stepping into my shoes.

"Well, have a good day, Abel." Claire gives me a half wave as I make my way toward the door.

"You too, Claire." I nod, exiting the apartment moments later.

"You were incredible tonight." Finley presses against my side as we make our way up to her apartment.

It's just after one-thirty in the morning and while I can tell she's trying to play it off like she's fine, it's easy to see how exhausted she is.

"Thank you." I kiss the side of her head when we stop outside her apartment door. "Here." I take the keys from her hand and quickly unlock the door before handing them back to her.

"I just don't get how you can do that," she says, following me inside.

"Do what?"

"Play in front of all those people. Isn't it nerve racking?"

"Maybe when I first started out, but now being on stage feels like second nature."

"Well you're a natural up there, that's for sure."

I snag her hand and guide her through the dark apartment, not flipping on any lights until we make it to her bedroom.

She holds her hand over her mouth and tries to stifle a yawn as she slides out of her coat and shoes.

"You look like you're about to keel over." I chuckle, draping my jacket over the foot post of her bed before kicking off my shoes.

"I don't think I've been up this late in a long time," she admits, taking a seat on the edge of the bed.

Tonight has been incredible. Everything about it. It's the first time we've really gone out for any length of time since our first night together. It's kind of hard to process everything that's happened since then.

It feels like it was only yesterday that I sat down next to her at that bar and yet at the same time it feels like a lifetime ago.

"Come here." She holds her arms out to me and I don't hesitate in closing the distance between us.

Leaning down, I wait until she locks her hands around my neck before straightening, pulling her up off the bed with me.

"Why don't we get you ready for bed?" I pull back, grabbing the hem of her shirt before pulling it up over her head, tossing it somewhere behind me.

My eyes go to the spot where her chemo port was. Even though it's been two weeks since they removed it I can still see the traces that it was there.

"Or, we could do something else," she suggests, pulling my gaze back up to hers.

She wraps her hands around my neck and pulls my face down to hers.

"You're tired," I remind her, our faces so close our noses are almost touching. "You need your sleep."

"I need you more," she says, leaning further into me so that her body is pressed flush to mine.

"We don't have to do this tonight." I wrap my hands around her back, my palms flattening against her bare flesh.

"I have my whole life to sleep." She kisses my jaw. "I've waited too long to feel like me again to wait another moment longer." She trails her lips up to mine and presses a soft kiss to my mouth.

"Finley," I groan, my body already tight and aching for her.

I reach up and slide the pink wig from her head, smiling when she doesn't object. She's been experimenting with different colored wigs recently and even though I think she looks amazing no matter what, I have to admit I like her best with no wig at all.

It brings all her beautiful features to the forefront and I'd rather see all of her than just the parts she wants me to see.

I run a hand along her scalp where her hair has started to grow back. It's still very short but there's enough now that it looks like a buzz cut rather than her being completely bald, which she pulled off spectacularly even though I know she was self-conscious about it.

I just wish she could see herself the way I see her. Then she would know that there hasn't been a day that's passed where she hasn't been breathtakingly beautiful.

"You're sure about this?" I tip her chin upward, forcing her to meet my gaze.

"One thousand million percent." A slow smile spreads across her lips but it's only seconds before my mouth is covering it up.

I take my time, kissing her slowly, undressing her even slower. I touch every inch of her body from the top of her head down to the balls of her feet. Cherishing her in a way she deserves to be cherished.

I've never had a woman open up to me the way Finley does. She offers me not just her body, but her heart, and the way she does it is so fearless and unapologetic. Like there's not one thing she's trying to hide.

She lets me see her and fuck if she isn't the most incredible thing I've ever laid eyes on. So pure and innocent and yet wild and untamed at the same time. The perfect contradiction.

She drives me wild. Both physically and emotionally. And when I finally settle down on top of her and bury myself deep inside, I swear I never want to leave.

This is my home. *She* is my home. I've never felt more at ease than when I'm with Finley. Never felt more myself. She sees me for who I am and loves me in spite of my flaws. She brings out the best in me and I struggle to think about where I'd be without her.

It's funny how someone can walk into your life without any warning and completely change everything. After that first night I knew nothing would ever be the same again. I just don't think I realized at the time how right I was.

Finley and I move in perfect unison. She lifts her hips to meet each thrust, matching each movement as if we were made to fit perfectly together.

The room is quiet, only the softness of the lamp lighting the space, yet I feel like the sun is blazing down on my back and the sound of my heart pounding against my ribs is deafening.

And when Finley looks up at me, a whisper of *I love you* falling from her lips, I can't help but wonder if this is what perfect feels like. Having the girl I love beneath me, her hands in my hair, my name on her lips, as we both climb higher and higher until I swear I feel like I'm coming apart at the seams.

I can't imagine life gets any better than this. I want to bottle the moment, tuck it away and keep it forever because even though she's getting better, a part of me still fears the loss of her.

The thought has pain shooting through my chest while pleasure courses through the rest of me. I focus on that. On the soft moans Finley makes beneath me as her release teeters on the edge. On the way her supple skin feels beneath my palms. On the way her lips feel pressed to mine as I kiss her one last time before we both fall over the edge.

And there in that moment I realize that the way I feel about Finley isn't just a man loving a woman. It's a man finding the other part of himself. The person that completes him.

Because that's what Finley does for me. She makes me feel whole in a way I never have before.

I don't just love this girl. She's a part of me now. Down to my very core. Engrained into every cell of my body.

She is the air I breathe. The sunlight on my face. The wind in my hair. She is everything...

Chapter Twenty-nine
Finley

"It's so good to have you back." Heather slides up to the food counter next to me as we both wait for our orders to come out of the kitchen.

I've been back at work for almost two weeks now, but this is the first time Heather and I have been scheduled for the same shift. She usually works dinner and I've been taking lunch shifts because they're not quite as demanding while I ease my way back in.

"It's good to be back," I admit. "I still can't believe Henry gave me my job back after the way I left."

"I told you he would. Besides, if he didn't he would have pissed a lot of people off. It's not like you purposely got cancer." She gives me a sideways glance, grabbing two plates off the line the moment the cook sets them down. "We'll have to catch up after the lunch rush. I feel like I haven't talked to you in forever."

"Okay, yeah," I agree, feeling a twinge of guilt for being so far removed from Heather and some of my other friends from the restaurant.

Between surgery and chemo and Abel, I've been a little preoccupied. I guess that's what almost dying will do to a person.

It causes you to focus on yourself even when doing so isn't something you're necessarily used to.

"Order up." Josh's voice snaps me from my thoughts and I look up to see table thirty-six's order in front of me.

Grabbing the plates, I pile them on a tray before hoisting it up and making my way out into the dining room to deliver the food.

Stopping in front of the table, I get one of the four plates down when suddenly the ground sways beneath me. I don't know how it happens. One moment I'm on my feet and the next I'm on the ground, plates of food scattered all around me.

I blink and several people are grouped around me, including Heather who helps me into an upright position before getting right into my face like she's trying to determine the damage.

"Are you okay?" she asks, worry evident in her voice.

"I think so." I look around, feeling a bit disoriented and quite embarrassed.

"Come on. Let me help you back to the break room." She pulls me to my feet while two other waitresses work on cleaning up the mess of food on the floor.

I barely register the concerned looks on my customer's faces before Heather pulls me out of the dining room and through the kitchen, into the break room.

Only seconds pass before Henry steps inside, a glass of water in his hand.

"Are you okay?" He kneels down in front of me as Heather guides me into a chair.

"I think so." I shake my head, trying to shake off the thick fog that seems to be surrounding me.

"What happened?" Heather asks, taking the seat next to me.

"I don't know," I admit, taking a gulp of water. "One minute I was putting plates on the table, the next I was on the ground." I take another drink, the cold liquid feeling good on my suddenly dry throat.

"I'm going to call Claire," Heather says, quickly standing to retrieve her cell phone from her locker.

"Don't," I object, my voice weak.

"Finley, you just passed out in the middle of the restaurant. I'm calling Claire." Her tone tells me it's not up for debate.

"I didn't pass out. I just fell." I say what I think happened even though I'm not entirely sure.

"No, you passed out. You were unconscious on the floor for at least thirty seconds."

"I was?" I turn my wide gaze up to her.

She nods, pressing her cell phone to her ear moments later.

"Oh my god, Fin." Claire bursts into the small curtained off area of the emergency room. "Are you okay?" Within seconds she has her arms wrapped around me in a tight hug. "I was so worried."

"I'm fine, really," I reassure her, shaking off her embrace. "I don't even know why I'm here." I gesture around the room.

After Heather called Claire, she immediately called an ambulance. I guess my sister gave her specific instructions and my friend did not hesitate to do exactly as my sister told her to. Even though I felt like it was a wasted trip, I obliged because I knew Claire wouldn't be satisfied until I was given the all clear by a doctor.

In truth, I was really too out of it to argue. I felt fine leading up to the incident but since, I don't know, something has felt off.

"You're not fine. You passed out!" she exclaims, taking both of my hands and lifting them up as her eyes give me a thorough once over.

"I probably didn't get enough to eat or something. I didn't have much of an appetite this morning." I make the only excuse that I can stomach right now.

"Abel is on his way," she tells me, releasing my hands.

"You called Abel?" I bite, instantly irritated.

"Of course I did. You passed out!"

"I know I did. But you shouldn't have called him. It's probably nothing and everyone is getting all worked up for no reason."

"Sis, you have cancer. Or maybe you don't anymore. Regardless, you're still not a hundred percent. Things like passing out *are* a big deal in your situation." She plops down on the side of the bed, her body angled toward me. "Have you seen the doctor yet?"

"They took me back for a couple scans and drew some blood as soon as I got here."

"Well, at least they aren't dragging their feet." She blows out a breath.

"The ER doctor said they are going to consult with my oncologist as soon as they have my results back. Until then I guess I'm stuck here."

"This is the best place for you until we know everything is okay."

"I'm sorry I scared you," I say, realizing the concern etched into every feature of my sister's face.

"Don't be sorry. I just *need* to know that everything is okay." She gives me a tight smile, wrapping her fingers around my hand.

It seems like only moments pass before Abel comes bursting through the curtain, his panicked gaze finding me in an instant.

"Thank god." He lets out a relieved sigh as he crosses the small space toward me. "Are you okay? Claire told me what happened." He takes my other hand before dropping a kiss to my forehead.

"I'm fine. I just got a little light headed is all. Probably because I haven't eaten today." I give him the same excuse I gave my sister.

"What are the doctors saying?" he asks Claire instead of me.

She quickly recounts everything I just told her, the two talking as if I'm not sitting between them.

"Why didn't you call me the second it happened?" Abel's gaze swings back to me.

"Because I didn't want to worry you over nothing."

"Finley."

"I passed out. I know." I sigh audibly. "But I'm telling you, I'm fine." My gaze bounces between him and my sister.

"Well I'm not leaving until I hear a doctor say those words." He squeezes my hand, worry evident behind his brilliant blue eyes.

"I think I'm gonna track down a nurse and see if I can get you something to eat," Claire says, standing.

I know my sister and sitting around waiting is not her forte. She needs to be up doing something, otherwise she'll drive herself crazy.

"I'll be right back." She offers Abel a nod before she disappears behind the curtain.

"When she called me, I, I…" Abel looks down at our joined hands, his voice shaky.

"Hey." I wait until his gaze comes back to mine before continuing, "I'm okay," I reassure him.

"I was so scared," he admits, showing vulnerability in a way I'm not sure I've seen from him before.

Throughout this entire ordeal it's always been *when* I beat this, never *if*. It's strange to see him suddenly so unsure. Then again I can't imagine how scared I'd be if the roles were reversed. I try to keep this in mind.

"It's okay," I reassure him again. "Look at me. I'm right here and in one piece. I'm telling you it was nothing."

"I hope you're right." He blows out a breath.

"I know I am." I smile, watching him relax slightly.

I spend the next two hours with Claire and Abel fussing over me. As much as I love that they care so much, deep down I wish they'd let me be.

I may not have admitted it out loud to either of them, but what happened this afternoon scared me pretty bad. To the point that by the time the doctor finally shows up my stomach feels like it weighs a hundred pounds from all the knots inside of it.

I wait for him to tell me that it was nothing. Something caused by my medication or maybe a side effect from surgery, but the longer he talks the more I begin to realize that what I'm waiting for him to say isn't going to come.

I stop listening at some point after he says the cancer has spread. My vision blurs and the only sound I can focus on is my heart beat thrumming in my ears. I feel like I'm in the middle of a nightmare and am silently screaming for myself to wake up. *Just wake up!* I tell myself over and over again as if I can will it so.

Only it's not a nightmare, at least not the kind I can wake up from.

"So, what now?" I zone back in right in time to hear my sister ask.

"I'll need to run some more tests before we know the true extent. In the meantime, I'm going to admit her and we will go from there," he says, his hand settling on my shin moments later. "I know this isn't the news we were hoping for, but it's not uncommon with cases like yours. It's just another bump in the road." He pats my leg before removing his hand completely.

I'm in complete and utter shock. Abel's next to me, stiff and silent like he's trying to process this just as I am. We thought we were in the clear. After weeks we've finally reached a point where we're actually able to start living and now here we are, having the rug ripped out from underneath us.

I'm full of so many different emotions. Anger. Sadness. Fear. And yet not a single one really registers. It's like I'm numb from the inside out, and even though I know I should react, I can't seem to figure out how to.

"It's going to be okay, Fin," Claire says, her hand sliding over mine. I blink, realizing that the doctor is gone and yet having no recollection of him actually leaving.

"The cancer spread?" My voice finally breaks the surface as my gaze finds Abel.

Chapter Thirty
Finley

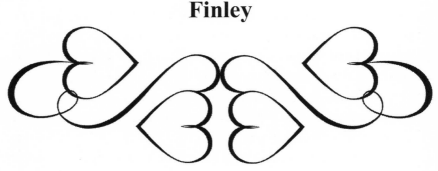

My eyes flutter open and I look around the room. It takes me a moment to remember where I am and why. Heaviness settles down over my chest the instant I do.

I turn my head to find Abel in the chair next to me, his head tilted back slightly as he sleeps. I take a minute to look at him. The scruff on his jaw, the fullness of his lips, the tiny dip in his chin. He really is the most beautiful man I've ever seen. My heart hurts just by looking at him.

Tears sting the backs of my eyes. I spent the first three days feeling numb and the last two crying at that drop of a hat.

We've found out so much over that time. Things I still don't think I've fully processed.

First it started with the news the cancer had spread and it only spiraled further out of control from there. Learning that you have a brain tumor you may not survive is one thing because there's a chance. Receiving a terminal diagnosis and having the doctors tell you there's nothing more they can do is quite another.

I thought I had gotten a second chance at life when I survived the surgery. Now I'm finding out we only delayed the inevitable.

Three months. That's how long they've given me. Six to twelve with chemo, and that's if I'm lucky. I've spent the last two days weighing every option that's been given to me and yesterday, I finally made the decision. While Claire was at work and Abel had run home to shower and grab a bite to eat, I informed the doctor of my choice.

Neither of them know yet. They don't know that I've refused chemo. That I've chosen quality of life over quantity. I'm not sure either of them will agree with me, but at the end of the day it's my choice to make. If I'm going to die, I'm going to do it on my terms.

"Hey." Abel's groggy voice fills the air as his eyes flutter open to find me watching him.

"Hey." I smile, emotion so thick in my throat it's a wonder I'm even able to speak.

"How are you feeling?" He stretches, turning his head from side to side as he pushes himself completely upright.

"I'm okay." I reach for his hand which he immediately gives me, scooting closer to the bed as he does.

"Has the doctor come in yet?" he asks, checking his watch for the time.

"No, but the nurse was in earlier this morning and said he should be in before lunch to release me."

"They're releasing you?" He sits up straighter.

"There's nothing they can do for me that they haven't already done."

"What about treatments? When do you start them?"

I take a deep breath, realizing this is something I can't keep from him.

"I'm not having treatment." I push past the lump in my throat.

"What do you mean you're not having treatment?" His brows draw together in confusion.

"I'm not going to do the chemo."

"Why?"

"Because I don't want to spend what little time I have left sick and weak."

"But what if it works? It could work. You won't know unless you try."

"Abel, you heard the doctors. Chemo might buy me a few months, but it's not a cure. I'm dying, whether I get treatment or not."

"No." He pushes to a stand, dropping my hand as he does. "No." He runs his hands through his hair, letting out a loud breath through his nose as he paces the room.

"Abel."

"No," he repeats, stopping in the middle of the room to look at me. "I won't stand by and watch you choose to die."

"I'm not choosing this," I say, tears filling my eyes.

"But you are. You can get the treatment. You can have more time. You can have a future."

"What future? One where I'm too sick and too weak to function before I die anyway? There is no future for me, Abel. Not anymore."

"That's bullshit!" His voice echoes off the walls around me and I immediately draw back in surprise. In all the weeks we've spent together he's never so much as raised his voice, let alone yelled. "You're giving up." He points a finger at me, anger the one emotion on his face I can read clearly.

"What part of this is me giving up? I'm dying. What don't you understand about that?"

"You are not dying!" he screams again.

"Yes I am!" I push myself further upright, my tone matching his. "You were here. You heard what the doctor said."

"I heard the doctor say you could try chemo," he interrupts.

"To buy me time. Not to cure me," I say, wondering if this whole time he's just been hearing what he wants to hear and not actually accepting what they've been saying.

"You're getting chemotherapy. You're going to fight this. Or you're going to die without me." His voice is eerily calm as he stands facing me, his arms crossed in front of his chest.

"Are you saying you'll leave me if I don't get chemo?" I question, my heart beating so hard and fast it's a wonder it hasn't worn a hole in my chest at this point.

"I'm saying I won't sit around and watch you die."

"Well then you better leave now because I hate to break it to you, I'm dying, whether you like it or not."

"Is that what you want? You want me to leave?" His nostrils flare.

"I want you to accept the decision I've made when it comes to *my* life."

"It's not just *your* life anymore." He throws his hands up in the air.

"Maybe not, but I'm the one dying!" My temper flairs and emotion swells in my chest.

"You have to get the chemo, Finley. You have to." He takes a deep breath and lets it out slowly, trying to calm himself. "I won't watch you die."

"Then leave."

"Is that what you want?" He draws back like I've physically slapped him.

"Of course it isn't. But I'm dying. If you don't want to stick around to watch, then leave," I grind out, my tears breaking free and moving in quick succession down my cheeks.

"You want me to leave. If you didn't you wouldn't be refusing treatment. Is this your way of pushing me away?"

"I'm not pushing you away. I want you to support my decision."

"I can't support your choice to die."

"You think I *want* to die?" My tears flow harder. "You think this is what I want?" I sob.

"Finley." He takes a step toward me but I hold up a hand to stop him from coming any closer.

"You know what, you should leave."

"Finley," he starts again.

"I said leave!" I scream, all of the emotion I've been holding in for the past five days boiling to the surface.

He stands there looking at me for a long moment, indecision dancing behind his eyes, but then he does something I never expected. Without another word, he turns and walks away. His fists clenched at his sides is the last thing I notice before he disappears into the hallway.

Abel doesn't come back to the hospital. He's not there when the doctor releases me and he's not at my house when I arrive home that evening.

I've picked up my phone to call him a hundred times over but then talk myself out of it. I don't know why. I don't know why talking to him feels so impossible.

"Fin." Claire pops her head into my room as I lay curled in a ball in the center of my bed. "I made some grilled cheese and soup if you're hungry."

"I don't want anything." I try to mask that I've been crying by burrowing my face into the sleeves of my sweater.

"You haven't eaten anything. Would you at least try?"

"I said I don't want anything."

Her footsteps grow closer as she crosses the room, the bed dipping under her weight moments later.

"Are you going to tell me what's going on?" Her hand settles on my back.

"I'm dying. That's what's going on." I sniff, my face hot with tears that I try to keep hidden.

"I meant with Abel," she says hesitantly.

"Nothing is going on with Abel," I bite, wiping my cheeks with the sleeves of my sweater before using it to cover my face again.

"Don't shut me out, Fin. Tell me what's going on."

"I refused chemo," I blurt, preparing myself for the backlash I know is to come.

"What do you mean?"

"I mean, I told the doctor I don't want to do it again," I say, pushing myself upright before tucking my legs underneath me.

Claire's gaze dances over my red cheeks and swollen eyes and she immediately reaches for my hand.

"Are you sure that's what you want?" she asks softly.

"If I thought I could beat this, if I thought there was a chance, of course I would have treatment. But you heard what he said. Chemo may buy me some time but that's all it will give me. I'd rather have less time and feel like me than more time feeling so sick I can barely get out of bed."

"Quality over quantity." She says the very thing I was thinking when I made the decision to refuse chemo.

"Exactly." I sniff, wiping my cheeks with the sleeve of my sweater again.

"And I'm guessing Abel didn't like that choice?"

"He completely lost it. He was acting like I was making the choice to die by refusing the chemo. It's like he doesn't understand that I'm dying regardless and no matter how many times I said it, he wasn't hearing me."

"He's in denial, Fin. He loves you and I'm sure the thought of losing you is beyond terrifying to him. I know how it makes me feel and I'm just your sister."

"You're not *just* my sister," I disagree. "You're my family. My best friend. One of the most important people in the world to me."

"I know that. But what I'm saying is that he's more. And you're more to him. Put yourself in his shoes. How would you feel if he was the one dying?"

"Like I was dying right along with him." A fresh onslaught of tears well behind my eyes and no matter how hard I try to fight them back, they spill over.

"Exactly." She takes my hand. "I don't know what happened between you two because I wasn't there. But what I do know is how much that man adores you. Give him time to process."

"Time to process?" I question. "Shouldn't I let him go? Save him from having to watch me die?"

"Do you really think there's any way he would let *you* go? This isn't something you walk away from and hope it hurts less. This is something you face, accept, and then spend what days you have left loving each other as fiercely as you can."

"I don't want to die," I sob, choking on my words. "But more than anything I don't want to leave him."

"I know you don't, honey. And doing so will seem impossible. Saying goodbye to you feels impossible to me already, and yet I know I'm going to have to do it." Claire blinks and two tears trickle down her cheek.

"Claire." I cry harder, my emotion getting away from me again. I hold out my arms and she immediately goes into them.

I don't know how long we sit like that. Arms tangled around each other, crying like we may never stop, but eventually we do stop and when we do, I feel a little lighter.

I know this is only going to get harder. I know that there's no fixing this. But I also know I don't want to waste a single second I have left fighting with the people I love.

I want to spend it laughing, loving, and living. I want to look back as I take my dying breath and know that I lived every minute to the absolute fullest for as long as I could.

Some people don't get that chance. The chance to accept what will happen. The chance to live and love while they still can. The chance to say goodbye when their time comes to an end.

Life is unpredictable and at times, highly unfair. But that's life. There's no rhyme or reason to it.

Messy. Heartbreaking. Cruel. Beautiful life.

Some people just get a lot more of it than others. But time doesn't define how much life we live. What we do with the days we have does. And I plan to spend every second loving my sister, my friends, and most importantly, Abel. Until my dying breath I will love them with everything I have. And maybe even after…

Chapter Thirty-one
Abel

"Can I come in?" It's the first thing I hear when I pull open my front door and find Claire standing on the other side.

It's been two days since I left Finley in the hospital. Two days that I've spent half out of my mind with alcohol and grief.

"I guess." I sigh, slinging the door further open before walking away without bothering to see if she follows me or not.

The door closes right as I grab my beer and plop down on the couch.

"So this is where you've been hiding out?" Claire looks around the messy room, littered with empty beer bottles before honing in on the half empty bottle of Jim Beam sitting on the coffee table in front of me.

"I haven't been hiding out," I say, taking a long pull of beer. "This is where I live." I gesture around.

"My sister has been crying herself to sleep for the last two nights and you've been sitting here getting drunk and sulking?" She picks up the bottle of whiskey and for a moment I wonder if she's going to chuck the damn thing across the room.

"She made her choice. She doesn't want to live and she doesn't want me. What would you have me do?"

"Are you listening to yourself right now? She has terminal cancer. She's not making the choice to die. She *is* dying."

"She's not getting chemo."

"Because she wants to enjoy the time she has left. Not spend it too weak and sick to get out of bed."

"It could save her."

"It won't."

"It could."

"It won't!" she interjects more forcefully. "She only has a few weeks left on this earth, Abel. To you, two days getting drunk and trying to drown your sorrows may not seem like a lot, but to Finley it's like a lifetime. Every day matters now. Every single minute. And here you are, wasting it away like it means nothing."

"It means everything!" I explode, jumping to my feet.

"You sure have a funny way of showing it! I know you're hurting and I know you're scared, but think about Finley. Think about how scared she is. She loves you and you're leaving her to face this alone."

"Because I can't face this." I crumble back onto the couch, killing off the remainder of my beer in one drink before throwing the bottle across the room. It soars a few feet and shatters against the wall, shards of glass scattering all over the floor. "I can't watch her die." I lean forward, sinking my face into my hands.

The couch dips as Claire takes a seat next to me.

"So you'd rather let her die alone?" she asks, her voice barely above a whisper.

"What can I do?" Emotion tightens my throat. "How can I stand by knowing there's nothing I can do to save her?"

"You just do." She puts her hand on my arm and squeezes. "You take it one day at a time. You love her as hard as you can for as long as you can. Give her a lifetime in the matter of weeks, because Abel." She tugs at my arm, causing my hands to fall away from my face. "That's all she has left. Whether you want to accept it or not, it doesn't change that she's leaving us."

"I don't know how to live without her." Tears fill my eyes.

"Neither do I," she admits, her own tears bubbling to the surface. "But I do know that I won't waste away what time she has left worrying about how *I'm* going to survive. It's not about me. It's about her. And I will do everything in my power to make sure what time she has left is the happiest time of her life. But I can't do that without you. I need you to get it together. For her."

"This isn't fair." I shove my emotion down as deep as I can, refusing to let it take me under.

"You're right. It isn't. But that doesn't change it either."

"Fuck!" I roar, pushing to my feet. "Fuck! Fuck! Fuck!" I pace the room, pulling at the ends of my hair. "I can't fucking lose her, Claire. I can't." My stomach churns and every ounce of alcohol I've pumped into it over the last forty-eight hours threatens to come back up. "What can I do? What can I do?" I repeat, the grief I've tried so hard to ignore swarming me like a thousand bees. I feel every sting of pain as it pricks my flesh.

"Be there for her." Claire stands, crossing the room toward me. "Love her. And when it's time," she stops directly in front of me, "let her go."

I sag forward, a pain riddled scream ripping so loudly from my chest it echoes back in my ears. Claire presses into me, her arms wrapping around my middle, supporting my weight as I slump forward. Her soft words blend with my sobs as I finally let the pain in.

I let it seep into my pores and I force myself to feel every ounce of it. Because no matter what I'm feeling, Claire's right, what Finley is feeling is so much worse.

So I let myself cry. For the first time in as long as I can remember I let myself go, and Claire is there, holding me as I do.

I knock lightly on Finley's bedroom door. I don't wait for a response before pushing my way inside.

She's in the same position I've found her in countless times before. Back pressed to the head board, legs stretched out across the bed, a thick paperback book in her hands. She peers up over the tattered pages, her eyes going wide when she sees me enter.

"Hey," I say, shoving my hands into the front pockets of my jeans.

"Hey." She sets her book face up on the bed beside her.

"How are you?" I ask, rocking back on my heels. I feel like I say the same thing every time I see her. I wonder what it would be like to not have to ask her how she's feeling or how she is from day to day. I wish I didn't have to.

"I'm hanging in there." She gives me a soft, emotion filled smile. "How are you?"

"I'm hanging in there. Finley, look, I'm so sorry."

"No, I'm sorry." She pushes out of the bed and crosses toward me. "I made the decision on my own and I didn't let you have a say. I should have talked to you. I should have let you in instead of shutting you out."

"I shouldn't have yelled at you the way I did. I was angry and scared."

"I know." Tears fill her eyes and she reaches up to cup my face. "I know and it's okay."

"Forgive me?"

"I already have." She slides her hands from my cheeks to the back of my neck, pulling my face down to hers. I rest my forehead against hers, taking a slow, steadying breath in.

"I'm scared," I admit, forcing myself to meet her gaze.

"So am I." She blinks and one solitary tear slides down her cheek. I instantly move to wipe it away with the pad of my thumb.

"I will never walk away from you again; I need you to know that."

"I won't ever ask you to," she whispers back, pressing up on her tip toes to kiss me.

The second the contact is made I'm a swarm of emotions. Want. Need. Fear. Love. Anger. It all bleeds together until I feel like I can't breathe without pulling her closer. Kissing her deeper. Loving her more fiercely than I ever have before.

"Tell me something you've always wanted to do but never have." I slide my fingers gently up and down Finley's bare back as we lay naked, tangled in bed together.

"I don't know. There's a lot of things I'd like to do I guess." She snuggles her cheek against my chest, her palm flat on my stomach.

"If you had to pick one thing, what would it be?"

"Well, I've always wanted to rent a big van and road trip around the country." She lets out a breath.

"And where would you go?"

"I don't know. Everywhere. I just want to explore the land. Not big cities or touristy things. Just see the country. The fields, the mountains, rivers, and caves. I'd spend my days exploring, eating at different restaurants, and really getting a lay of the land. And at night…at night I'd sleep on the mattress in the back of the van with the doors open so I could look up at the stars."

"A mattress in a van, huh?" I chuckle.

"I saw it in a movie once."

"Then let's do it." I smile when she lifts her head up and gives me a questioning look.

"I can't." She shakes her head like it should be so obvious.

"Why not?" I ask. "We could go. There's nothing stopping us."

"I can't leave Claire. And what about your mom?"

"Claire wouldn't care and you know it. She'd want you to go. And my mom will be fine. She has plenty of people to help take care of her. Besides, we can go for a couple of weeks, maybe a month. You know, while you still feel good enough to go." I shove away the sick feeling that forms in the pit of my stomach at the thought of when she gets to the point that she's not well enough.

"You're serious?" A smile snakes across her mouth.

"I am. Let's do it." I shift upward, taking her with me. "We can do it exactly as you said. We can rent a van with a mattress in the back. We can drive from state to state, sleep under the stars. The weather is getting warmer so now is the perfect time."

"It sounds amazing, Abel, but I just don't think I can. I don't have the money and I need to stay close to my doctors."

"I have the money. Let me do this for you. Let me give you this adventure. There are doctors everywhere. And you said so yourself, there's nothing they can do for you now." I swallow back the emotion that filters into my voice. "Let's do it."

"Okay," she agrees, laughing when I pull her on top of me and hug her to my chest.

"I'll make all the arrangements. We should leave tomorrow."

"Tomorrow?" She pulls back, eyes wide with surprise.

"We don't know how many tomorrows we have left together, Fin. I don't want to waste a single one."

"Okay, we leave tomorrow," she agrees, tears in her eyes and a wide smile on her face. "I love you, Abel," she whispers, lowering her face to mine.

"I love you too," I say against her lips just as her mouth closes over mine.

Chapter Thirty-two
Finley

"You're sure you have everything you need?" Claire asks me for the hundredth time as she slides my duffel into the van.

"I do. And if I forgot anything we can always stop and pick it up," I tell her, smiling as Abel comes bounding down the stairs toward us dressed in a dark t-shirt and black baseball cap, a large cooler in his hand.

"You'll check in every day?" Claire continues.

"Every day. I promise." I nod, pulling her in for a tight hug. "Are you sure you're okay with this?" I whisper into her ear.

"More than okay. I think this is just what you need," she tells me, pulling back to give me an encouraging smile. "Go live your life, little sis. I'll be here when you get back."

"I love you. You know that, right?" I fight against the sting of tears that threaten to form.

"I do. And I love you." She steps back as Abel pulls open the passenger door and holds his arm out to help me inside.

"I promise I'll take good care of her," he says as he closes the door between us.

I watch through the window as they share a few words, but because of their hushed voices I can't actually make out what they're saying. Abel rests a hand on Claire's shoulder and says something else. She nods before her gaze comes to mine.

She steps back onto the curb as Abel climbs into the driver's seat, giving us a small wave.

I wave back, blowing her a kiss as the engine rumbles to life.

After leaving Chicago we headed north into Wisconsin. Because I grew up on the east coast, I wanted a chance to explore more of the mid-western states. We stayed the night in Chippewa Falls, but because of the temperature we ended up having to get a hotel room for the night. Which turned out to be a lot of fun. We ordered in room service and spent the evening watching old re-runs on television. It was a good day.

After that, we spent six days driving through Minnesota, and North and South Dakota, before deciding to head south into Wyoming; which has been my favorite state so far. Not only do they have some of the most beautiful sights, but we also saw some incredible wildlife. Including a bison that forced us to stop in the middle of the road to avoid hitting it. I nearly had a heart attack when Abel hopped out of the vehicle and attempted to shoo it away. We both had a pretty good laugh about it afterward.

In all the places I've lived, people ruled the land but out here? Out here the world belongs to nature.

"You hungry?" Abel asks, pulling my gaze from the window.

"A little." I smile, loving how handsome he looks this morning with his messy hair and bright eyes.

"Okay, pick a letter." He waits patiently as I think about it.

We started this little game our third day on the road. I pick a letter and he'll stop at the first restaurant he can find that starts with the letter I chose. This way there's no discussion about where we'll eat and it forces us to try something we may not have otherwise tried. So far every place we've eaten has been a win, with the exception of the vegetarian Korean restaurant we went to in South Dakota. Turns out I don't like Korean food. Who knew?

"Hmmm." I tap my chin dramatically. "B."

"B," he confirms. "That shouldn't be hard or anything." He rolls his eyes playfully.

"I'm sure there are plenty of restaurants that start with the letter B. We just have to find one." I smile, unbuckling my seatbelt before sliding across the bench seat toward Abel.

"What are you doing?" He gives me a sideways glance.

"I just want to sit close to you," I tell him, laying my head on his shoulder.

"Well then, by all means." He turns and kisses the top of my head before turning his attention back to the road.

We sit like that for several minutes, music playing softly in the background as we take in the sights of Colorado. We'd crossed the state line a few miles back and out of every place we plan to visit, I'm looking forward to this state the most.

We plan to spend at least three or four days in Colorado. As cheesy as it sounds, some of my all-time favorite books take place here and I've starred several things I want to see. We quickly determined all of the places couldn't all be seen in the span of a day or two.

It's so easy to pretend out here. To pretend like everything is okay and we're just two people on an adventure. Two people who will eventually return to their normal, everyday lives. Only I don't have a life to return to. Not really. Because I'm on borrowed time, something Abel has chosen not to bring up once since we left Chicago. He said he didn't want this trip to be about me dying. He wants it to be about me living.

In truth, there are moments when I forget. Moments when it feels like we have forever. And it's during those times that I feel more perfect than I ever have before. But eventually reality sinks back in and I'm forced to face the truth. This trip may be about me living, but the fact still remains that I *am* dying. Other than a few minor headaches and a couple bouts of dizziness, I feel totally normal. I guess that's why cancer can progress so far before you realize you have it. Sometimes symptoms don't show up until the later stages, by which point it's too late.

"There." I jump, pointing at a road sign for Barrett's Bistro. "See! I told you we'd find something that starts with a B." I smack his thigh lightly.

"Hopefully it's open. I'm starving."

"How can you be starving? You had a huge cup of coffee and three donuts from the gas station less than an hour ago." I laugh.

"Which is precisely why I typically don't eat stuff like that. It's full of sugar and doesn't keep you satisfied for long."

"This is true. But damn are they good in the moment."

"As are most things that are bad for you." He grins, turning left as we enter the main center of town.

"Where are we anyway?" I look for a sign or something to tell me what town we're in.

"Walden I think." He glances at his phone that's mounted to the dash, the GPS pulled up on the screen.

"It's cute," I observe, thinking this is exactly how I would have pictured a small town in Colorado. "And look, they're open." I smile as he pulls into Barrett's Bistro – the open sign lit up in the window.

"Now let's hope it's good." He parks the van, killing the engine moments later.

"As long as it's not Korean food I think we'll be good." I wrinkle my nose.

After lunch we spend the next four hours driving to Colorado Springs, one of the top stops on my ever growing list of things I want to see.

When this trip started I only wanted to explore but the further out we go, the more places I realize I actually want to visit. So much so that after the second day of our trip I started making a list so I wouldn't forget.

"This is it," I say as we make our way through beautiful Colorado Springs. "This is where Jaxon and Mia fell in love." I look out the window, able to picture them walking down the sidewalk holding hands as if it was something that actually happened in real life. "I wonder if Tam Thompson spent a lot of time here before she wrote *It Begins Here*. She described the city so well that I feel like in a way I've already been here." I turn, smiling at the sweet way Abel looks at me.

"If she were alive today, what's the one thing you would ask her?" Abel asks, turning his gaze back to the road.

"God, I wouldn't even know where to begin. I guess I'd want to know more about her personal life. It had to be incredible. There's no way someone can write a love story like that and not have experienced it first-hand."

"I think you'd be surprised. Maybe she was a lonely woman who used her imagination to create the world she wished she was living in."

"I refuse to believe that." I turn my nose up at the thought. "She was beautiful and talented and there had to have been a very special man in her life."

"What happened to her?" he asks after a long moment of silence passes between us.

"She died of an autoimmune disease a few years ago. She was only forty-two."

"I had no idea you knew so much about her."

"She's my favorite author. I make it a point to know things about people that impact me the way her books have. She was a literary genius." My heart picks up speed when I see the sign for *Circus Ink* – the tattoo shop where Jaxon had Mia's name tattooed on his chest. "Pull over." I bounce excitedly in my seat.

"What?" Abel throws me a questioning glance.

"Pull over." I point to the tattoo shop. "I want to go in there."

"Into the tattoo shop?" he questions.

"It's where one of the characters in the book got a tattoo." I bite my bottom lip to contain my excitement.

Abel smiles and shakes his head, having learned at this point to roll with it. He knows how crazy I am about my books.

He finds a vacant spot on the street a block away from the shop and parks, laughing when I jump out of the van before he's even killed the engine.

"Slow down, would ya?" He chuckles, climbing out of the driver's seat.

Snagging his hand, we make our way toward the tattoo shop. I've never actually been inside one before but I've always wanted to. Seems pretty fitting that my first time would be in a shop that's featured in one of my favorite books.

When we step inside, I look around the small space. From the various pieces of artwork on the walls to the countless tattoo books and magazines spread across the counter. Everything about this place is exactly as I pictured it in my mind.

"Let's get tattoos," I say, looking up at Abel right as a middle aged man appears behind the counter.

"What?" He smiles.

"You heard me, let's get tattoos." I turn my attention to the man as he stops in front of us. "Do you have time to do two tattoos?" I gesture between me and Abel.

"I think I could squeeze you in depending on what you're wanting." He nods, scratching the back of his shaved head. For some reason this reminds me of my head and I quickly move to adjust my beanie to ensure it's in place.

"A name," I blurt without giving it much thought.

"A name?" Abel arches a brow at me, humor dancing on his face.

"Script tattoos typically only take a few minutes depending on the size. If you'll tell me what you're wanting I can pull up some fonts for you to pick from."

"Abel," I say, turning my attention to the man. "I want it to say Abel."

"Finley," Abel starts but stops when he catches the look on my face. "I want mine to say Finley."

I can't contain the smile that lights up my entire face. I know it's silly but there's something so comforting about the thought of my name permanently tattooed on his skin. Like he will carry a piece of me always, even long after I'm gone.

Tattooing someone's name on my body isn't something I ever thought I'd do, but given the circumstances, it seems fitting. What does it matter anyway? Before long the tattoo will be gone, as will my body.

I push the thought away, refusing to let myself go there right now.

"Okay, let's get the font and size dimensions worked out and we can get started." He nods once before swiveling the computer screen toward us, a variation of fonts displayed across the screen.

I select a basic cursive script for my tattoo and to my surprise Abel chooses the same font. I don't know if it's because he liked it the best or because he wants our tattoos to match. Either way it makes me extremely happy.

Abel insists on going first so I can see what getting a tattoo entails before actually going through with it. I watch in complete fascination as Carl, the tattoo artist, etches my name in large cursive letters on Abel's chest. Right above his heart.

I didn't question why he chose to get the tattoo there instead of putting it on his arm that's already covered in tattoos.

But I like that my name is all by itself – close to his heart, where he can always keep me tucked away just for him. Of course, I don't tell him that Jaxon got his tattoo in the same spot. It seems silly to compare a fictional character to the real thing.

It only takes Carl about forty minutes to finish up Abel's tattoo. When he wipes away the excess ink and shows off the finished product I'm a ball of emotions. There's something to be said about seeing your name etched into someone's skin. And while I've known all along that Abel loves me, I feel it now more than ever.

"You ready?" Abel grins at me as we switch places and I climb into the tattoo chair. Sliding his shirt over his head, careful not to disrupt the clear wrap taped over his tattoo, he plops down in the chair on the opposite side of Carl and takes my hand.

"I think so." I give him a nervous smile. While the whole process seemed pretty painless for Abel, I have a sinking feeling it's going to hurt a lot more than he led on.

"You'll do great," he reassures me, giving my hand a gentle squeeze.

I decide to get Abel's name on the inside of my wrist. I want it somewhere I can see anytime I want.

"What do you say after this we go grab some dinner and check out the night life? This is, after all, one of the places you wanted to see the most. We should make the best of it while we're here."

"I'd love that," I admit, jumping slightly when the needle touches my skin for the first time.

Abel keeps me talking the whole time Carl is working, no doubt trying to distract me. And while it definitely hurts, it isn't nearly as bad as I expected it to be. It takes him less than twenty minutes to finish and when he's done and I get my first real look at the tattoo I'm not sure if I want to laugh or cry.

To some it's just a tattoo. To me, it's something so much more. A memory. Another stolen piece of time that I get to take with me when this life is over.

As we make our way out of the tattoo shop hand in hand I feel freer than I have in a very long time. There's something so liberating about finding acceptance. About making peace with what you cannot change.

I'm not ready to die. I don't think I ever will be. But I've accepted that I am and that my days with Abel are numbered. Which only makes me want to make each moment count even more.

Some people get entire lifetimes to love each other. To make mistakes and learn from them. To start families and watch them grow. But I only get this. This small fragment of time where everything is temporary. And maybe I should be bitter that this is all I get. But then I look at the man next to me and I can't feel anything but blessed.

I've lived more in the last few weeks with Abel than I had in the nineteen years before him. He saved me in ways I don't think he'll ever truly understand. In ways I'll never be able to tell him.

"Pick a letter." Abel knocks his hip against mine as we make our way down the sidewalk in the opposite direction of the van.

"P," I announce without thought.

"P," he repeats, looking around.

There are several restaurants and shops lining the street and it's only moments before Abel locates a restaurant that starts with a P.

"Paragon." He stops, pointing across the street.

"Fish Market." I smile up at him. "We haven't had seafood yet."

"Here's hoping Colorado has good seafood." He chuckles, pulling me across the street toward the restaurant.

Chapter Thirty-three
Abel

"Do you see this?" Finley holds her arms out, her face turned up to the sky as the ocean waves crash around her feet. "It's so beautiful here," she says, eyes closed as the warm sun shines down on her face.

I stand next to her, not able to take my eyes off of her. She hasn't worn a wig the entire time we've been on the road and she abandoned the beanie she's been wearing a couple of days ago. The further south we drove the warmer it became and eventually she took it off.

I like her better without it. I like seeing her exactly as she is. Young. Beautiful. Alive.

We spent the last week exploring parts of Colorado, New Mexico, and Arizona. Watching Finley's expression every time we came across something incredible or we find a spot she wants to see has become my new favorite thing. The way her eyes light up, the way she bounces in her seat with excitement, how she kneads her bottom lip between her teeth. I swear I could spend the rest of my life watching her.

We arrived in Southern California this morning. We decided to drive straight to the beach because Finley couldn't wait to see the Pacific Ocean. And she wasted no time tossing off her shoes and running into the sand the moment we arrived.

"I've always heard that the Pacific Ocean was prettier than the Atlantic but I never believed it until now." She turns her gaze back out to the water, her eyes fluttering open. "But look at this." She gestures in front of her. "Look how blue this water is. Have you ever seen anything more beautiful?"

"No, I haven't," I say, my eyes on her and not the water. Her gaze slides to me and a knowing smile spreads across her lips.

"I love you so much," she announces, looking so happy I feel like my chest might burst open at the sight.

Finley has changed me in ways I'm still trying to figure out. One look and I had to know her. One smile and I knew I had to make her mine. One kiss and I knew I'd never be able to live without her. She is the heart beating inside my chest. The air that fills my lungs. The blood that pulses through my veins. She is all of me. Everything that I am.

I've never cared for another person the way I care about her. I've never looked at someone and felt like I was looking at my whole life. But when I look at her that's what I see. The stars, the moon, the sun, and the ocean. She is my world. Plain and simple.

"I love you too," I return, taking the hand she stretches out to me.

I don't know how long we stand like that. Hand in hand, the waves rolling up over our feet, the sun warming our faces. Time is no longer how I measure each moment. Instead I measure them in heartbeats. Because as long as her heart is still beating then I'm still living. And that's all I want to do with her. Live.

Eventually we make our way back up the beach where we change in the back of the van before grabbing some food from a taco truck set up near a populated part of the beach.

We eat on the edge of the sand and watch the sun dip lower and lower in the sky as the evening wears on. We don't talk much. There's something so beautiful about just existing together in the moment.

"Can I ask you something?" Finley breaks the silence between us, and I turn to see her eyes locked on me.

"Anything."

"Do you believe in Heaven?"

I want to change the topic, talk about anything besides death or what comes after, but something in her eyes tells me she needs this, so I answer as truthfully as I can.

"I think so." I blow out a slow breath. "I mean, I've always believed there was something more. A place where we go in the end."

"So you don't think this is all there is?" she asks, pulling her knees to her chest before resting her chin on top of them, her eyes sweeping back out to the water.

"I refuse to believe that this is all there is. Look around you. There has to be a bigger purpose for all of this. There has to be."

"I used to believe in God and Heaven. I read about it in books and heard about it from friends who went to church every Sunday. Even though I was never religious, I always believed. But then I got sick and I wasn't sure anymore. I kept thinking, if there is a God then why? Why make me suffer for nineteen years just to rip my life away from me before it really even had a chance to begin? But then I met you." Her gaze comes back to me, unshed tears in her eyes. "And you made me believe in so much more than just God. You made me believe in miracles."

"I'm still holding out for one," I tell her. I don't think I'll ever be ready to accept that I'm losing her.

"I already found mine." She reaches for my hand, entwining our fingers together as her head finds my shoulder. "I'd rather live a short life with you than a long one without you. I keep thinking that if I was never sick I wouldn't have met you. Maybe things really do happen for a reason."

"Finley," I croak, so many unspoken words clogging my throat.

"I know you don't really want to talk about it. And that's okay. I just want you to know that I'm okay with it. All of it. Because you gave me something to take with me. A lifetime worth of love wrapped into a few short months. I'll never be able to tell you how much that means to me. You gave me a reason to fight when I needed one the most and you'll give me peace in death when my time comes."

"Marry me." The request is out before my brain has time to process.

Finley lifts her head and hits me with wide eyes that are brimmed with tears.

"What?" she chokes, blinking rapidly.

"Marry me," I repeat. I may have not really thought it through but that doesn't mean I regret saying it. "I want you to be my wife."

"Abel." She lifts her hand to muffle a sob, fresh tears pooling in her eyes.

"I'm not asking you because you're sick. I'm asking you because I know that there's no way I'll ever love someone as much as I love you. I want to tie myself to you in every way humanly possible. I want you to be my wife. What do you say?"

She slowly lowers her hand, revealing the widest smile I think I've ever seen before enthusiastically nodding, tears streaming down her cheeks.

"Yes," she whispers. "Yes." She flings her arms around my neck and straddles my lap, hugging me tightly. "Yes," she repeats, burying her face into my neck.

Chapter Thirty-four
Finley

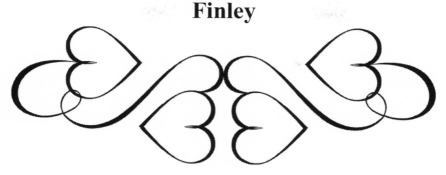

After three days of California sun and making love under the stars, the waves crashing in the background, Abel and I made the six hour drive to Las Vegas and said I do in a small wedding chapel right off the main strip.

It wasn't the wedding I had pictured when I was little but it turned out being so much better. Because it wasn't about where I was. It was about who I was with.

"I can't believe we're married," I say, holding my hand up to look at the small white gold band on my left ring finger. We picked our rings out at a little jewelry shop in California, and while they may not look like much to most people, to me they couldn't be more perfect. Simple. Understated. Beautiful.

"Believe it." Abel rolls into me, flinging his leg across mine as we lay tangled in the bed sheets.

Even though I was perfectly fine staying in the van, Abel insisted that we spend our wedding night in a fancy Vegas hotel.

We've spent the last three hours drinking champagne and making love. And while we've had some pretty incredible days together, I think today is my favorite.

"Claire is going to kill me for not telling her first." I smile when he lifts his head and kisses the side of my neck.

"She'll get over it."

"I'm married," I say again, just to hear myself say it out loud.

"You are."

"And so are you." I smile, still not able to grasp that Abel is actually my husband now.

"I am," he murmurs against my skin.

"This has been the perfect day."

"Well, it's not over yet." He abruptly rolls away from me, climbing out of the bed moments later.

I watch his bare backside as he leans over and snags his boxers off the floor, sliding them on moments later.

"What are you doing?" I laugh when he tosses his t-shirt at me.

"You'll see. Put that on."

"O-k-a-y," I draw out, sitting up to slide his t-shirt over my head. It smells divine – just like Abel – and I find myself taking a deep inhale.

Crossing the room, Abel grabs his phone from the dresser and fidgets with it for a moment.

I watch him curiously as I climb out of bed and slide my panties on, taking a swig of my champagne just as music suddenly fills the space.

I recognize the song blaring from Abel's phone immediately. It's the first song we danced to that night at the bar.

He turns, a slow smile pulling at his lips.

"What are you up to?" I plant my hands on my hips.

"Time for the bride and groom to share their first dance." He stalks toward me, pulling me to his chest the moment he reaches me. "What do you say my, little ballerina? Will you dance with me?" He pulls back, running a soft hand down my cheek.

"As if you even have to ask." I roll my eyes, laughing as he pulls me away from the bed to an open space in the room.

Pulling me back into his arms, he waits until I have my hands locked around the back of his neck before he slowly starts to sway in place.

"Remember when you said you couldn't dance?" He chuckles, stepping back to give me a twirl before pulling me back to him.

"Still true." I smile at him.

"I beg to differ. I think you would have been an incredible dancer."

"I think you're just being nice." I crinkle my nose and shake my head.

"One of these days, Finley, one of these days you're going to see yourself through my eyes and when you do, you're going to see just how special you truly are."

"Will you promise me something?" I ask, not waiting for him to answer before continuing. "Promise me that when I'm gone, you won't shut yourself off from the world."

"Finley." His expression drops.

"I'm not going to go there tonight. I just need to say this one thing. I want you to promise me that you'll keep your heart open to the possibility of loving again. Because I want that for you, Abel. I want you to find someone that makes you happy. Someone you can have children with and grow old with. Someone that makes you as happy as you make me. Find your person. And when you do, don't ever let her go."

"You're my person." He drops his forehead to mine, his movements stilling.

"For now." I reach up, tangling my hands in his hair.

"Forever," he whispers.

"Can you please just promise me?"

"I can't even fathom loving someone else right now, Fin. I just wanna love you."

"But one day you will. One day you're going to meet someone that makes everything you've lost seem like a little less and when that day comes, I need to know that you'll be willing to reach out and take it. Just promise me."

"Okay. I promise." He lets out a slow breath.

"Thank you." I push up on my tip toes and press my lips to his.

"You're the love of my life, Finley Collins," he murmurs against my mouth.

Goosebumps erupt across the skin at hearing him call me by his last name. My heart feels so full I'm not sure it can take much more.

"And you're mine," I reply before deepening the kiss.

"Good morning, Mrs. Collins." Abel snuggles the back of my neck, spooning his body against mine.

"Good morning, Mr. Collins." I smile, not bothering to open my eyes.

"The world is waiting for you." He lays a light kiss to my shoulder.

"It is, isn't it?" I stretch my legs, peeling one eye open and then the other, the morning sun peering in through the van windows warm on my skin.

"Today we're going to visit Zion National Park, remember?" he reminds me and I instantly perk up.

It's the only place I have on my list to visit in Utah. I mean there are tons of other things I want to see, but this was the main one I knew we had to see. We're going to hike the trails and enjoy the outdoors for a while. Then we're going to stay at a campground in the Park for the night. I've been looking forward to this stop for a while.

"That's right." I sit up too quickly and get a little lightheaded.

"You okay." Abel sits up, his hand going to the middle of my back.

"Yeah, I just sat up too fast."

"You sure you feel up to hiking today?"

"Yeah, I feel great." The lie I've been telling myself and him over the last couple of days falls easily from my lips.

The truth is, I've been feeling a little off since before we left Vegas. There's nothing major happening, but I don't feel quite right. I keep telling myself it's all in my head but now I'm starting to wonder if that's really the case. Regardless, I brush it off and quickly slide to the end of the mattress, pushing open the van doors a moment later.

We stopped at a small camp site not long after we crossed into Utah, and much to my delight they have real bathrooms, which I am desperately in need of at the moment.

"I'm going to run to the bathroom and freshen up. Brush my teeth. Then we can get on the road," I tell him, sliding out of the van.

The instant my feet hit the ground another wave of dizziness washes over me. I grip the door to steady myself and quickly recover before Abel seems to notice.

"Hurry back. I want to have time to stop and eat breakfast before we head to Zion," he calls from behind me.

"Okay." I nod once before setting off across the grounds toward the restrooms.

"You sure you're okay?" Abel slows next to me as we make our way along the trail leading back from where we visited some amazing waterfalls.

After looking over many of the different hiking options available, we decided on this one. It was hard to pick because there are so many things to see here. As soon as we reached the water I knew we had made the right choice. But the hike, even though not very long, has definitely taken it out of me.

"Yeah, I'm fine." I force a smile. "Just a little tired." I shrug.

"Come here." Abel steps in front of me and crouches down.

"What are you doing?" I laugh.

"Giving you a piggy back ride," he states like it should be so obvious.

"So you want me to get on your back?" I question, not moving from my spot behind him.

"Have you never had a piggy back ride before?" He straightens, turning to look at me.

"I can't say that I have," I admit truthfully.

"What?" He gives me a weird look.

"What?" I repeat. "Is that so hard to believe? Are piggy back rides something people do often?"

"I couldn't possibly count the numerous amounts of times I've taken a piggy back ride." He smiles like a kid. "When I was little I used to purposely pretend to get tired anytime we did anything that required us to walk for any period of time just so my dad would carry me around on his back."

"Well, you and I clearly had very different childhoods."

"Well, there's no time like the present." Turning back around, he says, "Come on, hop up."

"I'm not sure I know how." I bite my lower lip as I try to figure out my angle.

"Just jump up." He crouches down further. "I'll catch you and hoist you up."

"Okay." I laugh, placing my hands on his shoulders.

"Ready. One, two, three."

I jump and Abel catches me effortlessly, locking his arms around my legs as he hoists me higher up his back.

"See, that wasn't so hard, was it?" I hear the smile in his voice as he begins walking again.

"This is kind of nice," I admit, resting my cheek against his shoulder as my arms tighten around his chest.

"Glad I could be your first." He chuckles.

"Me too. My first at a lot of things it would seem."

"I like it that way. I like being the one you get to experience these things with."

"Me too." I lift my face, kissing the back of his head.

It only takes us about twenty minutes to reach the lodge from where we departed. Abel carries me the whole way and never once complains or acts like he's in any discomfort. Even though I can't imagine it's easy to carry someone on your back for very long.

Even though he did most of the work, when he slides me down to my feet my legs wobble slightly. I feel fine until I take a step back, then suddenly the whole ground goes sideways.

Before I know it, I'm on my side on the ground and Abel is standing over me with a terrified look on his face.

"Are you okay?" He crouches down, helping me into an upright position.

"I'm fine." I brush the dirt off my legs and reach my hands out for him to help me up. "I just lost my balance. I think my legs are asleep from how I was positioned." Such a lie.

"You sure?" He pulls me to my feet before leaning around me to brush off my backside.

"Yeah, I'm sure." I force a carefree smile even though deep down I'm a little panicked.

"Come on. Let's get out of here and grab a bite to eat. You're probably starving." He wraps a hand around my shoulder and tucks me against his side.

It's been hours since we've eaten and even though I know I should feel hungry, I don't. In fact, suddenly, I feel a bit nauseous.

Of course I tell Abel none of this because I don't want to worry him. He's already worried enough as it is. I refuse to add to that over something that is probably nothing.

Only if it's nothing, then why am I so hell bent on hiding it from him?

I know the answer to that question without even having to ask it. Because deep down I know it *is* something, and once he knows this little adventure of ours will be over and I'm not ready for that yet.

Chapter Thirty-five
Abel

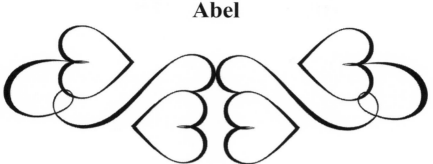

I wake with a start, the sound of Finley whimpering next to me pulling me from sleep. I shoot upright and turn my gaze on her, watching her curl into herself.

"Fin?" I question, resting my hand on her hip. "You okay?"

"My head," she cries, palms pressed to her forehead.

I lean forward and click on the interior lights in the van, a soft glow filtering into the back moments later.

"Finley." I try to roll her toward me but she resists. "Hey, talk to me. What's going on?"

"My head," she repeats and only then do I realize she's crying.

"What can I do? Do you want some ibuprofen?" I ask, not sure what she needs.

"I've already taken some. It's just getting worse." She groans.

"Do you want me to take you to the hospital?" I ask, panic stirring in my chest.

"Yes." Her sobs break through the quiet and I realize this is serious.

Finley is the strongest person I've ever known and even though I can tell she's been struggling with headaches recently, she's never once complained. She's also not one to go to the hospital voluntarily, either.

"Okay, baby. Just hang in there. I'm going to get you to the hospital." I lay a kiss to her shoulder before climbing into the front seat of the van.

Even though I'd feel better with her in the passenger seat with a seatbelt on, I also know she's in too much pain for me to move her.

Pulling up the GPS on my phone, I search the nearest hospital. The closest is right under thirty minutes away.

I fire the engine to life, pulling through the bumpy campground roads as gently as possible, trying not to shake her.

"Abel," she groans seconds before I hear the unmistakable sound of vomit.

I look back to see her head draped into a plastic bag with some drinks from the gas station still in it.

"Hang in there, baby. I'm going as fast as I can." Pressing my foot down harder on the accelerator.

"It hurts so bad." She sobs behind me, the sound damn near splitting me in two.

I've never felt so fucking helpless in my entire life. I wish there was something I could do. Someway I could take her pain onto myself, but I can't. So I do the only thing that's in my control at all. I drive faster.

We arrived at the emergency room a little over an hour ago. As soon as we pulled in, some of the ER staff came out and transferred Finley onto a gurney before rushing her inside.

I did my best to fill the doctor in on everything I knew, including giving him the name of her oncologist in Chicago. And even though the last thing I wanted to do was leave her side, they insisted I stay in the waiting room while they assess her condition. And that's where I still am, staring at the same fucking drab four walls for the last several minutes trying like hell not to imagine the worse.

I called Claire shortly after we arrived. I tried to reassure her that everything was fine but it was hard to sound convincing when I wasn't sure myself. I promised to update her as soon as I know anything.

"Mr. Collins?" I look up to see an older nurse standing in the doorway.

"That's me." I quickly stand and cross the space toward her.

"I can take you to see your wife now," she provides and I swear for the first time in nearly sixty minutes I pull in a real breath.

"She's okay?" I ask, following her down a long vacant hall before crossing through a set of double doors.

"She's asleep, but yes, she'll be okay. We gave her a pretty heavy pain killer to help manage her pain so don't be surprised if she sleeps for a while." She stops next to a closed door across from the nurses' station. "The doctor will come in and speak to you shortly. In the meantime, you can go sit with her." She opens the door.

The room is dimly lit but my eyes find Finley in an instant. She seems peaceful, her breathing even as her chest rises and falls. I close the distance between us, taking the chair next to her bed. My hand immediately goes to hers.

I hold her fingers up and kiss the back of each one, careful not to disrupt the I.V. drip connected to the underside of her forearm.

"Finley." I rest my forehead against her hand, all the fear and worry that's been building in me for the last hour and a half finally boiling over.

I swear I've never been so fucking scared in my entire life. I can still hear her pain riddled words in my ears, playing on repeat. *It hurts*.

I take a few calming breaths, trying to pull myself together.

"She's okay," I say to myself, repeating my words over and over. I rest her hand back onto the bed and lean forward, laying my face next to it.

I'm not sure how long my eyes had been closed for by the time the doctor comes in. I feel like I shut them for a minute but something tells me it was much longer.

"Mr. Collins." The white haired man steps further into the room, a tablet in his hand. "I'm Dr. Stevens. How's she doing?" He gestures to Finley.

"Still sleeping," I grumble tiredly, rubbing my eyes with the backs of my hands.

"I'd say she'll likely sleep a few more hours." He nods.

"Can you tell me what happened?"

"Product of the cancer, I'm afraid. She experienced a very severe headache, which also explains why she was throwing up."

"From the pain?" I question, having not really put the two together.

He nods, flipping across the tablet screen.

"We gave her a combination of pain and nausea medication which seemed to alleviate a good deal of her discomfort rather quickly. Unfortunately given her condition, there isn't much more we can do for her." He gives me a sad smile. "I'm going to write you a prescription for pain medication. That should help with the headaches until you can get her back to see her doctor in Chicago."

"We weren't planning on going back for a few more days," I say numbly.

"I would advise that you get her home sooner rather than later. Someone with her condition can go from completely fine to barely functioning in the matter of days. I reviewed her charts and based on what I saw I'd say it's only going to get worse from here."

"What are you saying?" I look up at him.

"I'm saying she needs to be home, with her doctors. They will come up with the right form of treatment to make her as comfortable as they can."

"You're saying she's going to die?" I choke on the words.

"I'm guessing you already knew this. But yes, she is dying," he confirms, his expression neutral but not uncaring. "We will wait until she wakes up to evaluate her. As long as she feels up to it, she'll be free to go."

"Okay." I nod, my brain working over time trying to process how quickly everything changed.

She was fine yesterday. She's been fine this whole time. It was so easy to pretend that she wasn't sick, but it would seem my days of pretending are over.

I need to find a way to accept what's to come. No matter how much I don't want to. I have to. For Finley.

Chapter Thirty-six
Finley

"It's so good to have you home." Claire tucks the blanket around me after helping me into bed.

I'm exhausted in a way I've never been before. An exhaustion that goes way beyond just being tired or wore down.

After the night I spent in the ER, Abel gave me no choice about coming home. He drove us straight through, only stopping twice to get a little sleep before he continued on. And while he did his best to try to act like things were normal, something in him shifted that night.

I don't know what it was or why but the last couple of days everything feels forced. His smile. His laugh. None of it feels real anymore.

"Did Abel say when he'd be back?" I ask, looking up at my sister.

"A couple of hours. He said he was going to go check in on his mom for a few minutes."

"She seems to be doing well. His mom."

"Thank god for that." She gives me a sad smile.

"Yeah. I can't imagine him having to lose us both. At least one of us might make it." I frown.

"Hey. Don't talk like that." Claire sits on the edge of the bed and takes my hand.

"Why not? It's the truth."

"Let's talk about something else. Tell me about the wedding. I still can't believe you got married without me." She puts on a brave smile for my sake.

I indulge her, filling her in on all the details of not only our wedding, but the entire trip. Details I left out over the phone because I was too anxious to get back to Abel to stay on the phone with her for too long.

Claire hangs onto my every word like she's never heard anything more exciting in her entire life. At first I think it's because she's happy for me, but then I realize that it's because she realizes what I've known all along. That up until three days ago I was living a fairytale. A fairytale that I never wanted to end.

Unfortunately for me, my real life fairytale isn't going to get the happy ending that they do in books. But I guess that's what makes mine special. Time is more precious when you have less of it to spare.

"I'm so happy you have him," she tells me once I'm finished, reaching out to squeeze my hand.

"So am I." I try to smile but the action feels too difficult at the moment.

"I hope one day I can find a man that loves me even half as much as Abel loves you."

"You will. One day you'll find someone that loves you more. Because that's how much you deserve to be loved. You deserve everything, Claire."

"Don't go getting all sappy on me. You're going to make me cry." She fans her face with her free hand.

"I'm serious. You are the most incredible person I've ever met. You saved me from a life that would have destroyed me. You brought me here. You gave me a chance at something normal. And it's because of you that I have Abel in my life."

"You're my sister. All I ever wanted was for you to be happy."

"I *am* happy. Despite everything I'm happier than I've ever been. And I have you to thank for that."

"I love you, Fin. So much."

"I love you too, Claire," I say, my eyes suddenly feeling too heavy to hold open.

"I'll let you get some rest. I'm going to make us some dinner for later."

Her lips pressing to my forehead is the last thing I remember before sleep takes me under.

It's been almost a month since my trip with Abel. A month longer that I've gotten to spend with him. A month more of memories we've gotten to make, even if most of them exist within the four walls of my bedroom or the hospital, which I've been in and out of several times over the course of the last month.

I wish I could say I've gotten better, that my body magically started fighting off the cancer, but that's simply not the case.

Abel's parents hired an in home nurse a couple of weeks ago to help take care of me at the request of their son. While he and Claire haven't left my side, there are some things only a medical professional can really do. He arranged the whole thing without my knowledge. I think he knew I would have fought him on spending the money so he left me in the dark.

Imagine my surprise when in walked Janet, a middle aged nurse who looked so much like my old next door neighbor from South Carolina that I had to do a double take.

Things haven't been easy and some days are definitely better than others, but I wouldn't trade a single one of them. Because even on a really bad day, I still get to look up and see Abel next to me. See his brilliant ocean blue eyes and that dimple that still makes my heart pick up speed.

Sometimes I feel selfish. Like I'm holding him back. But other times I know deep down that there's no other place he'd rather be and that outweighs the doubt.

"You're awake." I lift my gaze from the book I've been attempting to read for the last few minutes to see Abel enter the bedroom.

My focus has not been what it used to be and as such I have trouble reading. I still try every day though. I can't remember a day that has passed since I learned to read that I didn't open a book and at least read a few paragraphs. I'm not about to let that streak end now.

"Yeah." I smile when he sits down on the bed next to me.

"Is it any good?" he asks, pointing to the book now closed in my lap.

"I'm not sure." I shrug. "I didn't get very far. It's hard for me to focus on the words," I admit.

"Want me to read it to you?" he asks, handing me the milkshake I asked for.

"Maybe later." I place the book on my nightstand before lifting the straw to my lips.

Eating isn't something I really enjoy anymore. I get a lot of my nutrients from an I.V. drip that Janet set up last week. Even still, there are things I crave from time to time. Ice cream being the main thing.

"You look like you feel better today." His blue eyes sweep over my face.

"I do."

"Is there anything you need?"

"Actually there is." I sit up further in bed. "I need to get out of this room."

"Finley."

"I know, I know. We've been over this. But I'm going crazy in here. I just need to get out of here for a little while."

His eyes bounce between mine as he thinks on my words.

"Did you have some place specific in mind?"

"I want to go to the beach. It's warm enough now and I want to go one more time while I still can. When I moved here one of the first things Claire did was take me swimming at the lake."

"But your I.V."

"I've already talked to Janet and she agrees that a couple hours outside would do me good. I can take my pills with me for pain if I need them."

"Are you sure you feel up to it?"

"All I have to do is sit in a beach chair and soak in the sun. I think I can handle it," I tell him, leaning forward to lay a light kiss to his jaw. "Please." I pout out my bottom lip.

"Fine." He rolls his eyes with a chuckle. "The beach it is."

It's the perfect day. The bright sun warming my skin. The sound of the water as it hits the sand. The laughter of kids playing around me. The feeling of Abel's hand on my leg as we lounge side by side in fold out beach chairs. It's everything I had hoped it would be and exactly what I needed.

I'm not naïve enough to believe that I have much time left. Every time I look in the mirror I see myself fading further and further away. But then days like today make me hopeful that I still have more good days to come.

"Your face is getting red." Abel's voice causes my eyelids to flutter open and I turn my head, meeting his gaze through the dark lenses of my sunglasses. "Here, let me put a little more sunscreen on you."

"I can do it," I say, taking the bottle from his hand the instant he retrieves it from the beach bag. "I'm not entirely helpless, you know." I give him a sideways glance as I slide my glasses onto my head and squirt some sunscreen into my hand.

"I know that."

"Do you? Because between you and Claire I feel like you two think I'm incapable of most things." I spread the lotion across my face, paying special attention to my cheeks and forehead which is where I usually burn the easiest.

"I'm sorry we make you feel that way." He gives me a sad smile, taking the sunscreen bottle when I extend it back to him.

"I know you do it out of love, but sometimes it's frustrating. If I need your help I'll ask for it. If I don't, let me do what I still can do by myself. I'm your wife, not your patient."

"I'm sorry." He relaxes back into his chair.

"Don't apologize for wanting to take care of me. I love you for it, truly I do. And I know this isn't easy on you."

"Don't do that," he cuts in. "I'm here because I *want* to be. You are my life, Finley Collins. Do you hear me?" He takes my hand, lifting my fingers to his lips. "I don't regret finding you. I don't regret marrying you. And I sure as hell don't regret loving you." He kisses my knuckles before allowing our joined hands to fall to the space where our armrests are pressed together.

"Sometimes I just think it would have been easier if I had died during surgery. It would have saved you from having to watch me die. But then I wouldn't have gotten this time with you and that's not something I would take back in a million lifetimes."

"I would rather live one day with you like this than live my entire life without you."

"I'm going to miss you." My voice catches in my throat. "If missing someone is possible wherever I end up once I'm gone."

"Finley." Emotion covers his face. The anger, fear, and the pain he works tirelessly to keep hidden from me. I see it now so clearly and it nearly guts me from the inside out.

"We don't have to talk about it. I just want you to know that even though I'm dying, I've never felt more alive. And I have you to thank for that. You brought light into my life when I was shrouded in darkness. So when I'm gone I need you to remember one very important thing. You've made me happier than I ever dreamed possible. Because of you I know what it truly means to be loved. All of my life that's all I've ever wanted. To be loved. To belong. To feel wanted. You did that for me." I pause, pulling in a breath. "I love you more than I ever thought it possible to love another person. And you've made me happy. Abel, you have made me so, so happy." My chin quivers as I fight to keep my emotions in check.

"You've made me that happy too, you know." He smiles, his glossy eyes visible through his glasses. "My wanna be ballerina who always has her nose in a book. And no matter how bad things get, always has a smile on her face. You are so much stronger than you realize, my love. And I'm going to be lost without you when you're gone." He tightens his grip on my hand.

"You might be at first." I force myself to smile. "But eventually you'll find your way." I sit upright, untangling my hand from Abel's. "I have a favor to ask."

"Anything."

"My mom."

"You want me to try to track her down?" He sits up, angling his legs toward me.

"No. Not yet anyway. I don't want to know if she's alive and still killing herself or if she's clean and happy and I missed time getting to know the real Monica or if she's dead. I don't want to know any of it. But she is my mom and *if* she's still alive, I want her to know that I'm gone. I want her to know that I forgive her."

"And you want me to be the one to do it?"

"Only if you can find her. I wish I could give you something to go on but all I have is her name and date of birth, and for someone who never had anything in her name, that won't be much to go on. But I know you have a friend in the PI business, so I thought maybe if he could track her down then you could get the message to her."

"I'll contact Chuck. See what I can find out."

"You may never find her."

"That doesn't mean I won't try."

"Thank you. I know it's a lot to ask. I just feel like she should know. I don't even know if she'll care, but it'll make me feel better either way."

"There isn't a thing I wouldn't do for you, you know that, right?"

"I do." I lean in and kiss his cheek. "Now, what do you say we go for a swim?" I say, finished with this depressing conversation. We've had far too many recently and right now I want to enjoy this beautiful day.

"You sure you feel..." He stops himself, his eyes trained on me as I shakily push to my feet. "Let's take a swim," he agrees, quickly standing.

Looping his arm through mine, he helps me to the water. I smile the instant the cool waves hit my feet. Abel allows me to walk until the water is around my knees before swooping me up into his arms.

He waits until the water is at his chest before lowering me back to my feet. Because of our height difference it's quite a bit deeper for me than it is him, hitting me almost at the neck. It feels amazing. The cool water on my sun heated skin. The weightlessness of my body. The feel of Abel as he presses against me, both arms wrapped around my shoulders as the gentle waves lap around us.

"You know, one day I'd like to rent a boat," I say, keeping my gaze away from Abel. "We could pack lunches and spend the entire day on the water. Wouldn't that be amazing?"

"Yeah, it would be," he agrees, kissing the side of my head.

"Promise me we will do it one day," I say, knowing that one day will never come but I need to pretend like it will.

"Finley." I look up to meet the incredible gaze of my husband, the love of my life. The man who gave my life meaning.

"Promise me." I reach up, cupping his face with both of my hands.

"I promise," he finally concedes, dropping his forehead to mine. "I promise."

I close my eyes and breathe in Abel's incredible scent which blends with the smell of the water, overwhelming my senses in the best way possible. Things may be hard right now, but it's moments like this that make it all worth it. Moments where Abel and I can disappear into our own little bubble where we're safe from anything and anyone. Nothing can hurt us here.

I only wish we could stay here forever.

We spend the remainder of the day on the beach. Abel doesn't press me to go home and not until I say I'm ready does he even mention leaving.

It's been a great day. The perfect day. A day I'm so glad we got at least one more of. I don't know how many good days we'll have left. Maybe none.

Maybe this is all we'll get. I don't try to rationalize how that makes me feel like I normally would. I've accepted that while leaving Abel feels impossible, it's not something I get to choose. I *am* leaving him but instead of focusing on our impending goodbye, I'm trying to enjoy what little time we get before I go.

"Thank you for today," I say as Abel lowers me to my feet next to the car. "It was exactly what I needed."

"For me too." He runs the back of his hand down my cheek. "No one will ever love another person as much as I love you. I've decided it's not possible."

"Is that so? You've decided, huh?" I smile at him.

"I have." He nods.

"Well I hate to break it to you, but there is no way that's true. Because I love you more."

"Let's agree to disagree on this one." He winks, pulling open the passenger side door before helping me inside.

Leaning over, he grabs the seatbelt and starts to pull it across my chest, stopping mid motion when he catches my expression.

"I'm doing it again, aren't I?" He chuckles, letting the seatbelt snap back into place before backing out of the car and shutting my door.

I smile, snapping my *own* seatbelt right as Abel slides into the driver's seat next to me.

"Can I ask for one more favor?" I lay my head back on the headrest, my face tilted in his direction.

"Anything." He meets my gaze.

"Take me back to your apartment."

"What?" He seems confused by my request.

"I love it there and I haven't been there in so long. I want to lounge on your couch and soak in your big tub. I want to make love to you without having to worry about Janet or Claire walking in. I want to feel like me again and I can't do that at home." I take in his conflicted expression. "Oh, and I want to stop and get a burger from Jack's on the way."

"You know if we go to Jack's we may end up stuck there for a while."

"And that would be a bad thing, why?"

"Because you're sick, Fin. You need to get home and get some rest."

"All I do is rest. Today I feel better than I have in a very long time and I plan to take full advantage of it. Now, if you don't mind, husband." I point at the road in the distance. "Jack's, please."

The smile that spreads across Abel's face is enough to make my insides swirl in delight. It doesn't matter how many times he smiles, because every time he does it's like seeing it for the first time. He just has one of those smiles that makes everything feel okay, even when it isn't.

"Yes, wife," he agrees, firing the engine of the car to life.

Chapter Thirty-seven
Abel

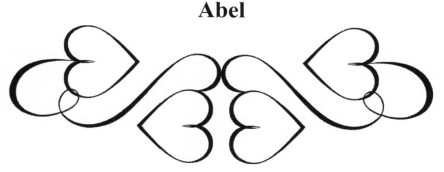

"Hey." I look up from the notepad in my lap at the sound of Finley's voice.

"Hey." I smile, glad to see she's awake. She's been sleeping for hours, like she does most days.

"What are you doing?" she asks, her gaze going to the notebook.

"Oh nothing, just playing with a song I've been working on."

"Is it any good?" Her eyes close for a long moment before reopening slowly.

Finley's health has declined rapidly over the last couple of weeks. Most days she's too weak to get out of bed, and when she does she can no longer walk on her own. Her legs aren't strong enough to support her weight, even though she's withered down to almost nothing. It's hard to think that just a few weeks ago we were on the beach, laughing and smiling. It feels like a lifetime ago and yet like it was yesterday at the same time.

"Define good," I say, leaning forward to touch her face. "How are you feeling?" I ask, feeling to make sure she doesn't have a fever.

We brought hospice in three days ago at the advice of her doctor. He said it was time, and while neither Claire nor I wanted to admit it, we both knew he was right.

She's been less and less herself as the days have gone on. Some days she seems entirely herself, sick, but still herself. Other days it's like she can't tell the difference between dream and reality.

That became apparent when I walked into her room the other day to find her having a conversation with someone named Joan. I tried to intervene but it was like she couldn't see me. She just kept talking to this person that wasn't here.

We knew from the doctor that episodes like this are very common in brain cancer patients and to not be surprised if it gets more frequent or worse at times. Though up to this point that's as bad as it's been.

"I'm okay." She gives me a weak attempt at a smile. "Can I hear it?"

"Hear what?" I ask, not following.

"The song."

"Oh." I chuckle. "It's not ready yet."

"I don't mind." She tucks a hand under her cheek as she gets more comfortable on her side.

"You might once you hear it." I give her a knowing look.

"You couldn't sound bad if you tried." Her voice is frail and breaks on the end, sending another crack through my already splintered heart.

"You sure I can't get you something first? Something to drink maybe?"

"I just want you to play for me."

"Okay," I cave, reaching for the acoustic guitar that's propped against the nightstand next to me. I brought it over a few days ago after Finley had asked me to play for her. It seems to be the one thing that settles her when she's in a lot of pain or feeling restless.

It helps to have something that makes me feel less powerless, like I'm helping her in some small way.

Propping the notebook on the stand, I make sure it's angled so that I can see the words, before settling the guitar in my lap. While I know most of the song off the top of my head, I've spent a lot of the afternoon switching up the lyrics.

I strum a few chords, making sure the guitar is in tune.

"What's it called?" she asks when I pause to fiddle with one of the strings.

"A Place Without You," I tell her, emotion clogging my throat when I see the understanding expression cross over her pale face.

I've been trying like hell to hold it together for Finley's sake, but that task has become almost impossible. Every time I look at her I want to hit my knees and sob like a child. I want to throw my hands up and beg God to make her better.

My fingers move along the strings before I realize what I'm doing. I take a deep breath in and let it out slowly, hanging onto the one thing that helps me empty out my emotions without completely falling apart. The one thing that's always gotten me through. My music. Sadly, I'm not even sure music is powerful enough to get me through this once she's gone. The further she fades, the less meaning life has. Some nights I lie awake watching her sleep, wishing God would take me too so I would never have to say goodbye.

"*Life has a way of taking you down the path you're meant to be,*" I begin to sing. "*I didn't know I wasn't living until you looked up at me. You smiled and right then I knew that you were the one. You stole my breath and my heart before the first song was done. But now you're leaving me here and I'm not sure what to do. I keep asking myself how I'm going to live in a place without you. A place without you.*" I hum out a part at the end of the chorus, not looking at Finley as I continue into the second verse.

"You took my hand and in that moment I felt like I could fly. I never stopped to question it or even to ask why. I knew with you was where I was meant to be. That's where I'd spend my life. There was no greater feeling in the entire world than when you agreed to be my wife. But now you're leaving me here and I'm not sure what to do. I keep asking myself how I'm going to live in a place without you. A place without you."

My fingers move effortlessly along the strings as the song builds into the bridge.

"You gave me purpose. You gave me meaning. You gave me a place to belong. You made me see that I was enough. You are my perfect song. I'll play you over and over again until my fingers bleed. Because you are the only thing in this world that I truly need. You are my world, my light, my life. You are my dream come true. I didn't know that real love existed until I found you. But now you're leaving me here and I'm not sure what to do. I keep asking myself how I'm going to live in a place without you. A place without you."

I strum out the final chords, emotion stinging the back of my throat as I open my eyes and my gaze lands on Finley.

Tears slide down her cheeks in quick succession and she immediately reaches for me.

Setting my guitar to the side, I slide into bed next to her, pulling her close. She buries her face in my chest and for the first time ever, she falls apart in my arms.

She cries like I've never seen her cry before. The kind of cry that pours deep from your soul and completely takes over your body. It's gut wrenching to witness and yet at the same time, I want it. I want all her pain. I want to absorb it into my own body and take it away. I want to save her, even though I know I can't.

So I do the one thing I can do. I hold her. I hold her until long after her body stops trembling and her tears have dried. I hold her until she sleeps and even then I can't bring myself to pull away.

I don't know how many moments we have left. How many times I'll get to hold her like this before she's gone. How many days, or hours, or minutes I have left to feel her warm against me. To feel her breath hot on my neck. To feel her heartbeat pound inside her chest.

I blink, in an attempt to hold back the tears. Push them away like I have done so many times before, but this time I can't find the strength to do so. I feel like I'm dying, being ripped apart from the inside out. I struggle to breathe, to pull in even the smallest amount of air, but it's like my lungs have forgotten how to work.

I hold Finley tighter. Holding onto the only thing tethering me to this world. I can't bear to think about her not being here. I can't imagine a world without her smile and her laughter. I can't picture who I'll be without her.

As if sensing I'm fighting a losing battle, Finley stirs in my arms and her eyes flutter open, landing on my tear stained face.

"Abel," she whispers, wincing as she reaches up and cups my cheek. "I love you."

"I love you." I choke on a sob, trying to reel it in, yet feeling like there's no way to do so. This pain, this fear, has been building for weeks and now the flood gates are open and there's no way to close them again.

"It's going to be okay." She lays her head on my chest and slides her arm across my stomach.

It feels so wrong to have *her* comforting *me*, but right now I need her to. I need her to tell me that everything will be okay. I need her to tell me that I won't totally fall apart once she's gone.

"How is any of this okay?" I rest my face against the top of her head, my tears flowing harder now.

"I'm grateful for the cancer because it led me to you. I'd die a thousand times over if it meant I could have even one day by your side. You told me that I was the love of your life. Well you, Abel, are mine. You are my everything. And when I'm gone, I won't really be gone. I'll still be here." She kisses right above my heart where her name is etched into my skin. "I'll be with you always. To experience everything. The highs and the lows. The failures and triumphs. I'll be here to watch *you* live, Abel. And you're going to have an incredible life. I just know it."

"Not without you." I grip her tighter. "Nothing will ever mean anything without you."

"Then make it mean something." She pauses. "Make it worth it. And one day, when you're ready, open your heart to someone new. Let them help heal the wounds I left behind. Let them love you the way you deserve to be loved and don't for one single second think that your happiness is somehow a betrayal to me. All I want for you is happiness. So when you feel it. When you really feel it, look up to the sky and know I feel it too. Because that's what it means to love someone, Abel. You taught me that."

"I can't even think about loving someone else, Fin. I can't imagine looking at someone else and not seeing your face, hearing your voice, feeling your soft touch."

"I know it seems impossible right now. But one day you will find someone new and I need you to promise me right here and now that you won't push it away. Embrace it, even if it scares you. Hold onto it and don't ever let it go. Love is such a rare gift, Abel. Don't keep yours bottled up inside. Promise me you won't. Promise me that you will love again. Promise me that one day you'll find happiness. I can't leave you until you promise."

"I don't want you to ever leave me."

"I'm so tired, Abel. I want the pain to stop. I want it all to stop. It's time. You know it's time. Now promise me. Promise me you won't shut yourself off from the world. Promise me that you'll live. For the both of us."

I choke back the fresh tears that pool in my eyes and press my lips to the top of her head.

"I promise," I whisper. "I promise."

Finley died two days later. Claire and I were by her side when she took her last breath. It was the hardest thing I've ever done in my life. Watching her go.

Every day since has been like a nightmare. Whether I'm awake or asleep, I'm trapped. Trapped in the endless cycle of mourning that I can't seem to escape.

I managed to pull myself together long enough to attend the service earlier this afternoon that Claire helped Finley prepare before she got too sick. But even then I didn't feel like I was there. It's like everything keeps moving around me but my entire world is standing still.

My parents decided to host a dinner at their house for Finley following the funeral. I think it made my mom feel better. To be able to help in some way.

Claire came, along with a lot of Finley's co-workers from the restaurant. My brothers were all here and Adam even flew in from California.

I know they all just want to help. That they want to be here for me. But how can they? How can I let them when I feel like my very reason for existing is gone?

"Knock, knock." Seconds later the door opens, and Claire peeks her head inside my childhood bedroom. "Hey." She steps in and closes the door behind her. "Your mom said I could find you up here." She turns, dropping down onto the bed next to me.

"I just can't be around everyone right now," I tell her, keeping my face pointed down toward the ground. I tighten my grip on the edge of the mattress in an effort to stop myself from doing what I've wanted to do since the moment I walked into this room twenty minutes ago. Which is take my old baseball bat and smash every last thing in sight.

"I understand. But it's nice – having everyone come together for Fin. It would have meant so much to her to see how many people showed up. She never understood how easy it was to love her and just how many people did."

"Yeah."

"So about Finley's ashes," she starts, my gaze shooting to her.

"What about her ashes? We buried her ashes today."

"No, we buried some of her ashes. I have the rest."

"Why?"

"Because Finley told me to. She wanted half of her ashes buried with her headstone so that we would have a place to sit and talk with her whenever we wanted. The other half she wanted me to give to you. I left them downstairs with your mom. When you're ready."

I guess I shouldn't be surprised that I'm just hearing all this now. Finley never stopped trying to protect me, even up until the very end.

"She left you a note too, so you'd know exactly what she wanted you to do with them. I'm sorry I'm just now giving it to you," she says, reaching around to pull out a small white envelope from the back pocket of her dress pants. "But she made me promise to do it this way." She slides the envelope into my hand and stands. "Finley loved you so much, Abel. So much that all she wanted was for you to be okay once she was gone. So do us both a favor and be okay. Okay?" She squeezes my shoulder.

When I struggle to find words to say, she continues, "It's going to take time. For both of us. But I know one day I'll get there. And I think you will too. Until then, take comfort in how happy you two made each other. Remember her smile, her laugh, all the things you loved most about her. Then instead of mourning those things, celebrate them. It's what Finley would have wanted." She releases my shoulder and crosses the room toward the door, pausing with her hand on the knob. "If you ever need me, Abel, for anything, please know that I will always be here for you," she says, tugging open the door before disappearing into the hallway moments later.

I stare at the sealed envelope in my hand for what feels like an eternity. The only sound in the room is my heart drumming in my ears and the rip of the paper as I tear the envelope open and pull out the letter.

Unfolding the paper, it takes several seconds for my eyes to clear enough for me to make out the words on the page.

My dearest Abel,

I've written this letter so many times in my head that it almost feels rehearsed as I put it on paper for you now. There are so many things I want to say and yet there aren't nearly enough words to do it.

First, I want you to know how much I love you. Because of you my life ended with happiness and love, which is much different than the way it began. Thank you for that.

I never admitted this to you, but I fell in love with you the very first night we met. How could I not? You took one look at me and I felt my entire world shift. We only spent ten hours together. Thirty-six thousand seconds. Six hundred minutes. However you break it down, those ten hours changed everything. You changed everything.

I've told you before that I was grateful to the cancer because it brought me to you. No matter how much I wish our ending had been different, I wouldn't change one single thing about our story. Because it was the perfect story. Maybe it didn't end in the

traditional version of happily ever after, but I think we came
pretty close.

I left Claire with instructions to leave you with half of my ashes. I
want you to take me with you, Abel. Keep me close. And when
you're ready, I want you to let me go. You'll know when the time
is right. And when that time comes, take me to the beach where
you asked me to be your wife and sprinkle me into the water that
will dance around our feet. Let me go, Abel. Let me go, and live.
Live your life fully, fearlessly, and without limit. Live for us both.
And never forget how much I love you.

Until we meet again,
Just Finley

    I want to ball the letter up. I want to scream at the top of
my lungs. I want to make sure she hears me when I tell her that I
won't ever be ready to let her go. But instead, I hold the letter
against my chest and let the tears flow. I let the grief and sadness
pulse through me like a heartbeat, not sure if I'll ever find the
strength to pick up the pieces now that she's gone.

Chapter Thirty-eight
Abel

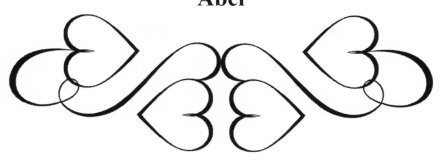

Two months later…

I spot Claire as soon as I round the corner. She's sitting at a small round table outside, a few feet from the street. It's the table where her and Finley used to always sit. The thought causes my chest to tighten but I push past it, forcing a smile to my face when Claire looks up and sees me crossing the street toward her.

"Abel." She stands, wrapping her arms around my middle the moment I reach her.

"Hey, Claire." I breathe in the scent of her hair, emotion clogging my throat when I realize it smells exactly like Finley's used to. They must use the same shampoo and I never noticed before now.

Then again it's been almost two months since I've seen Claire. Since the day after the funeral to be exact. It was never my intention to separate myself from her the way I have. I guess after everything I needed some time.

"How are you?" I release her and take a full step back, sliding into the seat across from her as she reclaims her own.

"I'm doing okay." She lets out a small sigh. "Some days are better than others."

"Yeah, for me too."

"I knew I'd miss her. I just didn't realize how much." Her eyes well with unshed tears but she quickly pulls herself together. "I ordered you a water. I wasn't sure what to get you since you don't drink coffee and this is a coffee shop." She gestures to the glass in front of me.

"Water is perfect."

"So how are you, Abel? Really?"

"I'm taking it one day at a time," I admit.

"That's really all you can do." She reaches for her coffee cup, lifting it to her lips. After swallowing and setting her cup back down, she continues, "I have to admit, I was surprised when you reached out."

"I shouldn't have waited so long. I'm sorry about that." It feels hard to meet her gaze. Her eyes are so much like Finley's that I'm not sure if I want to get lost in them or avoid looking at them all together.

"You needed some time. I get that." She leans forward, resting her elbows on the table in front of her. "I stopped at your parent's house the other day to visit. Your mom told me the news. She's in remission. You must be so relieved."

"I am." I nod slowly. "I didn't realize you were on a drop in to visit basis with my mom."

"We've stayed in touch since the funeral. We talk every couple of weeks or so. Just check in with each other."

"I see."

"She's worried about you. We both are."

"There's no need to be. I'm okay, really." But it's a lie. I'm nowhere near okay. But I don't feel guilty in my dishonesty because I have to believe that one day it won't be a lie anymore. It's the only thing that gets me through. "Listen, the reason I asked you to meet me is because I wanted to tell you face to face—"

"Tell me what?" she asks before I can finish.

"I'm leaving Chicago."

"Oh." She draws back, clearly surprised.

"I'm going to stay with my brother in California for a while. I'm hoping getting away will help me clear my head a little. Maybe figure out my next move."

"Your mom said you haven't been playing."

"I just need some time. Time away from all of it."

"I can't begin to understand what you're feeling, Abel, so I won't pretend that I do. But Finley loved how much you loved to play. She would be devastated to think that she might have taken that from you."

"I've been writing and stuff. I would never be able to give up music completely, but like many things, it reminds me too much of Finley. Most days it hurts too damn much. When I pick up my guitar and start to play, I look up expecting to see her sitting across from me, wearing that goofy smile she always wore when I'd sing to her."

"The one where she looked so stupid happy you'd wonder if her face might split apart."

"That's the one." I smile at the thought, something I wish I could do more often.

"God, she could listen to you for hours on end and never get tired of it."

"I could play for her for hours and not tire of it. I loved watching her watch me."

"You know, I used to think I knew what it meant to love someone. I've had boyfriends over the years, people I thought I was in love with. But it wasn't until I saw you two together that I realized what true love really looks like. The way you two would look at each other, my god, it would take my breath away watching you together. Every relationship I've ever been in has been a struggle, an uphill battle trying to figure out the ropes, but you and Fin, you made it look so effortless."

"Because with her it was effortless. I never had to try to love her. I just did. From the moment I met her all I wanted was to be near her."

"She felt the same about you, ya know?"

"Yeah, I do."

"So, when are you planning to leave?"

"My flight is tomorrow morning." I lean back in my chair.

"And how long will you be gone?"

"I don't know yet," I admit.

"Would it be too much to ask if you'd text or call every now and again just to let me know you're doing okay?"

"I think I can handle that," I agree, knowing that's what Finley would want me to do.

Claire is an amazing girl and we became good friends through Finley's illness, but since Finley died I can't stomach the thought of being around her. She reminds me too much of Finley and right now it's too hard. Even sitting across from her for these few moments makes it feel like daggers are stabbing into my chest. On one hand I want to pull her to me, inhale her scent, pretend for one moment that she's her sister. On the other, I can't do that to myself or to Finley's memory. I won't. I won't substitute her for even a second. I can't.

"I've been meaning to ask you, have you had any luck tracking down Monica?"

"Not yet. Chuck's monitoring the situation. Waiting to see if she pops up somewhere. If I find her, you'll be the first to know."

"Thank you." She pauses. "By the way, I have something for you." Claire grabs her purse off the back of the chair and rifles through it for a moment before pulling out a long silver chain with a compass charm attached to it. "I gave this to Finley when she first moved to Chicago. Told her it would help her find her way." She extends the necklace in my direction, dropping it into my outstretched hand.

I stare down at the necklace for several long moments, not sure what to say.

"I think maybe you could use a little help finding your way." She gives me a soft smile when my gaze comes to hers.

"Thank you," I say, unclasping the chain before slipping it around my neck.

"She'd want you to have it."

I run my thumb over the small compass charm, the weight of the necklace feeling foreign around my neck.

"I miss her every single day."

"Me too." Claire reaches across the table and takes my hand.

My instinct is to pull away from the contact but for some reason I don't. I let her wrap her fingers around mine and I take a small piece of comfort in feeling connected to someone who understands my loss.

"You'll find your way, Abel. And you'll do it because it's what Finley wanted. She's with you, even if you can't see her. Let her guide you. That's what I try to do."

"Does it help?" I ask.

"A little." She shrugs. "Some days more than others. But even on the bad days I push through. I do it for her. And you need to do it for her too."

"I'm trying. I think getting away for a while will help me clear my head. There's just so many memories here."

"Trust me, I know." She releases my hand, sitting back in her seat.

"Well, I guess I should probably get going. I have a lot to do before I leave tomorrow."

"Will you text once you land? Let me know you got there okay."

"I will," I promise, pushing to a stand.

"And don't forget to call me here and there. It would be nice to hear your voice. I know it sounds strange, but you make me feel closer to her."

"It doesn't sound strange at all," I admit, feeling reminiscent of that at this very moment.

"Take care of yourself, Abel." She stands, once again wrapping her arms around my middle. This time I return the hug, embracing her in a way I haven't since Finley died.

It feels good, freeing almost, and in a way I wish I hadn't waited so long to see Claire. She meant a lot to Finley, and because of that, she means a lot to me.

We hold each other a little longer than we probably should. Each of us clinging to the parts of Finley wrapped up in the other person. Several seconds pass before I pull away, pausing to look down at her again.

"Don't get into too much trouble while I'm gone," I tease, tipping her chin.

"I make no promises." She laughs, taking a full step back. "Have a good trip. And Abel," she calls just as I move to leave. "I hope you find the peace you're looking for."

"Yeah, me too." I give her a small smile before turning and quickly walking away.

I don't know what the future holds. It's hard to think about tomorrow let alone weeks or months from now. But deep down I know I'll be okay. I know it down to my very core because I can feel her there. In everywhere I go, in everything I do, she's with me. Just like she said she would be.

No matter how badly it hurts, no matter how much I miss her, I'd do it a hundred times over again. I'd relive every moment from beginning to end if it meant that I could see her face again. See her smile again. Hear her voice when she says she loves me.

I'll never understand why I had to lose her right as I found her. And I don't think a day will go by that I won't think of her. Of how our lives could have been if she were still here.

Finley was my axis. Now I have to find a way to keep my world turning without her in it. And one day I will. One day I will find my way because I know that's what she wanted for me. And one day, one day, I'll find the strength to let her go, just like she asked me to.

The End

Acknowledgments

Thank you so much for taking the time to read Ten Hours. I truly hope you enjoyed Finley's story. I know it probably wasn't the easiest to read but in the end I hope you felt like it was worth it.

Having lost my father to a brain tumor in 2008 I know first-hand what these characters were going through. I felt every emotion. I laughed with them, I cried with them, and by the end I felt a little better because it allowed me to leave a bit of my own pain within the pages. Thank you for taking the journey with me.

To everyone who helped make this book possible*- thank you.*
*My editor **Rose**, for being a master with a red pen.*
*My friend and teaser extraordinaire, **Angel**- I adore you!*
***Melissa Gill**- for designing the PERFECT cover for Abel and Finley.*
*My book besties **Joni** and **Jackie** for always being there to cheer me on and for being the most kick ass event assistants a girl could ask for.*
*My **husband** and **children** for always supporting my dreams and pushing me to be the best version of myself.*
*My **family** and **friends**- your support means more than you will ever know.*
*To my **readers**- thank you. If I could hug each and every single one of you in person I would. It's because of you that I'm able to live my dream and I will forever be grateful. From the bottom of my heart- thank you.*

XOXO

-Melissa

57459878R00179

Made in the USA
Middletown, DE
03 August 2019